"McLaughlin capitalizes on his insider's knowledge of the biz, creating a mix of characters so authentic it's hard to tell which are pulled directly from *Daily Variety* and which are pulled from thin air." —*The Advocate*

"Slyly amusing . . . a delicious and gossipy behind-the-scenes peek at daytime TV. . . . McLaughlin's immensely likable hero will surely grab readers' funnybones and hearts." —*Publishers Weekly*

"Wild, witty, and laugh-out-loud funny, incredibly romantic. . . . McLaughlin has populated his book with characters who are immediately familiar without being complete stereotypes." —*Bay Windows*

"Hilariously funny, unabashedly romantic, and very sexy . . . a novel that is as easy to devour as a box of chocolates. McLaughlin's sense of humor and style never fail, and the writing is crisp." —*Southern Voice*

CHRISTIAN MCLAUGHLIN moved to Hollywood minutes after graduating from the University of Texas at Austin. He writes for television and is currently at work on his second novel.

"Humorous and touching. . . . The worst thing that can be said of this book is that it's not long enough. More, more!"
—*Entertainment Weekly*

"Wonderfully funny . . . entrancing. . . . McLaughlin takes his place with novelists Robert Rodi, Joe Keenan, and Eric Shaw Quinn: writers who are restyling the comic novel with their own decidedly gay bent."
—*Genre*

"Outrageous, amusing. . . . McLaughlin has a gifted comedic sense and his pleasant jump-start narrative style keeps the book zipping happily along."
—*Pittsburgh NewsWeekly*

"Torrid, dishy, and outrageously romantic, *Glamourpuss* is both an irresistibly dewy-eyed love story and a satiric skewering of star-studded Hollywood."
—*Gay and Lesbian Times*

CHRISTIAN MCLAUGHLIN

Glamourpuss

A PLUME BOOK

For Chris

PLUME
Published by the Penguin Group
Penguin Books USA Inc., 375 Hudson Street,
New York, New York 10014, U.S.A.
Penguin Books Ltd, 27 Wrights Lane, London W8 5TZ, England
Penguin Books Australia Ltd, Ringwood, Victoria, Australia
Penguin Books Canada Ltd, 10 Alcorn Avenue,
Toronto, Ontario, Canada M4V 3B2
Penguin Books (N.Z.) Ltd, 182–190 Wairau Road, Auckland 10, New Zealand

Penguin Books Ltd, Registered Offices: Harmondsworth, Middlesex, England

Published by Plume, an imprint of Dutton Signet, a division of
Penguin Books USA Inc. Previously published in a Dutton edition.

First Plume Printing, October, 1995
10 9 8 7 6 5

Ⓟ REGISTERED TRADEMARK—MARCA REGISTRADA

The Library of Congress has catalogued the Dutton edition as follows:

McLaughlin, Christian.
Glamourpuss / Christian McLaughlin.
p. cm.
ISBN 0-525-93866-4 (hc.)
ISBN 0-452-27265-3 (pbk.)
1. Television actors and actresses—United States—Fiction.
2. Gay men—United States—Fiction.   I. Title.
PS3563.C38364G57   1994
813'.54—dc20
94-9308
CIP

Printed in the United States of America
Original hardcover design by Steven N. Stathakis

BOOKS ARE AVAILABLE AT QUANTITY DISCOUNTS WHEN USED TO PROMOTE PRODUCTS
OR SERVICES. FOR INFORMATION PLEASE WRITE TO PREMIUM MARKETING DIVISION,
PENGUIN BOOKS USA INC., 375 HUDSON STREET, NEW YORK, NEW YORK 10014.

Part One

I had put a lethal dose of poison into Cyrinda's milk shake two weeks before, but the bitch had lived through it. Still, she was a hell of a lot more likely to segue from coma patient to corpse than she was to write any more prize-winning investigative journalism for the *Crossing Herald*. That meddling blonde know-it-all . . . How I wanted to be in that hospital room when her fat parents decided to pull the plug and she sank into the dark eternal slumber she deserved for *daring* to get in my way—

"Simon?" I turned my reflective gaze from the window to my half-sister Natalie, framed in the doorway, looking ever so upset. Hard day at the dental office? Someone write a bad check for a root canal? I just looked at her. "Simon—they've arrested Sean Nortonsen. For trying to murder Cyrinda." What a surprise. Poor, tearful Natalie.

"How interesting," I remarked. "Your little playmate Sean

tries to knock off his ex-girlfriend, who just happens to be the one woman in Harts Crossing you can't stand. Aren't you flattered?"

"How can you talk to me like that? My life is falling apart," she complained through clenched teeth.

I crossed over to an armchair and picked up a magazine. "Just be glad you and Nortonsen never got to take that romantic getaway to Hawaii. If you'd started dating him like you wanted to, you'd probably be wearing stripes, too."

"You're so damn smug. Don't think for one second I believe that he did this!" Of course he didn't do it, you hysterical bleeding-gum maven. I framed him. So beautifully he's going to fry like a funnel-cake.

"He did it, Natalie. It makes perfect sense. And I'd keep any other theories to myself if I were you, or the police might want to sit you down for a little chat."

"You are despicable sometimes," she spat, sobs boiling to the surface.

My expression softened. "I'm just trying to protect you from becoming involved in a very ugly situation. With somebody capable of murder."

"I loved him," she stage-whispered, then clattered away to her room, composure in shreds.

"Then you deserve each other," I said to myself aloud, tossing the magazine to the floor and retrieving my jacket from the bedpost. I opened the closet and took out two suitcases. "This place is starting to bum me out," I snickered. I flicked off the lights and walked out with my luggage. I *was* Simon Arable, diabolical young son of the unstable late scientist Dr. Jules Arable and an utterly ruthless sociopath with no redeeming quality but cuteness. So in character as I strode off the set I barely heard the stage manager call, "Clear! That's a wrap!"

A perfect second take. Allison Slater Lang, the Annette Bening-via-Tawny Kitaen who played Natalie slapped palms with me then administered a full-body squeeze.

"Thank you very much everyone," executive producer Reese Jacobs intercommed from the booth. "Welcome aboard, Alex. See you in three weeks."

"You were wonderful. Have a great trip, Alex," Allison said. She checked her watch. "Goddamnit, 12:45. I'm ready to drop. I'll see you soon." She pecked my cheek and took off.

I said bye to the hastily dispersing crew and practically pranced to my dressing room. My last day as a "recurring" character on *Hearts Crossing*, the number-five rated daytime drama, was over. When this episode aired in approximately two and a half weeks, the general viewing public wouldn't realize my character would soon be sneaking back into Harts Crossing, the town, this time to stay, as a three-year contract villain, at a satisfying $1350 per episode (up $350 from my day rate).

It wasn't as if the decision to make Simon a permanent character had been a surprise; when I was hired they'd made it clear it could go contract depending on "how the storyline played," which of course meant how deliciously, indispensably evil I could play it. Still, I'd been in The Biz long enough (fifteen whole months at that point) to know better than to count on it. So I hadn't. And when the call came three weeks ago, it was more than just great news—it proved that Belinda Carlisle had been absolutely right . . . Heaven *was* a place on Earth.

I threw off my clothes and dove into the shower with cold cream, soap from the gift basket delivered yesterday from Network Daytime, and a bottle of Pellegrino I'd been saving all day. Minutes later, scrubbed, changed and carbonated, I was behind the wheel of my Accord, heading toward Del Taco for a drive-through feeding frenzy. But when I hit Sunset, I hooked west and instead ended up at Ralph's market, open twenty-four hours for Hollywood's grocery needs, but I was sure they turned up the fluorescent lights after midnight to create a harsher shopping environment. I wasn't intimidated.

I emptied the dainty little red plastic basket onto the conveyor belt. One loaf of French bread, a green pepper, Sure unscented solid. A woman and a kid around six walked into the store. When I was six, I would never, never have been allowed to be awake at 2:00 a.m., much less taken to a grocery store. My parents hadn't even let me visit California till I was fifteen. I wondered if I was a happier adult because I'd usually been in bed by

8:30 when I was little. As the zombified cashier picked up the pepper and scanned it, I tossed a *Soap Opera Digest* down, too.

I was filling in *Pay To The Order Of Ralph's* when I heard the girl in line behind me snarl, "Put those fuckin' cupcakes back." She was Sunset Stripped in a leather bustier and miniskirt and stiletto pumps, a dripping dagger tastefully tattooed down the side of one shin, the dye job on her glam-metal mane reasonably fresh. She dropped her carton of whole milk and can of Ultra SlimFast Chocolate Royale on the conveyor belt and turned on her smaller, look-alike boyfriend.

"I want 'em, man," he whined.

"You don't need any more sugar tonight, goddamnit." She snatched the package of Hostess cupcakes out of his hand. I looked at the cashier.

"Six seventy-nine," she repeated.

"I got money, Veronica. I'll pay for 'em," the boyfriend mumbled. Veronica lobbed the cupcakes over his shoulder. They smacked against a big cardboard Teddy Graham bear, who swayed but did not topple from his position over the Teddy Graham creme sandwich cookie display.

I balanced the groceries, my gym bag and pop-out cassette deck on one arm while opening my mailbox. I shoveled the mail into the grocery bag and noticed a yellow postal slip stuck to the back of the box. It said that I had a package that had been left at Apartment 102. It was too late to get it now and tomorrow morning I had to leave for the airport by 8:00, which would be too early. I started up the stairs, irritated, when a door opened. An Asian teen came out of 102, trying to squeeze a hand into the pocket of his jeans.

"Excuse me," I said. The teen turned around. The resident of 102 peeked out his door.

"Oh, *hi*," he said to me. He was around fifty, homosexual, with close-cropped hair and a little beard. He was in a short silk kimono. "You haven't met Chang, my student." Right. "Chang, this is my neighbor, Alex." We nodded at each other. I'd been in 102 once before, when I moved into the building four months ago. One wall was nothing but framed Herb Ritts prints. He had a giant-screen TV that had been tuned to a *Facts of Life* rerun when I was there.

I brandished the yellow slip half-heartedly. "Do you think I could get my package from you? I know it's late, but—"

I didn't have to finish. "Of course!" He disappeared into his apartment and came out with a long, thick envelope. The teen extracted his car keys and left. My neighbor handed me the envelope. It was from the network.

"How's the show going? I saw you the other day. They're turning you into such a little villain."

"I'm really enjoying it. Thanks for watching. And thanks for—" I waved the envelope at him, not about to say "my fan mail," although I was sure that's what it was.

"Anytime," he said. Then he winked. I made a quick getaway.

In my kitchen I made a huge sandwich with cold chicken breast, peppers, tomatoes and mayonnaise and ate it while pawing through the contents of the network envelope. There were seventeen letters addressed to me, Alexander Young, and eight addressed to Simon Arable. I opened a Simon letter first. Those viewers so driven to write they couldn't even take the time to come up with my real name usually produced the most enjoyable fan letters.

Dear Simon,
You evil prick. What you did to Cyrinda is beyond belief. You are ruining life in Hartz Crossing. I am seriously considering boycotting the show until you are inprisoned or killed. Tell me —are you really Natalie's half-brother or is this just another one of your damn lies.
Sincerely,
Arlow Shank
9115 Wagon Wheel Lane
Carson City, NV 89701

I used to quickly and personally answer all such letters because I got a real kick out of it, but lately the *Hearts Crossing* producers had forbidden us to respond to any "weird, threatening or abusive" mail. I regretfully tossed it aside and tried an Alexander Young. This one was from Delaware.

> Dear Alexander Young,
> I watch you all the time on <u>Hearts Crossing</u> and recently rented your movie <u>Teenage Brides of Christ</u>. I was wondering how long you've been performing and if you are single or married (if you don't mind being asked).
> Thank you.
> Your friend,
> Elaine Cloonan
> P.S. Could I also have a color autographed picture of yourself (if you don't mind being asked)?

Now that I was under contract, the studio would start answering my mail for me, but right now it was just Elaine and me (if I didn't mind being asked). I hoped black-and-white would be acceptable. I thought my family would enjoy the mail, so I decided to answer it in San Antonio.

I went into my room and put the envelope on top of my packed bag. I started to take off my clothes, then remembered my answering machine. There were four calls. My mother. My agent. A hang-up. Then, "Hi there, Alex." It was him. My eyes darted to the wall. If this had been a movie, there would have been a slow zoom-in to the photo hanging there, while his deep voice filled the soundtrack. "Sara tells me you're leaving tomorrow and I wanted to make sure we got together for at least a little bit when you come to Austin. So call me and we'll give you a hard time about being a TV star. Okay? See you soon." He sounded so friendly, almost folksy, so easygoing. I slowly sank to my bed, weak and clad in Perry Ellis briefs, my hand already reaching for the rewind button.

April 1990

He was driving me so crazy that at first I put the videotape in backward then stood there stupidly waiting for it to start playing. I'd just given my best performance as Starcat in *Psycho Beach Party* at Capitol City Playhouse in Austin, fueled by nervous energy and Nick's presence in the audience and my resolution to actually kiss him tonight. Kenneth Anger's *Fireworks* started. I sat down on the floor in front of Nick's chair. "Is it okay if I sit here?"

"Sure," he said, as if I'd asked if he wanted a glass of water. I leaned back and he put his legs over my shoulders. I pulled off his Topsiders and ran my hands over his bare feet and up his calves. After months of forbidden longing, he was touching me and I was touching him. I felt like I had been starving and was now being presented with an exquisite gourmet meal that I would be allowed to finish, course by course, only if I exhibited perfect table manners.

I waited as long as I could, then turned around, still between his tan, muscular legs. We kept talking about the play and my final exams and I slid my hands under his shirt and slowly and carefully stroked his stomach and hard, hairy chest. His hand stayed on my shoulder and I looked into his eyes, which were fiery blue steel. It didn't matter that he had been living with a guy for years and that we could never spend a night together. I whispered the words I'd waited six months to say to him: "Nick, I'd really like to kiss you."

"We'd better not," he said.

I was undaunted. "Just a little one," I pleaded. He closed his eyes as I leaned in for the kill. Kissing him was like hot rain in a tropical forest. I was the virgin sacrifice, he the pagan love god with movie star-sensual lips.

"You're falling in love with me, aren't you?" he breathed afterward. Jolts of pleasure ran down my body as those lips brushed against my ear. I couldn't tell him I'd been in love with him since the second I saw him. But I squeezed him as tight as I could, my face pressed against his chest, opting for tasteful unspoken assent.

"It feels good to have a man hold you, doesn't it?"

I thought this question was safe to answer. "Yes," I half-panted, "it feels so good to touch you."

My hand on his thigh, then my fingertips just under the leg of his neon-red nylon running shorts. I was no longer in control. Someone else was sliding his hand farther and farther, until he encountered Nick's huge, rigid penis encased in the mesh lining of his shorts. Someone else was squeezing it, making him close his eyes and sigh a shuddering breath of pleasure.

"Alex . . ." he said. So I guess it *was* me. I withdrew my hand.

His big dick slapped against his stomach after we wrested off his pants. I looked at him, not believing this was happening. I could barely talk. "You're so beautiful," I said. He held my hand. I kissed him all over. He went home to Barney at 11:55.

Dear *Alexander*,
You're one of my favorite actors! *Hearts Crossing* is one of my favorite shows and I especially like the scenes with *Simon*. A personally autographed photo would really mean a lot to me! I've enclosed a SASE.
Ruth Velverson
Tacoma, WA

I couldn't sleep. I snapped on the light, not caring that it was 3:20. I could sleep on the goddamn plane. I played Nick's message again. I closed my eyes and ran a hand over my pecs and biceps, imagining it was Nick showing affection in our enormous bedroom in Nichols Canyon. I hopped out of bed and grabbed my fan mail. I went through it quickly, wondering if any guys besides Arlow Shank had written. Didn't look like it. I noticed one letter had a San Antonio postmark. It was her again. I ripped it open.

Dear Alex,
H̲i̲! It's me again. Thanks for the autograph! I didn't even mind cutting up my yearbook, because now I have a great, wallet-size reminder of you that I show everyone I work with. They're pretty impressed when I tell them I was in your algebra class at Roosevelt! Your mom said she didn't know when you'd be home again when I called today, but when you are, I hope you'll let me take you to lunch! Congratulations on getting that yicky Cyrinda out of the picture! I'm sure not going to miss one single episode of <u>Hearts Crossing</u> now. Please write if you have time.
Sincerely and God Bless,
Juliana Butts
4950 Royal Glen Dr.
San Antonio, TX 78239

Question 1: Why didn't my parents have an unlisted phone number? This was Juliana's seventh letter in the fourteen weeks I'd been recurring on *Hearts Crossing*.
Question 2: Who the hell was this girl? I had no idea. I'd

have to look her up in an old yearbook when I got to Texas.

I turned on the TV and must have fallen asleep immediately, because when I woke to my blasting alarm clock, the Trinity Broadcasting Network was still on. In a pretaped segment, Jan Crouch was bouncing her wacky-looking grandbaby Kalin on her hip and cooing, "Can you say Jesus? Jeee-zus?" The stylishly dressed Christian tot batted Jan's rock-stiff, silver, angora-kitten coiffure with a tiny fist. "Deeza!" he gurgled.

I quickly switched to a Madonna Rock Block on MTV and hopped out of bed.

When Trevor rang me, I was making my bed—returning from a trip to an unmade bed was a really depressing image. I buzzed him up, grabbed my bag and a Coke and met him in the hall.

Trevor was a slightly offbeat, kind of gorgeous and one of those striking model types that looks most natural dripping wet in a tank top, which he had plenty of practice at in photo layouts for Hawaiian Tropic, Nautilus and International Male. Not to mention his more private and special appearance in an *Advocate Men* centerfold the year before.

We'd met last January at Risa Bramon's casting office, the day's last two appointments for a part in a Tom Cruise summer fluff movie. I was sneaking glances at him in the waiting area while scanning my sides and trying to decide how I was going to add some zing to the nine-line role of Todd (which Trevor ended up almost getting, even though he'd picked up the wrong sides and kept calling Risa "Rita"). Trevor was listlessly perusing *Dramalogue.* He tossed it down and we made eye contact. Then he spoke: "Remember *Highlights for Children?*"

Pretty and quirky, too? Intriguing. "I used to look at it at the dentist's office," I said.

"Yeah," he said. "It was always in somebody's waiting room. Like they only allowed industrial subscriptions or something. Even when I was real little, it always seemed like it came from another universe. Especially the part called 'Headwork,' which was supposed to be these tricky brainteasers, right? 'Does a baby have teeth?' 'How many shoes in a pair?' Jesus, it should have been called *Highlights for Retards.* And how about Goofus and Gallant? 'Gallant always applies plenty of spermicidal foam.' 'Goofus makes his girlfriends take the bus to the abortion clinic.' Oh, my God, you're in *Teenage Brides of Christ*."

He got up very quickly and sat down next to me. *Teenage Brides* had been my first movie, a low-budget sickie about a crazed former altar boy knocking off the wayward novitiates at a Dallas convent. I played a CCD leader tempted by the impure Sister Bernadette. We both ended up pitchforked. Trevor loved the film. I introduced myself. "Alex Young. Hi."

"I'm—" He was cut off when Risa's assistant peeked in.

"Trevor Renado," she announced.

"Don't go away," Trevor told me. He got up, still shaking my hand.

We became best friends for a few weeks and had a torrid micro-romance that ended when he started hitting the club scene with a chiseled airhead from a Janet Jackson video. I felt like dog shit only briefly, realizing that Trevor's zany and energetic hunkiness didn't come à la carte. His entrée-size middle-school-level emotional immaturity was the real staple of the menu. Not to mention every time we wrestled shirtless on the apartment floor or achieved a record combined total of nine safe orgasms in an eight-hour period or I discovered a hickey in some outlandish place, I felt like I was cheating on Nick. Talk about emotional maturity.

We remained in contact just enough for it not to seem totally prickish of him to ask me for a ride to the airport a couple of months ago. I was glad to reciprocate the imposition. "Hi, Trevor." I couldn't believe he was wearing one of those one-piece tank top–gym shorts unitard numbers. Sans underwear, too, from the way things were hanging up front.

"Good morning!" He took the Coke from me. "That's not a very fortifying breakfast." He handed me a bag. Croissants, orange juice, little containers of butter and strawberry jam.

"Hey, thanks."

"You can eat in the car," he said, grabbing my flight bag and sliding down the banister. "You look great, Alex."

We walked down to the street and got in his Miata. He was in a real chatty mood. "International Male is sending me to Rio for the spring catalog shoot. I'm real excited. . . . Have you seen those Kristen Bjorn videos? Yeeow! I'm going to be on *The Bold and the Beautiful* in two weeks. Are you still on *Hearts*?" He pulled into the thickening morning traffic on Sunset.

I finished a croissant and carefully wiped my fingers and the corners of my mouth with a moist towelette. "Haven't you seen it lately?" I enjoyed toying with him.

"No . . . I've been kind of busy. I'm sorry," he offered, looking at me with this wide-eyed expression and coy smile more suitable for the Gish sisters, or others similarly less buffed.

"Actually, they just put me under contract."

Trevor choked off the Divinyls and gaped at me. "Are you joking?"

"No," I said, grinning in spite of my affected detachment. "Three years."

"That's amazing," Trevor said. Not *that* amazing, you little tramp. "How much?"

"Thirteen fifty a show."

"That is *soooo* great. And you're playing that wonderful psychopathic character. And you have your own dressing room and get to make all those personal appearances. . . . Yeeow! . . . So what are you going to be doing in Texas?" Muscles bulged as he whipped the car down the 10.

"Relaxing mostly. Hanging out. Visiting friends."

"Nick, too?"

I looked at him, genuinely surprised. He glanced at me, now expressionless behind Ray-Bans.

"I don't know," I said. "Why?"

He got a little defensive. "I don't know . . . it just seems pointless for you to get embroiled in that again. He's still with What's-His-Face, isn't he?"

"I don't know. Maybe not."

"Did he tell you they broke up?"

"Trevor, I've barely spoken to him in almost a year. I'm not making this trip to see Nick."

Trevor popped in a cassette. An obscure Book of Love remix started rocking. It was a tape I'd made for him a long time ago. "Good," he said. "Because you have a hell of a lot more going for you now than he deserves." He'd never met Nick, of course, but hated him. Not that it was now or ever had been any of his fucking business.

We overtook one of those family truckster minibus suburban torpedoes. It had Utah plates and lots of bumper stickers: MOM'S TAXI, WE SUPPORT PROVO'S FINEST. Plus a hot-looking Bart Simpson license plate frame. As we passed it, a pubescent chick with a goony grin waved at Trevor while her sister or cousin or lucky best friend slapped her shoulder and giggled and stared. Trevor slid the strap of his unitard over his left shoulder, revealing an erect nipple. He licked his lips lasciviously while the girls went berserk. Mom's Taxi put on speed. A boy about eight years old was jumping around in the back window, and when they moved in front of us, the little scamp shoved his bare ass against the Saf-T-Glass.

"Goddamn kids!" Trevor snarled. He sped past them, flipping the whole family off.

"You're really a scream," I said.

He flashed me a sand 'n' surf smile. "If you have a week off, maybe you can come to Rio with me."

"Yeah, maybe." I was politely aloof, tastefully unexcited. I filed the idea away for future consideration.

We hit the airport. Trevor pulled into a red zone. "I'll pop the trunk," he told me.

"Thanks, Trevor."

"I hope you have a great trip." He put one of his big hands over one of my smaller yet normal-size ones. Then he leaned over and kissed me on the mouth. I didn't exactly protest.

"The top's down," I reminded him.

"That's okay. You're not a star yet, you know."

"I am, too." I got out and hoisted my bag out of the trunk. He took off, waving, in a cloud of disco.

The plane was full. Luckily I had an aisle seat. A couple in their fifties separated me from the window. The husband had his hat, a Tom Clancy novel and a Zip-loc bag of pistachio nuts on my seat. He moved them when I showed up but didn't seem too damn happy about it. I had just squeezed myself in and was trying to slide my legs under the seat in front of me when the wife reached across her husband and accosted me. "Hi! We're Buzz and Bernice, from China Grove, Texas." The husband, Buzz, I presumed, grunted. I introduced myself. They asked me what I did and I told them I was studying to be an astronomer.

We headed down the runway. I pulled out a pack of spearmint gum and offered Buzz a stick. This did the trick. Now we were pals. I looked past Bernice as L.A. dropped into a flat urban stain against the Pacific. I had kept a promise to myself, that I wouldn't return home until I was a success. I wondered how much fortune and fame it would take for me to want to confront my most significant failure.

November 1989

If I had decided to go home to take a nap or had felt like hanging out at the Fine Arts Library instead of the Undergraduate, or if I had taken one minute to get a drink of water or had chosen another study table, or if the Jansport backpack on that table hadn't been unzipped and resting at the right angle, it never would have happened. It was the most randomly perfect alliance of cosmic variables that I could ever hope to be a part of.

The floor was pretty deserted as I pulled the complete works of Voltaire from the stacks and carried it over to a table that was vacant except for a navy-blue backpack. It was open. As I walked past, something inside caught my eye. It was about a half inch of magazine cover that seemed to feature the unmistakable tarty smirk of porn star Joey Stefano. I glanced around, intrigued. Nobody. Still keeping watch, I slid two fingers into the backpack and propped up the magazine. It was upside down, but easy to identify—the latest issue of *Jock*. I snatched my hand away as if scalded. The contents of the backpack shifted forward and a red folder popped out. *Nicholas Miller* was written on the upper right-hand corner. I quickly pushed everything back in, then sat down two chairs away as the cutest guy I'd ever seen stepped up to the table.

He was so dreamy all I could do was try not to stare, my brain so paralyzed it did not occur to me that it was his backpack and, by simple deductive logic, his copy of *Jock*. His hair was almost black. A dusting of five o'clock shadow made me wonder how it would feel to have that chiseled jaw rubbing against my ear while those muscled, hairy arms encircled my lean, blond torso. I shuddered. We made eye contact. "Hi," he said, in a deep, honey-smooth man's voice. He picked up his backpack, smiled pleasantly and walked out. I watched his ass move under Structure jeans. Nicholas Miller. I stared stupidly down at Voltaire. It was going to be a long night.

There were a couple of Nick Millers in the UT directory, but only one Nicholas, who was a third-year law student. I copied his phone number, then hit the yearbooks. Last year's *Peregrinus*, the law school annual, featured him on two separate pages. His individual second-year student head shot was mighty cute, but not as cute as the Human Rights Activist Committee portrait. He stood on the far left of the group, which I knew had a pretty gay agenda, not exactly smiling, but looking kind of amused and almost serene, except for those penetrating eyes. I closed the book and tried to snap out of it.

This was way out of character for me, the cute blond smart ass who went to the Bonham Exchange in San Antonio and danced wildly to Erasure but stuck real close to his female clubbing friends and never reciprocated male eye contact. The kid who'd been having locker-room fantasies since he was seven and spent high school jacking off to three or four chapters of Nancy Friday's *Men In Love* and a couple of strategically hidden *Playgirl* special editions. The sensitive and lonely twenty-one-year-old virgin so terrified of being just another stereotypical drama fag he had the romantic life of a lawn jockey.

"Hello?"

"Nicholas?" I asked. It was two weeks later. Things had not been going well. I had a crummy supporting role in the department's big fall production of *Measure for Measure* and had been recently chastised by the petulant grad-student director for not being "innovative" enough. I wanted to ask him if wearing that same Antioch College sweatshirt every fucking day of rehearsal and pronouncing every other word with a British accent made him an expert on innovation, but I instead bottled up my frustration and so was doomed to suffer further stress. Also, my dad had been attacked and beaten up in his office by one of the rich coke-addict patients he counseled at an exclusive rehab center, necessitating a fast drive south to San Antonio, where Dad was resting comfortably in between bouts of indignant rage. And to top things off, the swim team member who lived in the apartment across from mine finally installed window shades.

"Hold on. I'll get him," some guy said.

I was lying on my stomach in bed, gripping the phone so hard my knuckles were white. An eternity . . . then: "Hi, this is Nick."

"Hi, Nick. This is Alex Young. We met at Human Rights Activists. You may not remember me . . ."

"No," Nick cut in. "The name sounds familiar . . . Alex Young . . ."

"Anyway, I'm thinking of going to law school and I was hoping we could meet and I could talk to you about it." I held my breath.

"Sure," he said. He sounded real nice but butch. "When's a good time for you?" Today. This minute. Get over here right now.

"Maybe we could meet for dinner," I suggested, not innocently. "Friday night?" It was now Sunday.

Nick said, "Let me check. . . . That sounds fine. I'll call you later to firm it up."

He took my number. I hung up, incredulous. I had a date with a gorgeous man. I grabbed *Bananarama* and went to the gym, where I hit all major muscle groups. Just in case.

○   ○   ○

I went to the Measurement and Evaluation Center at UT and picked up a Law Services Bulletin and filled out the registration. I had been toying intermittently with the idea of selling out my acting talents to the courtroom since my humorous monologue from *Little Murders* had bombed at district competition in tenth grade, so I didn't feel like a complete liar. I studied the bulletin on the shuttle bus and did the practice test backstage at rehearsal. Even actually taking the LSAT would be worth it to get to know Nick. I imagined the study dates I could look forward to, with the emphasis on stud.

Wednesday morning, the phone rang. I snatched it up, a shag carpet of sleep still stapled to my head. "Hello?"

"Alex? It's Nick Miller. I woke you up, and don't tell me I didn't."

He sounded like a forest ranger in some comforting children's safety film. "Hi, Nick," I said, instantly wide awake and sporting a bone-stiff erection. "I have to get up in ten minutes so it's okay."

"Well, good. I wanted to catch you before you left for class so we could firm up Friday night."

I'll give you firm, Mister. "Do you want to come by around six-thirty?" I asked.

My stomach was in knots. I flicked my eyes down at the massive amount of food I had ordered, then quickly back up to meet Nick's. He was telling me about this psychotic professor he'd had his first year of law school. My mouth was on automatic pilot, smiling, asking pertinent questions, while my brain luxuriated in sensory overload.

I drank in his deep Texas voice and wondered what it would sound like in a low whisper. I stared at his incredibly sensual lips and had never wanted to kiss anyone more in my life. I watched the tendons in his hand as he cut his chicken-fried steak and imagined the gentle pressure of that hand on my shoulder, on my thigh. I couldn't eat another bite. My digestive system had been sabotaged by lust.

He asked me if I wanted to be a movie star. I told him about how I'd always loved acting, the plays I'd been in—what

I'd said a thousand times to everyone I'd ever met; this spiel was the only link between the grind of my daily existence and the reality of this amazing fantasy dinner.

He didn't bring up Human Rights Activists and neither did I. We talked about law school more. "It's such an all-consuming thing," he said, "especially that first year. It can be pretty rough if you have a girlfriend "

Oh, my God, was this it? Was he wondering if I was? Hoping there was no food on my face, I looked straight at him and said, "I don't have a girlfriend."

He took a bite. Was I expecting him to say, "That's good to hear"? We continued to chat, although dinner was rapidly drawing to a close. I had to make a move.

"Do you have plans for later tonight?" I asked.

"I'm seeing a movie at ten with my roommate and some friends." I smiled expectantly, thinking he would invite me, while simultaneously feeling my gut free-fall at the mention of the word "roommate." What were the chances he lived with a demure Hindu girl? He didn't ask me to join them. We left the restaurant, but hope sprang again when we got to my apartment and he suggested we go inside.

I made White Russians and showed him my video collection, hoping the presence of *Pink Flamingos* and *My Beautiful Laundrette* would tip him off. He remarked politely on everything then asked to use the phone. I pretended to retrieve a notebook while I peeked over his shoulder. He dialed his own number.

"Hi, how y'doin'? I'm still over at Alex's. . . . We've still got plenty of time. . . . Barney, it's only a few minutes away. . . . Okay. Bye." He hung up.

"Out of time?" I asked, knowing damn well he was.

"Afraid so, Alex," he said, clapping me on the shoulder. I resisted the urge to place my hand over his. "I did enjoy talking to you, though. Hope I didn't scare you away from law school. It's really not so bad. Especially for a bright guy like you." He headed for the door.

"Nick?"

"Yeah?"

"Let's do something again really soon."

"You got it." Then he was gone.

I was shocked at how suddenly crushing loneliness descended upon me. Desperate for companionship, I picked up the phone and left messages for four or five friends who were out having a good time somewhere. I sat backward in the chair Nick had just vacated. It smelled like him . . . this musky floral fragrance that could have been cologne or shampoo or maybe some body lotion he smoothed over his hairy, naked torso after stepping out of a steaming hot shower. I pressed my face against the upholstery and breathed him in.

Barney? Nobody was named Barney. Except Barney Rubble.

Dear Alexander,
I knitted you this sweater because you are so cold-hearted (ha-ha). I hope you like reindeers. I do. (My cat is even named Rudolph!) If the sweater doesn't fit, please give it to Cary Rietta, who I think is shorter.
Love,
Narda Hudson
Duluth, MN

San Antonio, where folks know what picante sauce should taste like, is a charming potpourri of historic Tex-Mex culture, right-wing religious zealotry and sleek suburban development. Its perfect representational image is a vacation Bible-school class enjoying lunch at The Sombrero Rosa, a pink adobe sombrero-shaped restaurant (equipped with drive-through capability) located smack-dab on Walzem Road.

We ate their Family Fajita Feast at home while I tried to explain to my dad that a three-year soap contract meant four thirteen-week and four twenty-six-week option cycles—the show's option.

"That's fucked," he said.

"It's standard," I told him, stuffing my face.

"What's to stop them from canning you every thirteen weeks?" Dad got right to the point, refreshingly.

My mother intervened. "They're not going to can him. If

you were watching the show, you'd see they're setting up a huge plot line for him."

"Hey," my father protested, "I watch the show. I saw the one where you tricked that blond bitch into drinking the poisoned shake."

The phone rang. My mom got up and answered it. For me. It had to be Sara. Or that girl Juliana. What if it was Nick? Shit! I couldn't believe I hadn't rehearsed anything to say to him. It had been eight months since I last talked to him. How the hell did he expect us to jabber on about my life as if we were nothing but a couple out-of-touch college buds? But what if he was trying to reach out to me? What if—

It was Sara.

"There she is. Juliana Butts." Sara pointed to a plain blonde with sweeping winged bangs and a dreamy smile. We were sitting on the rooftop deck outside Sara's apartment, the top floor of a converted Victorian house near Trinity University.

Like all the girls in the full-color senior section, Juliana was wearing one of those idiotic graduation wraps and displaying ample cleavage, I might add. Sara and I were not featured—she had gotten an alternative hairstyle at Curl Up And Dye the week before senior pictures and her mother had hysterically forbidden her to appear in the yearbook. We skipped school together that day and saw a triple feature downtown at the rat-and-gang-infested Aztec Theatre.

"I really don't remember her at all," I said. The night air was warm and humid, even though it was already October.

"I do," Sara said. "She was in my homeroom ninth and tenth. She was really into Duran Duran. She was always writing their names on the sides of her tennis shoes and notebook covers and stuff."

"You used to do the same thing."

"Yeah, but it was The Smiths. Big difference. So, are you going to call her?"

"No," I said. "I wrote to her four times and sent her a picture and that's enough."

"Whoa," she said, stroking my back obsequiously. "I forgot how important you are."

I took her arms and squeezed them to her sides, laughing a little. "I don't think I'm being an asshole. Am I?"

"Well . . ."

"Okay. I'll call her. But if I have to do anything with her you have to come and pretend to be my luv-uh."

"Wait a minute."

"Hey!" I interjected with mock spontaneity. "Nick said he talked to you." Sara squirmed away and went into the kitchen to load up a plate of tollhouse cookies.

"Yeah, he called me last weekend. I guess he's been watching you on *Hearts Crossing*. I told him when you'd be here. Is that okay?"

I nodded. "Did he say he wanted to see me?"

She poured me a glass of milk. "Yeah, I think so. He said something really vague about all of us getting together. You know Nick. He's not going to tell me or anyone what he's feeling. But, Alex, I don't think you can blame him for wanting to be your friend. He sounded so proud of you. We all are, y'know?"

"I'm so incredibly excited about this job, Sara. I love it."

"Then cheer the hell up."

My mouth popped open to protest, but she knew me really, really well. "Look, Alex, I know you need more than success and money and being a celebrity guest on the charity version of *Family Feud* to make you happy. You need romance. So do I. So does everybody. But I just don't think it's going to be with Nick. And if seeing him is going to be that hard for you, then fuck it. Let's not go to Austin."

"Okay," I said. "You and I can hang out downtown instead. I could pick you up at your office."

"You mean my cubicle."

"The Editorial Coordinator doesn't get her own suite?" I teased.

"I'm lucky to get one or two paychecks a month. No, really, the magazine's doing fine." She worked for *Paseo del Rio*, a bi-monthly targeting San Antonio's "hip, culturally in-tune, 21 to

47-year-old lifestyle" that stunned everyone a year ago by putting a nude Henry Cisneros (except for strategically placed bandolier and sombrero) on its first cover and had been serving up irreverent restaurant and nightlife critiques, local news and features ever since. "They keep promising me my own column. But I'm already in it a lot. Everyone was on vacation so I ended up with four things in the August issue."

"You'll be running it a year from now."

"I just got the assignment of editing the calendar—you know, the huge center section of every esoteric event between Austin and Corpus—so I guess they trust me. It's a fun place to work. The only person over thirty-five is Maxine the receptionist, who's about eighty. Next time Richard leaves town, I'm going to take her out to pick up men."

"Are you working on anything big right now?"

"A feature about sexual compulsives. By the way, are you available for an interview?"

I gasped. "Why you—"

The phone rang. I grabbed it. "Sara Richardson."

"This isn't Sara." It was Nick. "How are ya, Mr. Alex?"

"Okay . . . great, Nick." I looked beseechingly at Sara. She raised both hands in surrender and shook her head. She hadn't planned this.

"Your mom told me you were over here. Hope I'm not interrupting anything."

"No," I told him. "We're just catching up on a lot of stuff."

"You'll be coming up here before too long, won't you?"

I was helpless. "Yes, we're planning on it."

"I'm finishing up a big project tomorrow," he said. I heard pages riffling as he looked through his Daytimer. "How about we get together for dinner the day after that?"

"Okay," I said. "Do you want to meet at your office?"

Sara clasped her brow, giving up on me. I couldn't help smiling. "Is six o'clock good for you?" Nick asked.

"Yeah."

"Congratulations on your big break. I'm looking forward to seeing you. Bye bye."

"Bye."

$$\boxed{\text{December 1989}}$$

By the sixth week of our acquaintance, Nick was on my brain every waking second. We'd gotten together exactly once since our first "date"—an arty movie followed by a long, leisurely dinner, then a three-hour chat at my place that avoided any mention of sexual orientation, his relationship with his roommate, Barney, or physical urges of any kind. But when Nick left at 2:00 a.m. I knew the meaning of male bonding.

He wanted to see *Measure for Measure*. I comped him closing night, thrilled that the shitty production was over and that he was sitting alone in the audience watching me. My semester was at an end. The only final exam I had was the one tonight, after the play. And if I passed, it would mean graduation from virginity. And of course I'd been boning up for it a long, long time.

I bowed out of the cast party and met Nick in the lobby of

the B. Iden Payne Theatre. "Bra-vo," he grinned, shaking my hand vigorously. Electricity.

"Don't tell me you weren't bored out of your mind," I said, as we walked across the shuttle bus circle to Longhorn Stadium and the privacy of his car.

"No," Nick insisted. "It was interesting. I'd rather watch Shakespeare than read it any day."

"And I'd rather have my flesh shredded by wolverines than be involved in such a pretentious mess again." He laughed and looked at me with what I hoped was pure fondness.

We went back to my apartment and ate the cake Sara and her roommate Valerie had made me. We talked about Christmas and I wanted to give him a present, but knew how pitiful *that* would look if he rejected me later.

I got up and brought the dishes to the kitchen. As I rinsed them, he brushed behind me and for a second I expected to feel his arms encircle my waist and those pouty Greco-Roman lips on my neck. But he was only going to the refrigerator for more milk.

I followed him into the dimly lit living room. "That was some great cake," Nick said.

I couldn't take it anymore. The line I'd rehearsed for days came spilling out. "Nick," I said, "I'm so glad we became friends, and I don't want to do anything to screw that up. But I'm powerfully attracted to you, and I'm confused, because I don't exactly know how to deal with it."

Dead silence. But he never took his eyes off me. Please please please, let me get what I want. "That's very flattering, Alex. I *am* attracted to you, very much, but I'm in a relationship right now, and I can't do anything to jeopardize that."

I bet you say that to all the boys. "That's what I was afraid of."

He wasn't finished. "And I think if we slept together, it would make things really difficult for you and me."

The fact that he saw this as even a possibility pumped me full of an uneasy mixture of pride, wonder and despair. He didn't make it any easier with his next question: "So . . ." he began, looking at the floor and smiling in a cute, self-conscious way I'd never seen before, "what was your first experience with another guy?" I didn't say anything and he finally looked up at me, eyes dancing.

"I've never had that kind of experience," I practically stammered. His expression subtly softened, like he thought he'd embarrassed me. Nothing could be further from the truth—I was happy to let him know I was fresh, unmolested and 100 percent safe. What about Nick? I asked him.

"That was a real long time ago," he said, like some great-uncle launching into a story about voting for one of the Roosevelts. He settled back in his chair and clasped his hands behind his head, the short sleeves of his green rugby shirt pulling back to reveal hard triceps and tufts of dark underarm hair. "The summer I graduated from high school this old friend of my mom's moved in down the street. And she had a boy who was a year younger than me. Blond, massively cute. Tennis player. Me and my dad helped them move in and the kid and I started talking about the high school and what to do in town and where to hang out and all—not that I was ever any kind of social butterfly. We sorta became friends and went out and messed around in his brand-new truck and one day we ended up a ways out of town and hiked over to this quarry. And he asked me if I wanted to go swimming and before I knew it, he was taking off all his clothes." Between his Amarillo baritone and the *Penthouse Forum* spiel, I was becoming inexorably turned on. Transfixed, I waited for him to continue.

"So we went skinny-dipping at the old swimming hole. We swam out to some rocks sticking up in the middle and he just stretched out and relaxed. Even though that water was awful cold, it was easy to see he was hung like a horse."

My mouth popped open all on its own. He smiled slightly and raised his eyebrows, nodding. "I crawled up there on that rock and tried to relax myself but I got all excited. And he reached over and just helped himself."

This was unbelievable. Not the story—I bought every word of that. It was incredible that after I'd made a pass—well, a swipe, anyway—at him, he felt comfortable enough to sit three feet across from me and use expressions like "all excited" and "hung like a horse" while confessing a mouthful like that. Christ Almighty. My brain was still rewinding and scanning and freeze-framing what he'd just told me, only it was I who splashed into the quarry naked and watched Nick strip, the cold water barely keeping my raging erection in check. And it was me lying next to him on the sun-warmed rocks until I sat up and lifted Nick's robust penis from his stomach and began to caress it, his balls splayed beneath my other fist as I gripped—

I checked in long enough to ask, "So what happened?"

"Not a lot. We got together a couple more times and I thought I was in love and then he decided he didn't want us to be friends anymore." For two seconds, his face looked like it must have looked on whatever sweltering West Texas day he found this out. I wanted to touch him. It was out of the question.

So I said, "He was an idiot."

Nick smiled and nodded. Then he laughed. "So, all those pretty actors and you never . . . ?"

"No," I told him. Then, playing up the tender vulnerability angle: "I guess I was waiting for the perfect guy."

"Aw, Alex," he said, clapping me on the shoulder. I nearly squealed like a girl. "You're a hot-lookin' fella . . . you won't have any problem finding someone."

There was nothing to say to this, so I changed the subject. Nick suggested having more cake. I cut him another slice, but my appetite had been drowned in queasy disappointment. Somehow we started talking about Barney, and he told me how they met while living at the same co-op and "found out about each other" pretty quick and had been together four years. I felt like an idiot. He told me how much I'd like Barney—we had real similar tastes. Obviously.

The walk over to my front door was especially hard. There would be no good night kiss, no exchange of whispered intimacies. I'd never see him again. It would be too awkward, too unfair to both of us. He put one hand on the knob—the doorknob, that is—then said, "Thanks for the play. And the cake. And the company. I had a real good time." I believed him. "Have a merry Christmas. I'll talk to you soon."

I nodded, managing to get out a fairly friendly, "Goodbye,

Nick" before shutting the door and starting to weep. Big, wrack-
ing, hopeless sobs from the most sensitive depths of an artist's
soul. I lurched over to Nick's chair, but my nose was running
and I couldn't even enjoy one final fragrance sample. I went into
my room. Had I actually believed Nick and I were going to share
this bed? I couldn't bring myself to crawl between those crisp
and, yes, damnit, freshly laundered sheets alone, so I did a fast
packing job, hopped in my car and headed for San Antonio. I
cranked up a techno-pump collection of dance mixes to keep me
cheery and wide awake, but ended up listening to *Tusk*, realizing
for the first time what a heartbreakingly insightful poetess Stevie
Nicks really was.

I spent the week before Christmas acting like I was the same
person my family and friends had deposited in Austin at the
beginning of the semester. The main topic at home was the
lawsuit my battered, bitter dad was filing against the corporate
"douche bag" who'd snuck up behind him at his office at Shady
River Recovery Clinic, put Dad in a chokehold and started kicking the shit out of him. All while under the influence of some
très contraband coke laced with angel dust.

I thought unceasingly of Nick. Usually this took the form
of abstract daydreams—I'd constantly blank out and imagine he
was holding me, that nothing existed but the warmth and
strength of his arms and his face (eyes closed, dreamy lips parted
as they nuzzled my neck and cheek) and his beautiful hairy chest,
which I'd been able to infer from his open collar the last night
I'd seen him. Songs by Tracy Chapman and Journey attained
new heights of relevance; every happy couple I saw on TV or
in the street or in a restaurant were people oblivious to the dam-
nation of romantic rejection; the rest of my life, spent never
knowing true love, previewed continuously in the obsessive cinema of my brain. Realizing how much better off I was in San
Antonio, on vacation and away from it all, I made a titanic effort
to snap out of it and have a holly jolly Christmas.

December 27 I was back in Austin, which isn't exactly a
hopping town between semesters. I was auditioning for *Vampire
Lesbians of Sodom* and *Psycho Beach Party* at Capitol City Playhouse that night. I really, really wanted a big part. Not only was

Charles Busch my absolute favorite, but I'd purposely been borderline shitty at the University drama department's auditions a few weeks earlier so no one would cast me in a school show next semester and create a conflict. I knew the Busch plays backward and forward and planned to be hilarious.

As soon as I unlocked my apartment, I knew my hasty departure had been a mistake. Plates and forks sat in the sink, crumby, frosting-smeared remnants of my aborted lovefest. There was Nick's glass, the only property of mine his lips would ever touch. I plugged the sink, ran the hot water and glanced at the answering machine. I had one message. It was Nick.

"How you doin', Mr. Alex Young? It's Nicholas Miller. I wanted to see how your holidays were going. I'll be back in town on the twenty-eighth and I should have lots of free time to get together. Maybe you can come over for dinner or something. I'll talk to you soon." Click. The machine's robo-matron voice revealed that this message had come in at 9:37 Christmas night.

He was thinking about me enough to call from Amarillo on *Christmas*? I tried to reason through this. The worst-case scenario was that he really wanted me to be friends with him and Barney—hence the dinner suggestion. Seeing them together in their natural habitat would reinforce the reality of the situation in a firm yet gentle manner. Fine. Or . . . maybe he saw something in me one of those nights, a sweet, well-muscled innocence, a spark of mutual attraction, an intangible, powerful quality he didn't want to pass up too quickly. But even if it was some cheap hybrid of flattery and pity that prompted the call, I was going to be at my absolute best for Nick.

I mean, really. Does somebody who rejected you when you came on to them like a sledgehammer usually want to pal around together the next week? I certainly had no experience to draw from, but I didn't think so. Sara would know. It was time to confirm what she'd probably always suspected about my sexual orientation. I imagined us discussing Nick over a drum of Ben & Jerry's cookie-dough ice cream, and wished she wasn't on a goddamn ski trip.

I hit the gym and pumped up for my audition. Then I went down to the theater. I was hilarious, bouncing off the walls, *and* wearing a slutty tank top. They kept me there four hours, usually a good sign.

The next day, I prowled the apartment like a caged beast waiting for the phone to ring. There was no reason for me to expect Nick would call the minute (or even the day) he got back into town, but I was feeling hyper and positive and everything seemed possible.

The Cap City director phoned to schedule a callback. He told me I'd definitely be in the show, he just wasn't sure which role. Starcat Starcat Starcat, I telepathed into the receiver. I'd be happy with whatever I got in *Vampire Lesbians. Psycho Beach Party* was the real apple of my eye. An outrageous cross-pollination of *Gidget* and *Marnie* about a surfer chick with a dominatrix alter ego, it was the funniest of Busch's wacky plays, and the role of Starcat, the brainy beach hunk, was perfect for me. Surely they knew that. Wait a minute . . . what if I had been *too* campy, and they were planning to cast me in one of the female roles? It could happen. I squelched the thought and packed my gym bag for a blistering, masculine torso workout. I was closing the door behind me when the phone rang. I grabbed it just before the machine could. Nick was calling from the snotty law firm where he clerked—he'd driven into town that morning and invited me over for dinner with him and Barney and "a friend of ours" the next evening. I said sure.

At the gym, I watched a few really attractive guys and thought that any of them could be Barney. The duplex he and Nick shared was nearby—it made sense that he'd want to be flexed and hard to welcome his handsome lover home after a long day at the office. I was too tired and depressed after a grueling ninety minutes to worry about getting aroused sharing the showers with one of the Barney prototypes, a sandy-haired stud best displayed bending over lathering his big feet, perfect white ass taut and spread, making it much easier to picture him romping naked with Nick in their lovenest which, during the past two months, I'd slowly driven by five or six times just to torment myself.

I made up my mind to be friends with them. It was self-destructive to believe Nick had anything else in mind. After all, our little dinner foursome with their "friend" seemed like a setup. What the hell—I had my career. I'd get over my first crush gracefully and come out of it with two new friends and positive feelings about my sexuality. I really believed this. I went to Texas French Bread and bought a dozen cookies, then picked up a bottle of champagne and a couple of videos. What a guest. I drove over to Nick and Barney's, arriving precisely at 6:30.

I rapped on their door, assertive, confident. Dry and secure. Lights, voices. Their friend answered. Thanks a lot, Nick. He was tall but dumpy, with a crow's nest of bright red hair, shapeless clothes, and a face that could be tactfully described as bovine.

"Hi!" I said, all smiles.

"Hi," he said, quickly checking me over. The nerve. I went in and there was Nick, looking wonderful in jeans and a paisley shirt.

"What's up, Alex?" He had such a great smile. "Like you to meet my roommate, Barney Gagnon."

I was bracing myself for Barney's entrance when the red-headed dork stuck out his hand and I shook it and realized the horrifying truth. Before I could scream, Barney had left for the kitchen, mumbling something about Cokes.

"How's it going, Glamourpuss?" Nick kind of swiped at my bicep with his fist. "I guess congratulations are in order."

I was spacing. "For what?"

"Your big part in *Lesbo Beach Sodomy*," he laughed. "I promise I'll buy a ticket. Whatta you got there?"

I handed over my peace offerings and started to compliment the thrifty-hip decor when Barney came back in with two six-teen-ounce bottles of Coke. He sucked on one, then passed the other to me.

"Thanks," I said.

"You're welcome." He looked at Nick. "Oh, did you want one?"

"That's okay," said Nick, ever chipper. "I can get it myself."

"So . . ." I said to Barney, "are you going to UT, too?"

"I'm in my second year of the MBA program." Fascinating. Nick came back in. "Why don't we all have a seat?" he suggested. We all glanced at the furniture, mentally choreographing this maneuver. Luckily, a knock at the door saved us from going through with it.

"That must be Pete," Barney said and answered the door. I was introduced to a rail-thin, not-bad-looking Mexican guy with gold hoops in his ears and a ridiculous goatee.

My little matchmaking theory was quickly invalidated— Barney and Pete began a private conversation that continued out the door, into the car, and at the restaurant (Hut's, a retro-50s diner downtown). Pete and Nick sat on one side of the table, with Barney and me opposite them. It was a loud weekend crowd—Nick and I could barely hear Pete and Barney. Of course, they couldn't hear us, either. Not that anything incriminating was said or nonverbally communicated, although I had to constantly make sure I wasn't staring at Nick too dreamily.

Soon we were back at their house, where Nick broke out the cookies and we achieved the semblance of a four-way chat. The vibes were so completely unlike what I'd expected. Nick and Barney behaved like they barely knew each other. Were they acting so detached because they were uncomfortable in front of company? You'd think after four years they wouldn't feel the need to suppress natural loving chemistry and affection, especially in front of a couple of fags like myself and Petey-boy.

The evening got murkier when we cleared away the cookie plates and Barney announced he and Pete were going to take a walk. They threw on their jackets and left. What the hell was going on? I decided to just be grateful to be left alone with Nick.

"Feel like a movie?" he asked.

How about *Inch By Inch*? We can act it out right here on the couch. "Sure," I chirped.

He put in one of my selections, *Lair of the White Worm*, then sat down next to me on the futon couch. He got into the movie right away, relaxing for the first time all night. I'd seen the film enough times to fake involvement despite the distraction of being six inches from him. All I could think of was how easy it would have been to snuggle in close. I wanted to lie against him, to take his hand in mine and place it under my shirt and let every obstacle between us dissolve. . . .

Nick laughed at Amanda Donohoe. I had a hard-on. I checked my jeans. Not too obvious. I couldn't help it—I shifted my position slightly toward Nick. We both looked toward the porch area. Barney and Pete were goofing off outside. Nick zapped the movie to pause and said, "I think I'll put on a pot of tea. Want some?"

I politely declined. I tried to hear what was going on outside. Nick came back and we watched more of the movie, but it wasn't the same. He kept glancing at the door. Barney and Pete finally came in. Pete said he had to get up early to open the mall record store and split. Nick brought Barney a steaming cup. "I made you some tea," he said, handing it over. Barney chewed and swallowed two dollars' worth of cookies and took a sip.

"It's not strong enough," he bitched. "Didn't you let it steep?"

"Sorry about that," Nick said, visibly disappointed. I wanted to punch Barney's ungrateful mutt face.

Suddenly, I was glad that Barney had been so standoffish. I sized him up from my vantage point on the couch next to Nick as *Lair* galloped to its frantic conclusion: homely, sullen, socially inept, apparently quite resentful of me for no damn reason at all. Was I too cute and upbeat for Nick to be friends with? Or did Barney always act this way? After rewinding the video, I said my friendliest goodnight to Barney then asked Nick, "Wanna walk me to my car?"

"Okay," he said. "Be right back, Barney." Barney grunted something and shuffled into the kitchen.

I walked as slowly as possible without seeming impaired, wanting to prolong this moment, knowing what I'd be feeling as I drove back to my empty apartment.

"Pete's a pretty nice fella," Nick said. "He's really more Barney's friend than mine."

"Yeah, I liked him," I agreed. "I didn't get much of a chance to talk to him, but he seemed really cool." A bit of a stretch. Whatever.

"They hadn't seen each other in a while. . . ." Like Nick really had to apologize to *me*. We were standing by my car. Of course a kiss was out of the question. Still, neither one of us was making a move to go our separate ways. "Will you be going back to San Antonio?" he asked.

"Yeah, right after the callback. My mom's planning a big New Year's dinner."

"That's how moms are."

"Nick, do you want to have dinner with me before school starts?" I had to add it: "Just the two of us?"

"I'll be looking forward to it," he smiled. Chills. Had I just made an indecent proposal? And had he not minded at all? It was all so confusing. A few things, however, were crystal-clear as I drove home through the deserted streets. Nick deserved better. I was crazy about him. And, as any MBA student will tell you, the customer's ability to compare and choose the best-quality goods and services for his particular needs is the corner-stone of our free-enterprise system.

Alex:
Please sign this poster for <u>Teenage Brides of Christ</u>, the movie in which I first became aware of your overpowering charisma & star-quality. Please send it back to me in the enclosed mailing tube.
Magickally yours,
Ray Lanville
Silverlake, CA

In high school, Sara worked part-time at The Gap with a girl named Karla who was always bopping around to KITY during her shifts and singing along with the power hits of the day, like Stacey Q's "Two of Hearts," the refrain of which she continually mis-chirped as "I'm easy, I'm easy!"

Sara was doing a dead-on impersonation of that particular blast from the past when I hung up the phone.

"I just couldn't tell him no."

She nodded sagely, eyes condescendingly slitted.

"What? So I'm never going to see him again?" I scoffed, so well-adjusted.

She grabbed a handful of her full-bodied raven hair and corralled it into a phony ponytail. "There was a time when you thought so," she said quietly.

"I know." I flashed back to the hideously lonely months after my first Christmas after graduation. I'd been enjoying infrequent but regular telephone calls from Nick since I relocated in June. It's true he never said he was planning on following me to Babylon-On-The-Pacific, but the combination of his curiosity about L.A. and boredom with his job (and Barney, one would have inevitably inferred), and my own surging optimism—my busy year had climaxed with a five-episode stint on *General Hospital* and two weeks in December on a major-studio action thriller—led me to assemble a scrapbook of enticing L.A. material plus a few issues of key publications (like the *Weekly* and *Planet Homo*), wrap it all up with *Myra Breckinridge* and Bruce Weber's *Bear Pond* and ship it to my friend Valerie to drop off at Nick's office for Christmas.

And that was it. I spent the holidays with my parents and some cousins on Maui, covertly beeping in to my machine for the message I imagined Nick just *had* to leave after thoroughly excavating his box of goodies. But he didn't call. Or write. Or take out an ad in the personals column of *The Village Voice*, which we both subscribed to.

It was over. I spent dozens of hours and hundreds of dollars on long distance calls to Sara nursing my broken heart. I wondered how close I'd come to Nick moving here and what had been the fatal spark that torched the bridge between us. My fling with Trevor started on Martin Luther King, Jr., Day and was dead by Valentine's. Afterward, I didn't even look at another guy for months—and God knows they're everywhere.

"When was the last time you talked to him?" she asked.

"June, remember? After my big blockbuster opened. For about six minutes." The whole damn world had called that week. The movie, about a serial killer policeman (Matt Dillon) who targets a physically challenged romance novelist (Winona Ryder), did $8 million its first three days. I played a bookstore clerk and had one good scene with Matt and another with Winona and Laurie Metcalf. "I know you think I didn't come back to Texas all this time because of him."

"Well, jeez, Alex, why else? You've been making good money practically since you got there and your schedule's been flexible until this soap thing. I can't *believe* you've been away from here for almost a year and a half." She took the last half a cookie from the plate and compressed it between her fingers before popping it into her mouth.

"I admit it. The idea of being so close to him without . . . being with him . . . really upset me. But I'm back. And you can see I'm okay. Phone calls, faxes, meetings, I can take it. He can put on a live sex show for us at the Chain Drive if he wants to. No problem."

She laughed and flicked a gooey crumb from her Bundeswehr tank top and looked exquisitely beautiful. "Shit," she said.

"You're gorgeous," I told her.

"Thanks. Now there's something I've been avoiding telling you because I didn't think you'd take it the right way." She picked up the plate and glasses and I followed her back into the kitchen, asphyxiating from curiosity. The CD player was shuffling *The Queen Is Dead*, the *Pretty in Pink* soundtrack and something by John Wesley Harding. We went into the living room and sat on Broyhill furniture she'd inherited.

"You're toying with me, Missy. And I won't have it," I snapped, Simonesque.

"I went out with Nick and Barney this summer. In August." I forced myself not to lunge forward. "It was totally by accident. I was in Austin for *Six Degrees of Separation* at the Paramount, covering the opening for *Paseo*, and I had three house seats and Valerie and Chuck were supposed to go with me. It was a big benefit for the county food bank. Like fifteen dollars a ticket. Then Chuck was called to Chicago at the last minute to solve some software crisis and Valerie decided to go with him for a romantic weekend. So I was up there on my own. Anyway, I'm in Waterloo Records and who do I see through the window but Nick? And he sees me and runs in and hugs me and everything—it'd been almost a year—and we're just standing there talking and then I look out the window again and there's Barney, staring at us like a big dildo. And Nick waves at him to come in—they'd been next door at Sparks getting cards—and he just stands there until it starts to get awkward and I ask Nick something just to, y'know, break the evil spell, and when we stop looking at Barney he comes in, and I'm as friendly as a girl from San Antonio can be and he acts autistic, even though I've hung out with the two of them twice since you moved to Hollywood, and I just feel sorry for Nick and ask them to come to the play."

I felt a little gross hanging on every word of such mundane gossip, so I excused myself and retrieved one more cookie and another glass of milk. Sara had a full-color soap mag photo of me affixed to her refrigerator with a rectangular magnet advertising *The Unholy Wife*, a fifties shocker starring Diana Dors. ("Half-Angel, Half-Devil! . . . She made him Half-A-Man!")

"So then what happened?" I asked, my expression expectant and bemused but nonobsessive.

"Nick says they're planning to see a dollar movie, but he'd rather go to *Six Degrees*. And Barney asks if I have passes and I tell him no, they're fifteen dollars but it's for a good cause, et cetera, and he kind of shakes his head at Nick, which really surprises me because I figured Barney must have heard of the play and that it had sex and a naked guy in it. So Nick looks torn and uncomfortable and I tell them I don't mind buying one of them a ticket and Nick says no and pulls Barney kind of to the side and they start to whisper this argument and I pretend to be really interested in the used CD rack, but I overhear Nick say, 'It's not *that* much money,' and realize that this is all about Barney being incredibly cheap." I nodded. "Then Nick says they'll go and I say great and Nick tells me they'll meet me in front of the theater. What I thought would happen is that Barney would stay home and pout and I'd get Nick alone, but when I got there, no such luck. Nick had changed into jeans and a really pretty shirt and looked massively cute—I know you didn't ask, I'm volunteering that information—but Barney was wearing the same shorts and old T-shirt, except he'd thrown on a Members Only jacket."

"Eeeeuw! And in August?"

"Well, it was kind of cool and cloudy. Anyway. We were in the lobby waiting for the house to open and Barney doesn't say one goddamn word except to mumble these monosyllabic responses whenever Nick tries to include him in the conversation. It's more than just being a quiet person. It's like Barney has this fun-draining aura. Depressing. He finally perks up at intermission and goes straight to the buffet table and *plants* himself there and starts wildly shoving hors d'oeuvres in his face. Nick goes to get us champagne and it's so easy to see how mortified he is. I mean, Barney was out of control. People were staring. So after the show we're talking about your Matt Dillon movie and the soap opera which he apparently does watch and I ask Nick if they want to come with me to Oilcan's for a little while, and he starts to say yes, then checks with Barney, and they end up going home because it was 'so late'—ten-thirty. I talked to a few theatah people and hit the road. And the whole way to S.A. I thought about their relationship and how unhealthy it is."

"Why did you not want to tell me?" I asked.

"Because what disturbed me about it is that the bottom line here *isn't* that Barney's a colossal dweeb or that they're so miserable together. It's that Nick, who I think is a wonderful man in a lot of ways, chooses to stay in it. This goes beyond feeling compassionate or sorry for someone—it's been years and years. Nick is like a co-dependent, if I'm allowed to use an Oprahism. What kind of bright, sexy guy would take *that* over this?" She indicated me with a sweeping hand motion à la Janice Pennington. "Nick has a problem with self-esteem or masochism or something. And that's not good enough for the likes of you."

I smiled. There was no way in hell I could tell her how good it was to hear how rotten things still were chez Miller. "Don't worry. I'm not going to get all pathetic and abusive during dinner to entice him away from Barney."

"There've gotta be some boys around here to introduce you to. I bet Richard knows a ton of cute gay guys from his job." Her current paramour was an associate curator at the art museum (and played in a band called Bubonic Pest that I would thankfully not be required to experience in concert). "Should we give Richie a call?"

"No! I haven't even met him."

"It's all right. He's seen you on TV."

"Thanks, but I'm really okay. Believe it or not, just being with my best friend in the universe is enough."

"Of *course* it is," she laughed. Then in a dopey ingenue's squeak: "Hope I can get the day off to drive up to Austin . . ."

"You'd just better."

March 1990

Despite my *Psycho Beach* obligations (rehearsals, extra gym hours, mandatory tanning-bed sessions) and horrendous courseload, I still found ample time to obsess about Nick. We'd been like Tom Sawyer and Huck Finn since the semester started—he came over to use my state-of-the-art laundry room, we rented videos, went to dinner, hung out with Sara. And never discussed Barney or why he was glaringly absent from all our platonic fun. The bottom line was that the nicest, sexiest, most genuine guy in the world was so eager to be with me he never refused my invitations. I had to be content with that for the time being.

Sara ("I haven't been without a boyfriend in six years") was a font of wisdom on the subject, and advised me to just be the best friend possible to Nick, so that when he became comfortable enough to let the chemistry kick in, it would seem like we'd been in a relationship all along. She also made amazing mashed potatoes and had driven over in a downpour to help me finalize a major dinner I was going to surprise Nick with.

The apartment smelled like a country kitchen. I'd been microwaving a turkey-breast roll for hours and now the twin aromas of cinnamon incense and tollhouse cookies wafted forth into the evening as well. I prepared carrots and poised them on the stove, ready to steam, as Sara pulverized, whipped and seasoned.

"How do I know when it's time for The Kiss?" I asked her. I sank a toothpick into the pan-cookie mass. It came out gooey. Five more minutes.

She started to set the table. "When he grabs you by the shoulders and plants one on you. That's how."

"I'm sure I'm going to have to make the first move," I told her, pulling out a couple of wineglasses, then deciding that was too gothic for milk or Coke. "I just don't know when."

"Wait as long as possible," she said. "You have absolutely nothing to lose. He knows you want him. So relax."

"That's easy for you to say. You're not the one who has to live like a monk."

"No, I certainly don't," she vamped. "In fact, Evan is due at my place in about twenty minutes. So I'm going to scram." She pecked my cheek. "Oh, I almost forgot." She reached into her bag and pulled out a little bouquet of Indian Paintbrushes wrapped in plastic.

"You didn't have to buy that . . ." I began, touched.

She filled a glass and popped the flowers in. "I didn't. I stole them from the little gazebo in front of my building." She placed it on the table. "Now everything's perfect."

"Except for Barney," I pouted.

"I'd like to know when was the last time *Barney* did something like this."

She opened the door to the sound of rain splatting on the terrace and running off the roof. "Good luck. Maybe there'll be a power failure." She hugged me. "Mmmmm, those muscles drive me wild." She nipped at my neck.

"Hey. None of that."

She took off. I barely had time to assemble the Stove Top Stuffing before Nick arrived.

"Hi!" I practically cheered. It was impossible for me to quell my enthusiasm around him.

"Something sure smells great." He smiled.

"Thanks," I said, "it's a new cologne. It's called Rotisserie."

He laughed. I scampered over to the kitchen to coordinate everything. Nick checked out the spread. "You went to way too much trouble."

"Please, it's nothing," I said, removing the turkey from the microwave. I made sure the cookies were out of sight. Nick came in.

"How can I help?" he asked.

I allowed myself a borderline flirtatious look. "Everything's under control. Would you like Coke or milk?"

"How about a Coke?"

I broke out the drinks while he carried two heaping plates of food to my magazine-perfect dinette. We sat down. Our knees immediately bumped together and Nick made no effort to move his. Jesus.

It did my heart good to see him dig into his dinner, which was superb. "This is really superb," he said. "It's like Thanksgiving all over again."

"I'm glad you like it. Make sure to save room for dessert." I increased the pressure of my leg against his a tiny fraction.

He got that sparkle in his eye and said, "What did you do?"

"You'll see."

He smiled at me with such spontaneous warmth I felt giddy. He should be the movie star, not me. Then I imagined the effect he'd have on a predominantly female jury and knew he'd chosen the right career.

"You're looking pretty tan," he remarked.

"Orange is more like it," I said. "I'm only doing it for professional purposes. It's really awful. I'm sure it's like soaking in pure cancer. And you do it with all your clothes off, so I don't have a tanline." Why had I said that? Now he was probably picturing me naked. Maybe that wasn't so bad, orange genitalia and all. "The rehearsals have been fantastic. They're already talking about maybe extending the play and we don't open for two weeks."

"We're going to have to really celebrate the big premiere," Nick said. "I promise you won't have to cook." He pushed his chair back. "Although you're very good at it. I better slow down or I won't have any room for dessert."

He loved the cookies, topped not coincidentally with his favorite ice cream flavor, white chocolate. We sat at the table a long time after we finished eating, talking about his job and *Twin Peaks* and my classes. I realized that being able to make him dinner and look into his eyes while we had a long, easy conversation and listen to the rain together was like staring into the serene, beautiful face of my ordained destiny. How could I be so lucky to have someone like him two feet in front of me? Jesus, I was losing it. Suddenly, he jumped up. "That reminds me"— what does?—"I've got something for you. And it's down in my very wet car. I'll be right back." And he was out the door. Intrigued, I used the brief intermission to herd the dishes into the sink, then performed a quick handsome check in the bathroom. I heard the front door open and close and Nick call out, "Look who I found."

Expecting to see some unwelcome mutual friend crashing my quality time, I practically stumbled into the room. Nick was standing in the entryway holding a small plastic bag and a tiny, saturated black thing. As I came closer, the thing yowled miserably. A kitten.

"Hold on," I said, grabbing a towel from my cedar chest. Nick carefully wrapped the kitten, exposing only the golf-ball-size head. "Where was it?" I asked him.

"She was crying up a ruckus over by the Dumpster," Nick said, softly rubbing the kitty dry. It was wriggling around and mewling some.

I stroked its wet little forehead with one finger. "How about some milk?" I whispered. I warmed up a dish in the microwave and Nick lowered her to the floor and she started lapping it up, her tiny tongue flicking in and out in a pink blur.

"So . . ." Nick said, as we smiled beatifically at the tender scene, "want a cat?"

"Not allowed," I lamented, unable to make myself a hero

because the Duval Villa was strictly no pets. "Maybe I could sneak it . . ."

Nick picked up the satisfied kitten, who was now licking her whiskers. "Naw, I wouldn't want you to get in trouble if they came in while you were at school or something." He kissed the kitten's belly. "I think I can probably talk Barney into letting her stay with us a little while."

I bristled at the notion of Barney turning away the kitten, making Nick sad, figuring this would be a typically obnoxious and insensitive gesture of good ole Barn's. The kitten nestled down in Nick's lap, sleepy. It had had a busy evening. I petted it, deliriously conscious of the proximity of my hand to Nick's crotch.

"I used to have a kitty like this," he said. "Found him, too. I was riding my bike to the Seven-Eleven to get a Slurpee."

"How old were you?" We were both fondling the kitten now, our fingers lightly brushing together and moving apart, my pulse starting to race at the greatest erotic thrill I'd ever known.

"Twelve or thirteen," Nick said, then: "There was this construction site where I had to walk the bike over the torn-up sidewalk and I turned around and this black and white kitten, a little older than this one, was following me. I got kind of worried, 'cause he wouldn't let up coming after me and I was afraid he'd lose his way and not be able to get home. But he followed me all the way to the store and waited out by my bike while I got my Slurpee. When I came out, I took a look at him and he was all dirty and bedraggled and I knew he was a stray."

"So you popped him into that white basket on your handlebars with the plastic flowers on it and pedaled home," I teased.

Nick laughed. "Oh, no. I wasn't no sissy boy. I rode home no-handed, drinking my Slurpee. And he was such a good kitten, he just dug his claws into my shirt and held on." I was crushed when he took his hand off the kitten for a sip of soda.

"Did you keep him?" I asked, not moving my hand.

"Yeah. Named him Judson. My mom wasn't too wild about the idea, but I got him cleaned up and put a flea collar on him and she was okay after that. He'd always let me give him a bath."

"I'm sure he was very grateful."

"Till this one night. He used to sleep curled up next to me all the time"—smart cat, I refrained from saying—"and one night I woke up real late and I must have been having a pretty sexy dream. I didn't wear anything to sleep, so my thang was just standing tall under the sheet." There he went again. I felt my willpower weakening. "The next thing I noticed was Jud on the side of the bed, all crouched down like he was after something. And I was wondering what the hell he was looking at, thinking it was probably a beetle or something, then he started to slink forward and just as I figured out what was going on, he attacked my ding dong." He looked at me deadpan, then we both started laughing uncontrollably.

"What happened?" I finally got out.

"He got me good. I had to shove my face into my pillow so no one would hear me yell. I mean, that's not exactly a scrape you want to show your mom."

"No permanent damage, I hope?"

"It was okay. I just had to lay off my favorite hobby for a week or so."

He started tickling the kitten again, his hand coming to rest against mine. I felt the dusting of hair that trailed from his wrist to the knuckle of his little finger. "I'm in an interesting kind of fun class this semester," he said. "Trial Advocacy. All about cross-examining and discrediting witnesses and all the lowdown, sneaky things you can get away with in a courtroom. I was thinking maybe you might like to audit it with me once a week. If you have time."

If I had time? I would have given up a tour with Madonna to sit next to him in class every week. "That would be great," I told him.

"Well, good, then. Hey, we forgot about your present." He handed me the plastic bag. I took out a white jewelry box and opened it. It was a black leather thong strung with four dangling shark's teeth. "Picked it up while I was down in Galveston. Thought you could wear it onstage, playing a surfer and all."

"Thanks, Nick. I sure will." I wanted to hug him, but he was sitting down and the cat was sleeping. "Help me put it on?"

"Sure," he said. I had to resist arching my back at the feel of his fingers fastening it around my neck. I undid my top two buttons to give him a better view of the teeth against my nicely cut upper pecs.

"What do you think?" I asked.

"I think you're going to be the best-looking psycho on the beach."

Alexander Young,

My name is Tiffani Tarr! I'm 16 years old. I am a huge fan of Hearts Crossing! I have been for about a year or more now and I tell you it couldn't improve AT ALL!

My favorite story line is the Simon-Cyrinda-Natalie one. That's the BEST ever! Your character, evil Simon Arable, is perfect. I love it. I look forward to seeing what Simon will do next. He's so unpredictable but great. Your really a terrific actor & you just couldn't get any better. To be able to play that evil a character has got to be hard. I couldn't do it, for sure!

I also have a CRUSH on you. I have! Ever since you joined HC. You are just incredibly cute. I go nuts when I see you on the TV. I cut your pictures out of soap magazines and put them all over my locker. I have a lot. YOU ARE JUST REALLY CUTE, WOW! Simon Arable is the scariest, craziest character I've ever seen on a soap opera! He's my very favorite person in all of HC.

You are great. The best actor ever. You've got a great talent and are using it very well. I hope to meet you one day. It would be a dream come true for me. I would probably faint. Hearts Crossing is the ABSOLUTE BEST SOAP OPERA OF ALL TIMES! THE GREATEST! The Simon story line helps keep Hearts Crossing the #1 top on my list. That will NEVER change at all, NEVER!

You are the GREATEST & CUTEST ever! Thank you for reading my letter. Sorry to take up your time. If you have your own fan club, I'd love to join. I'd even pay! It would be THE BEST EVER!

Your newest friend,

Tiffani Tarr

Grosse Point, MI

A key pleasure in being home was raiding my mom's pantry for things I would never have had on hand in L.A. Sprawled on the couch, I dropped semisweet chocolate morsels into a jar of creamy peanut butter and dug out the decadent snack with a spoon. I listlessly flipped through the channels, stopping on a shot-on-video commercial for A-1 Mobile Homes. Employing cutting-edge Chromakey technology, the president of A-1 illustrated the luxuries of modern trailer life, then clinched the sales pitch by widening the shot to reveal his entire flabby family in their own A-1 Double-Wide deluxe model. Texas TV was great.

My mom peeked in. "Honey, are you sure you wouldn't like some lunch?"

"I'm probably going to have a huge dinner," I offered lamely, putting the peanut butter aside. The grandfather clock chimed.

"I can't believe it's this late! We're missing *Hearts Crossing*!" My mom changed the channel. On-screen, Gwen dabbed her eyes with a Kleenex then took a stiff drink, hoping to God that tonight she'd be able to overcome her clinical frigidity and be a real woman for Ollie.

"I'm getting pretty sick of that one," Mom said.

"She's going to start getting rape flashbacks real soon," I revealed. "Who do you think did it?"

"Probably you, dear."

"Mom, I'm shocked. It was Chip."

"That's what I thought." Gwen's doorbell rang. She pulled a dressing gown over her spiderwoman negligee and opened the door to Ollie, played by buffed but born-again Brent Bingham.

"He's really stupid, Mom. One time they were rehearsing a restaurant scene and he ordered a *carfay* of wine."

The scene switched to me and Natalie, the world's best-dressed dentist, in the middle of a vicious argument.

"I said take that back!" she barked.

"Not a chance. You never could face the truth, could you? Dad hated you for a damn good reason." I was being pretty vile, considering she was letting me stay at her ultra-modern penthouse apartment for nothing, not to mention the free cleanings and fluoride treatments.

"What reason?" Natalie started to sob. "I was just twelve years old!"

I shook my head, her self-delusion nauseating me. "You tried to break up their marriage, Natalie. You couldn't stand having a stepfather, especially one so brilliant and successful. Our mother may have forgiven you, but he never did. And I can't say I particularly blame him."

"You don't know what it was like, Simon, the emotional abuse—" Boo hoo hoo.

I got right in her face. "Don't tell me about abuse, you spineless amoeba. We're family, remember?" I hissed evilly, then turned and stomped out of the room. She wept.

My mom beamed at me proudly as the show's standard threatening music chimed in and Sara appeared at the back door. "How come you're watching this awful show?" she growled, after exchanging hugs and kisses with Mom. She flounced onto the couch and started to tickle me.

Somehow I was able to drag her upstairs so I could change into a sand-washed silk floral shirt and yarn-dyed silver tab Levi's.

"Not *too* flashy," she arched.

"It's a special occasion." I spritzed on some Grey Flannel.

She sniffed. "Isn't that *the* cologne?"

"Sure is."

"You're ruthless."

"Who knows what he's thinking . . ."

"Alex, you're doing it again."

"I'm not," I protested, pumping my hair full of spray gel. "Let's go dancing tonight."

"Okay. . . . You know, I think it might be a good idea if I had dinner with you and Nick."

"Sara, I can handle it. I just want to look good for him. You know?" She nodded, regarding me with such care and concern I felt like a neurotic jerk for making this Nick thing the focal point of my brief time there, and, as had always been the case, dragging Sara along into it.

The phone rang and I answered, eager to cut the Mr. Pathetic interlude short. "Young residence," I snapped, all business.

"Alex?" A female voice I couldn't place.

"Yes. Who's this?"

"It's Juliana Butts!" Shit.

"Hi, Juliana." I was friendly, yet unwarm and cautious. Sara smiled sweetly and made smooching noises. I shoved a pillow down on her face. She tried to escape before I ruined the little makeup she needed to wear. Juliana was babbling.

"*Hearts Crossing* just finished and I thought Alex is probably home watching himself with his family, if you were in town and your mom said you would be, so I thought, why not call?!"

"Ummm . . . you know I appreciated you writing. I'm sure all the letters helped them decide to keep me on the show."

"You do those shows in advance, don't you?" No, honey, I beamed in today's performance from my living room.

"Yes . . ."

"Well, I know you're busy, but I have the afternoon off, and I thought maybe we could go out for lunch and you could tell me about what's going to happen. I don't know if you've ever been to River Center Mall, but there's a Chinese restaurant with a two-for-one special—"

"Actually, Juliana, I'm just about to leave town for the afternoon."

"Maybe tonight, then. We could go to a movie. Have you seen the new one with Danny DeVito?" Sara smirked at my tortured expression. She tapped her watch with an index finger and started peeking into my luggage.

"Juliana, I won't be back until late tonight. I'm only in Texas a few more days and there's a lot I have to do."

"Would it be easier if I just dropped by your house tomorrow? I know where it is." Great. "I told all my friends I'd get to see you. . . ." She was whining now. I didn't even know who this girl was. Okay. Put a stop to it. Pronto. I stifled a sigh.

"I might have a little free time on Sunday. But I'm not really sure yet. How about I call you if I do?"

"Sunday . . ." Juliana had to think it over. "I usually go to Furr's with my family after church . . ."

Through clenched teeth: "Let's just see what happens, Juliana. I really have to go now or I'll be late."

"Oh, Alex? Could you just say hi to my mom? She's watched the show since it started."

"I don't really have time—" Too late. I heard the scuffle of the phone changing hands.

"Hello?" a new voice drawled.

"Hello, Mrs. Butts."

"Alex Young?!"

"Yes, ma'am, that's right. Thanks for watching the show and please tell Juliana I'll speak to her later." Before she could squawk, I hung up.

"*What* was that all about?" Sara asked.

"She just wouldn't let up." I started looking for my wallet. "Then she put her mother on the line."

"The public adores you," Sara said. "Let's get the hell out of Dodge before she calls back."

I said goodbye to my mom and we took off down the long, familiar road to Austin. I watched the odometer. When we left the driveway, Nick was seventy miles away. Then sixty-eight. Sixty-five. Fifty-nine. I-35 hadn't changed much in a year and a half. Maybe a few more "Luxurious Golf Course Living" condo developments marring the landscape between here and Schertz. We passed the reptile farm–whorehouse that had been an open secret since before I even knew what a whore was (age five, to be exact). I wondered what I'd be feeling when I watched this same scenery unreel as we drove back tonight. Not that it wasn't obvious: We'd pull off at the Wendy's after-hours drive-thru in San Marcos for a sugar boost, and the Frosty would slide down my throat, freezing me into further numbness as Sara tried valiantly to lift me out of my devastation, her memories of this time with me forever darkened and spoiled because the secret had been ripped wide open—I still loved Nick with all my heart. And seeing him again, being the bottom of a page in the personal appointment book that was his life in Austin with Barney, without me, had been a terrible idea.

April 1990

It had been laundry night at my apartment. Nick's clothes were neatly folded in his basket, a jug of Liquid Tide and a box of Bounce nestled among them. The TV was on. Sandra Bernhard was on Letterman. Nick was lying on the floor, his head and shoulders propped up on a cushion. And my head was resting against his stomach, where I'd casually laid it twenty or so minutes before. Just a couple of buddies chillin' out in front of the tube. I felt his breathing, deep and untroubled, like I'd imagined it would feel if we were in bed together. He didn't touch me and neither of us spoke. The only muscle that moved was my throbbing manmeat, imprisoned in baggy shorts. Next time I would kiss him. Count on it.

My dear Alex,
Thank you for autographing my movie poster. I'm having it
framed. Thank you for the 8 × 10 photo. What a surprise. I'm

sitting here, looking into your eyes as I write this, daydreaming about you, your penis and balls. Am I terrible?

Yes, in fact, I'm Astaroth, wizard. Please contact me soon RE: the spell you have cast on my heart.
Ray Lanville
Silverlake, CA

Austin seemed like a toy city, so clean and convenient, its half-dozen skyscrapers, one of them containing Nick, pristine against the huge blue Texas sky. We had a couple of hours before dinner, so Sara and I decided to cruise The Drag, adjacent to the UT campus.

We ended up at Quackenbush's, a cappuccino-espresso-cheesecake hangout favored by the cigs 'n' Sartre set. We both kept our sunglasses on. I had iced herbal tea and Sara ordered a chocolate croissant à la mode. She had the metabolism of a sand shark.

"Why are we here?" Sara asked. "We never came here in college."

"We're so much more sophisticated now, dahling. All right. Where are my fans? I vant to hold court at a private table."

"Let's go over to SRD, then. Those girls can appreciate a good soap star."

Snotty, anachronistic Scottish Rite Dorm, or The Virgin Vault, as it was unaffectionately dubbed, had been a running joke between us since a resident, one Staci Jane Henkel, had stolen Sara's high school boyfriend, Duke, our freshman year at UT. We took revenge on the despicable couple by taking out about twenty-five personal ads in smut rags both local and national, variously listing Staci as a leather mistress with a penchant for golden showers and tasty-looking Duke as a "dick-worshipping frat stud," complete with addresses and contact numbers. We were never exactly sure of any specific results, only that Staci moved out of SRD two months later *never to be heard from again*. Duke was now happily married to a fat girl in Grand Prairie. Sara even went to their wedding.

"We can't go to SRD," I said. "No men allowed."

"You're right. You'd hate it."

Sara finished her food while I picked up the Austin *Chronicle*, the city's oh-so-cutting-edge newsweekly that had once reviewed me in *Child's Play* at the Hyde Park Theatre as "a deadpan Aryan gerbil." I skimmed the paper. Except for the heat, Austin wasn't a bad place: a good crop of interesting movies, cool record stores, a politically active population, wonderfully cheap restaurants, and from the size of the "Men Seeking Men" column in the *Chronicle*'s infamous personals section, it was rapidly becoming Texas Queer Central.

"4–H Clubber (Hot, Hairy, Hung, Hard) seeks buffed J-O playmates 18–40." "Smooth freshman athlete, totally straight-acting, interested in discreet encounters with VGL blondes under 23. No fats, fems, freaks or mustaches." Talk about Aryan gerbils.

Still, I couldn't see myself ever living here again, and not just because you couldn't make a living as an actor. The main reason was the unbearableness of being in the same city as Nick, and I wouldn't be able to stand schlepping through the same territory as the world's most mismatched couple, knowing damn well Barney took all he had for granted while I was endlessly tortured by fantasies of elusive domestic bliss every time I walked into a grocery store alone.

I couldn't believe there was still an hour left before I was set to meet Nick. This was worse than waiting for prostate surgery. And the weather—October and eighty-nine degrees, not to mention the humidity that was dampening my studwear and making my bangs curl up like shrimp on a Sizzler platter.

We went over to Dobie Mall to get our parking validated. I was absurdly comforted that the little twin cinema still showed midnight movies every day of the week (even if one of them was *Tie Me Up! Tie Me Down!*). Sara and I had probably seen a hundred late shows here while we were in school, smuggling bottles of soda and homemade popcorn and feeling that invincible kind of college cool that comes from not having any classes before eleven the next morning. Nick and I had come here together, too. I'd always remember the time he'd taken my hand about twenty minutes into *Wild At Heart* and hadn't let go until every credit had rolled and we were sitting alone in the theater.

"Are you sure you don't want me to join you guys?" Sara asked from inside her car. I stood by the unlocked passenger door, making no move to open it, lost in a nostalgic haze. I checked back in and got in the car.

"Huh?" I asked Sara.

"I said, if you want, I can call Chuck and Valerie and tell them I can't make it. They're coming down to San Antonio for a vegetarian chili cook-off in a week or two, anyway."

"I'll be fine, I promise. Just meet me at Oilcan Harry's at nine-thirty."

We pulled up to Nick's building. The sunset splashed a beautiful golden glow over the plaza, the fountain, the big-haired secretaries on their way home.

"I guess I'll see you later," Sara said.

"Yeah, thanks." I unlocked the door and squeezed the handle.

"Alex, you're going to have a wonderful life no matter what happens. It's Nick's loss. Just remember that." I leaned over and kissed her cheek.

"Okay."

"You can get out of the car now."

I did. I felt a little dizzy. Excitement, sadness, dread—these I had expected. But what I was suddenly aware of, as I trotted toward the chrome-and-glass tower and a warm fall breeze bedeviled my hairdo, was that right now—tonight—I was standing on the cusp of my life as surely as I had been four months ago when I walked onto the *Hearts Crossing* set for my final network test with Cyrinda Blake herself, tiny, Tab-slurping soap diva Megan DuBois. It was one of those moments that defines the course of your existence. It puts in stark relief where you've been and what you've been working and waiting for, and everything that comes afterward seems to refer to it. I was about to write a whole new chapter in my autobiography—Life With Nick After Nick. I braced myself as I revolved into the building, afraid of stepping into the lobby and being face-to-face with him.

A few people walked from the elevators to the other revolving door, but the only one loitering was a chunky security guard at the marble reception desk, his big ass pointing heavenward as he leaned on his elbows over a newspaper, oblivious to the fact that I might have been a stylishly dressed agent of destruction sent to undermine Austin's corporate world. I assumed a post in front of a titanic bush near the elevators, arms folded, sort of hugging myself, eyes trained on the marble floor. A pensive attitude. No, that was ridiculous. I straightened up, thrust my hands into my pockets and kind of rocked back and forth in my Cole Haan loafers. That was stupid, too. Like I was waiting for my girlfriend to come out of the ladies' room. After trying a few leaning-against-the-marble-wall variations, I settled on standing perfectly still, my right hand in my pocket. I had just turned my attention from the burnished golden orb of a lobby clock—it was 6:04—back to the elevators, when the one directly in front of me opened and Nick was looking right at me.

I felt like those fifties sailors must have felt when they witnessed atomic tests from a mile away. He was radiant. He walked toward me, grinning, hand outstretched for a shake. I swallowed hard, not letting myself cry, blinking back the tears, definitely not allowing myself to lose it in the lobby of this fucking building, pulling in a long, deep, stabilizing breath as he took my hand and said, "Look who's here. A star. How y'doin', Alex?"

"Great," I answered. I could smell his delicious scent, never traced to any known cologne, soap or body lotion, exactly the same, like every detail of his unforgettable Texas face. The unquenchable desire to kiss him burned through me like a harlot's shameful secret. Which it was.

"You look so good," he told me. I watched his eyes unselfconsciously scan the length of my body. Oh God, I really was going to cry now.

Quickly, I said, "Thanks. You, too. I've never seen you look more handsome."

Now he was self-conscious. "What do you say we grab some dinner?"

"Sounds good to me."

"I'll make sure not to order a milk shake," he said, looking at me with sly amusement.

"You actually watch the show," I marveled.

"I have Barney tape it." He must *love* that. "How far in advance do you do 'em?"

"Right now, we're about two weeks ahead. I go back to work in about a week. I'm not exactly sure what Simon will be doing when he gets back into town. We don't get scripts until a few days before they tape. It's going to have something to do with my dead scientist father's sexual-potency drug, and my sister, Natalie and me keeping Sean in jail for poisoning Cyrinda. I have these porno photos she posed for while paying her way through dental school."

Nick laughed. "I never knew how many great-lookin' guys were on daytime TV. And they all seem to take their shirts off every couple of minutes. Well, except you."

"I'll have my turn. And believe me, I can't wait."

We found his car, a small, scrupulously maintained Mitsubishi. "Where's Sara tonight?" he asked, as we drove up to the street.

"She had some people to visit. She said to say hello."

"I sure miss seeing her. Seems like I never get together with friends anymore."

"How's To-bel?" I asked. The kitten Nick rescued from the rain was named after a character in *Scenes From the Class Struggle in Beverly Hills*.

"She's a handful." Nick smiled. "Last week, she tipped over the garbage in the middle of the night and I woke up to this horrible banging noise. You know what she'd done?"

I shook my head, smiling, starting to relax a little.

"She had her head stuck in a chicken soup can and was rapping her little noggin on the floor, against the wall, everywhere, trying to get it off." We laughed.

"I mean, it could have been serious," Nick continued. "I guess she could have suffocated or choked, but it was just so funny to see her thrashing around the kitchen, like she was slam-dancing with a helmet on. I had to wash all the chicken soup out of her fur, too."

"Did you ground her?" I asked.

"We had a little talk. She's a pretty smart kitten, though. Every time the phone rings, she runs right over to it."

We were driving north, past the campus. I felt a momentary clutch of panic—we weren't going to his house, *their* house, were we? You know, Nick, it's been lovely, but I have to scream now. He sped up Duval Street, toward my old apartment. Then I knew. Hyde Park Bar and Grill. We pulled up next to a huge pop-art fork with a baked potato skewered on it. We'd walked across the street from where I used to live to this very restaurant the first night we had dinner together. And we kept coming back, usually on those nights when he was most relaxed and what we had together was at its most uncomplicatedly romantic.

"I hope this is okay," he said sheepishly.

Obviously, my tears would be on ten-second call throughout the evening. "It's fine, Nick. It's one of my favorite restaurants in the whole world." I kept this speech light, even raising my eyebrows perkily at the end.

"I know," he said. "Mine, too. So . . . all set to eat hearty?" He opened his door.

"Let's do it," I agreed. Absolutely, Nick. Let's go right in. And by all means don't take me in your arms and ravish me in the privacy of your dark car.

The restaurant, a soothing, classy place built in a converted house, specialized in American standards prepared in fresh, innovative ways. To be shamefully honest, while I was in L.A., I'd dreamed of their thick, spicy, batter-coated French fries almost as much as I had Nick's penis.

We were led to a charming table immediately. The menu had changed slightly, but I didn't need to deliberate. I'd been waiting to end my self-imposed exile from red meat with a Hyde Park hamburger since I moved to California. Plenty of fries, too. Our waiter was cute and black-haired, with a couple of earrings and muscular forearms. Nick ordered. "I'll take the chicken-fried steak."

"Would you like succotash or carrot strips?"

"Carrots, please. And the gentleman will have a hamburger, done medium, and a large order of French fries."

The waiter was studying me a little intently. "Actually," I said, "*he's* much more of a gentleman." Nick smiled at me and I shivered.

"And what would you like to drink?"

I shrugged at Nick. "How about a couple iced teas?" he asked the waiter.

"Fine," he said, spinning on his heel and starting to march off. Then he stopped and froze as if slapped. He turned around. "Excuse me," he said to me, "but are you on *Hearts Crossing*?"

"Yeah," I said, flattered beyond reason to be recognized in front of Nick. "I play Simon, the evil prick."

"They watch the show in the study lounge at my dorm. Everyone stops talking when you come on. Definitely the most entertaining character."

"Thanks a lot," I said. He was *really* cute. If I wasn't desperately trying to win my one true love . . .

"Anyway, it's nice to meet you," he said. I remembered my manners and introduced myself and Nick. The waiter's name was Troy. He went to fetch the drinks.

"How does it feel to be famous?" Nick teased.

"That never happens," I insisted, coy.

"It's going to start happening a lot. You're going to be on TV five days a week for two years. That's more media exposure than Princess Di and Fergie put together."

"It's been fun. And amazing," I said. "You go to the studio in the morning and barely rehearse enough to get your blocking down, and then the cameras are rolling and you're making TV and it's on two weeks later. It sure doesn't feel like a job, even when I'm going in five days a week, ten hours a day. It's wonderful."

"I'm real happy for you, Alex." My hand was resting on the table, halfway between us. He moved his arm up onto the table and, I think, came really close to laying his hand on mine. Then some control mechanism clicked in his brain and he picked up his fork instead. "Where's that dinner?" he asked, mock-grumpy.

I didn't want it to come; after we ate, it would be over. I'd go on my way, nothing gained from this meeting but the proof that the relationship I'd strived for and cherished and kept alive in my thoughts every night since we'd last seen each other had dwindled to nothing more than a couple of college friends chatting about their careers over dinner. If I let that happen, there would be no turning back. A dull hopeless panic coated my stomach like metallic Pepto Bismol. I had to fight it.

"How do you like your job?" I asked.

"I guess it's all right. Seems more like busywork than brain-power. Real estate, financial, corporate crap. I get so tied up it's hard for me to stop by the GLSC." The Gay/Lesbian Services Center took on AIDS- and sexual orientation–discrimination lawsuits, lobbied for gay rights legislation and sponsored a counseling and therapy service for local homos. It was a small, insufficiently funded office working out of an old house down-town. Nick had manned the hotline there a couple of days a month since I'd known him, and now, as a lawyer, did pro-bono work for them. When he could.

"Right now, they've got a real tough case. This married couple, about twenty-one or twenty-two. He's gay, or bi anyway, real promiscuous, probably hustling, got AIDS and gave it to his wife. She works as a janitor over at the Air Force base. They're trying to screw her out of her health insurance. She's got two kids, too."

"Do they have it?" I asked, watching the hurt on his face that came from making every needy person's problems his own.

"No, the kids are okay. The husband's starting to get sick, though. It's a mess."

"And you're fighting the insurance company for her?"

"Me and a couple other attorneys down at the center. It's pretty grim, but I come back from working on that case at least able to fool myself that I'm making some kind of a difference."

"You are, Nick. How can you think you're not?" God, he deserved someone to treat him as well as he took care of ev-eryone else. The food came. I was hungry after all. We ate slowly and talked about the state of the nation's sodomy laws and *Hearts Crossing* and how Nick had gone to a luncheon at the state capital and sat next to Ann Richards. We talked about my small featured role in the major-studio killer-cop megahit that had been released that summer and I told him about my apart-ment and we discussed bicep-building strategies and the really awful new Aaron Spelling show and his sister's job at an artificial insemination clinic in Amarillo. We did not mention the fact that we had once followed up dinners like this with candlelit lovemaking at my apartment across the street. Another conversational taboo was apparently my romantic life, dating history in L.A., and if there were any guys I currently had crushes on. And Nick mentioned Barney exactly one time, to comment that he was still assistant-managing his father's furniture store, which he'd been doing for the past nine years, I believed. Gotta love those go-getting MBA kids.

When the bill came, Nick absolutely insisted on paying it. I did drop a hefty cash tip for the cute, soap-watching waiter, though. Maybe I'd see him later at Oilcan Harry's. When we got into the car, Nick said, "I hate to admit it, but I've got a few hours of prep left for tomorrow. I ought to be getting home before too long."

My heart was an egg that had just been cracked, and I could feel a pendulous glob of white swoop sickeningly downward, suspended over the pit of my stomach. All I could do was mumble, "Okay." To make matters worse, he turned on the radio for the first time since I'd known him, and we drove back to his office listening to the mournful ruminations of R.E.M. on KLBJ-FM.

Ten minutes later, we were at his building. I looked down at my watch for a split-second. An hour till I was supposed to meet Sara. I couldn't believe it was going to end like this. Months and years of pain and ecstasy and single-minded desire reduced to a casual, "friendly" goodbye on a street corner. I was amazed and disgusted that my dream could die so unmelodramatically.

"How about you come up and see the office?" Nick said, startling me out of my budding depression. "I left my briefcase there."

"Sure. I'd love to see it." A tiny, Satanic Jeff Stryker appeared on my left shoulder, wielding a pitchfork made of his custom-molded dildos.

"Git yer ass up there," Jeff growled. "Once you're alone in that fuckin' office, Nick's gonna whip out that big fuckin' dick and beg you for it. He's gonna tear those pussyboy clothes offa you and—"

He was cut off by a miniature Kyle Chandler from *Home-front*, who popped onto my right shoulder, clad only in angelic white briefs. "He wants to be your friend, Alex," Kyle cooed, "that's all. This is a law office, not The Meat Rack. It's entirely innocent and you know it!"

Torn and helpless, I followed Nick into the building. The lobby was empty, the elevator instantly summoned. We zipped to the eleventh floor in eleven seconds, just long enough for me to sigh over our shared reflection in the gilt-flecked mirror that covered one side of the car. Nick ran a plastic card through a detector and popped open the doors to his suite.

We walked into a reception area with a black modular sofa, smoked glass coffee table featuring issues of *Texas Monthly* and *Business Week* and a slick, hi-tech front desk where Nick must pick up his little message slips and melt the hearts of reception-ists both temp and perm.

We made a left and headed down a carpeted hallway to a door with a thin silver plate that said NICHOLAS MILLER. We went in. A small, neat oak desk, a bookshelf, a love seat (!), and a glittering view of Austin's nighttime cityscape.

"Pretty fancypants, huh?" Nick asked.

"Yeah. . . . Where'd they hide the bidet?" I pretended to hunt for it.

I heard him chuckle as I went to the window to enjoy the luxury of big, bright stars twinkling in a smog-free sky. Nick came up behind me and we stood together silently for a moment.

"People tell me I should get a telescope. Take advantage of the viewing opportunities." He was referring to the honey-comb of lighted windows blazing in the high-rise hotel across the street.

"You might get a little distracted," I replied. This was the perfect opportunity to put my arm around him, but it hung by my side, paralyzed.

"That's always a problem," Nick said lightly. Was he flirting? "Have a seat and I'll get us a Coke from the executive fridge. Perks." He vanished. I checked out his bookshelf. Lots of law. And a couple framed snapshots. One of his parents, looking sixty and happy at some restaurant, none of Barney, and one of Nick, Sara and me, taken at Lake Travis the weekend I found out I'd been cast in *Teenage Brides of Christ*. Sara was in the middle, wearing a bikini top and holding a can of Heineken. Nick and I were shirtless, in shades, our arms lying alongside each other's on her shoulders. Could it have been one of the happiest days of his life, too? I put the photo down and positioned myself on the miniature sofa. Nick came back in with two cans of soda. He transferred his jacket to a hanger, kicked off his shoes, and sat down next to me.

"Thanks," I said, popping open one of the Cokes.

"How about a toast?" Nick suggested. He pulled his leg onto the love seat so that his bent knee came into the slightest contact with mine. "To Alexander Young—my most successful handsome young friend." We bumped cans together. I realized my throat was dry to the point of constriction and I sucked back half the drink in one sip.

"How many hours a week do you put in up here?" I asked him.

"Let's see," Nick said. "I'm here at eight most mornings, usually take a half-hour lunch, stay till six or six-thirty, then do about two hours at home or the law school library. How much is that?"

"A sixty-hour work week. Not to mention what you do at the GLSC."

"It *can* be a grind sometimes." He complained less than Mother Teresa. "You know, Alex, it's never like you expect it to be." The sadness and resignation in his voice alarmed me. I had given up on getting any candid emotion from him tonight, and now here he was, alone with me on a love seat eleven stories up, practically crying out for help. Should I hug him and tell him everything would be all right? Did he think I was over him?

All I could say was, "I know it isn't." But of course in my case, *it* was a hundred times better than I expected after a measly year-and-a-half of kicking around Hollywood.

"Sometimes I just wanna walk in here in the morning and tell them I've had it with all the bullshit. When I finished law school, I thought I was really on the right track as far as my life went, y'know?" I nodded. Nick drank some Coke and looked around the office. "But lately I feel like I'm running a real tough maze and I'm stuck in this dead-end just a few feet away from the exit." He sighed. "I guess I'm lucky to even have a reasonably good job in the nineties."

Okay. Enough. It was talk like that that was keeping him exactly where he was. I could hear the complementary justification: "I guess I'm lucky to even be in a stable relationship." Watching Nick *settle* had always put the sharpest point on my despair, and here I was, finally able to confront these feelings of his in person. A surge of power coursed through me.

"They're lucky to have *you*," I said, simultaneously placing each of my hands between his neck and shoulders. I started to massage him, my hands working in firm, gentle slow motion, the blood rushing to my crotch, my eyes riveted on his face, nothing in the world mattering but whether or not he'd let it happen. He didn't look at me. He closed his eyes and his lips parted and I heard a soft sound somewhere between "ohhh" and "mmmmm," and his body went limp, swaying a little under my hands. I shifted myself for better leverage and worked my right hand under his Brooks Brothers dress shirt, kneading his T-shirted shoulders.

Nick put his arms up and my guts lurched and I thought it was over, but instead he unbuttoned his shirt, pulled it out of his pants, took it off and tossed it on his desk. I pressed my thumb and index finger beneath one of his shoulder blades and started to work his tight back. His hand dropped to my knee and he relaxed into me, my legs loosely cradling his waist. I tugged the T-shirt out of his slacks and my hands performed their unforgotten specialty on Nick's warm flesh with automatic precision. He lay back against me even further, putting delicious pressure on my big business, which he must have felt pressing into his buttock.

"It feels so good to touch you," I whispered, moving my hands down his arms, squeezing his biceps, wanting to lick them.

"It feels good having you touch me, Alex," Nick said. My head swam with lust, amazement, disbelief, hope. "I've missed you so. I was scared you hated me." Now he looked into my eyes, which were filling up with the sweetest tears I'd ever felt, but I couldn't say anything, so I just shook my head. He slowly rolled over on top of me, lowering his face to my neck, and I tingled with jolt after jolt of rapturous pleasure as his incredibly soft lips traveled from my throat up to my ear. I ran my hand over his hairy chest, then moistened one finger to caress his small, stiff nipple. Before I could fully savor the moment, his mouth found mine, and it was a kiss worth waiting eighteen months for. Hell, eighteen years would have been a bargain.

"You're shaking," Nick murmured in a low, confidential voice.

I was quivering like a baby bird. I held his handsome face in my hands. "I love you. I love you, Nick."

He wrapped an arm around my shoulders and stroked my hair. "You haven't changed a bit." Was he smiling? Yes, almost.

His T-shirt was already gathered around his neck, so it was easy to slip it off entirely. He reclined on his back, facing me, one arm behind his head. I bent to kiss every inch of his torso. The hand that I'd placed on his flat stomach moved down past his belt buckle to the oblong bulge displayed in stunning bas-relief in his greenish-gray trousers. I rested my fingers on it, feeling its weight, its power. The most gorgeous penis in the world, hooked onto the best boyfriend a guy could have. I spread open my fingers and started to close them around him.

Then I snatched my hand away, scared shitless by a loud series of pulsing, jangling beeps that pierced the office like a dog whistle. Nick jumped against the back of the sofa, then hopped off, toward his desk. The phone. The fucking phone.

"It's my personal line," he mumbled, scrabbling the receiver off the hook. "Hello? . . . Hi. . . . I'll be finished soon. . . . Sure, I guess I could. . . . Oreos or Pepperidge Farm? . . . Okay . . . Bye." He hung up. The most significant romantic encounter of my entire life was over because Barney Gagnon wanted something to stuff his face with while he was glued to the TV set. Armed with *The Bare Facts Video Guide*, no doubt.

I waited to see what Nick would do. He turned off the desk lamp and walked over to the love seat. He sat down beside me in the dark and put his arm around me, pulling me close. "My little Mr. Young. What are we gonna do." It didn't sound like a question.

I swallowed hard, not wanting my voice to quaver as I said, "I think we should talk."

He nodded, then exhaled a long sigh. "I wish you could hold me all night long."

Oh, Jesus. Was I hallucinating? "I can, Nick." Please let me. Better not say that. I kissed his neck softly.

"Not tonight," he whispered. "I can't. . . ." Okay, let's pull it together. Make a plan and don't beg and get out of there. He made it easy: "When are you heading back to L.A.?"

"Tuesday."

"How about if I come down to San Antonio on Monday? Sound like a good idea?"

"Yeah, it sounds great." I couldn't resist letting my hand stray over his crotch to see if things were still cooking. About halfway, I ascertained. He responded by lightly tapping me on the back, his long-established code signal for a requested end to friskiness. I complied, disentangling myself ultra-reluctantly from his manly embrace. "I'm due to meet Sara soon," I said.

"Where at? I can drive you."

"No, it's just down at the corner," I lied. I'd walk the half-mile to the club. I wanted our goodbye to be here in this room. We stood up, still holding hands.

"Thanks for dinner, Nick."

"Thank *you*."

"This is in case I don't see you again." I kissed him long and sweet.

"You'll see me." I couldn't tell if the glint in his eyes was tears or contacts. He hugged me. "Just remember . . ." he started to say, then trailed off.

I love you????? "What?" I asked, feeling the top of my head float away. "Remember what?"

He kissed my cheek. "That I'm thinking about you."

"Okay. Bye." I let myself out, practically running out of the lobby and across Congress Avenue so he wouldn't drive by and catch me walking the streets.

The implications of what had just happened were beginning to sink in through the heady, delirious glow that Nick had left clinging to me like pixie dust. The final piece necessary to make my life complete, fulfilling and eternally sun-drenched, could very well be ready to snap into place. Nick had been languishing in dull, underappreciated obscurity long enough. He was ready for a glistening new life with a remarkable young man—me. Or he had just been lonely and weak and didn't want to disappoint me. Naturally. This had been the question I'd tormented myself with since our sex life began. But everything was different now. It had to be. A car horn blared.

I'd stepped in front of a 4×4 barreling across 4th Street. Terrific. Get yourself run down because you can't focus on reality long enough to cross the goddamn street. "You dumb fuck!" the frat-boy occupants screamed. I hightailed it to the other side of the intersection. "Stupid faggot" I heard one of them bellow as the Suzuki Samurai took off. I would have given the finger, but the satisfaction wasn't worth getting shot at. These Texas kids had quite the tempers.

There was no line outside Oilcan's, just a few habitués eyeing the sidewalk traffic. Across the street at Capitol City Playhouse all was quiet as a demographically desirable audience watched the second act of *A Girl's Guide to Chaos*. The Ken doll at the club's door examined my exotic California license for just a moment before tying an alcohol bracelet around my wrist. No cover charge, of course. The competition among Austin's gay bars was almost as fierce as on Santa Monica Boulevard. And the music here was way better. Depeche Mode throbbed as I scanned the smallish, reddish, half-full club for Sara. I found her at a little table by the back bar drinking Coronas with her ex-roommate Valerie and Val's husband, Chuck, a Nicolas Cage look-alike computer engineer. I had trouble circumnavigating a middle-aged guy totally focused on a black muscle stud whose chest he kept tapping with a beringed finger to emphasize some hard-to-hear conversational point. Valerie spotted me and shoved past them. "Alex!" she squealed, trapping her "world-famous" breasts between us in an enormous hug.

Sara and Chuck quickly appeared. "What are you guys doing here?" I shouted, really pleased, wanting to see everyone tonight, eager to spread my happiness like rich creamery butter.

Chuck handed me a Cape Cod with a lime wedge bobbing in it. "We heard a soap star was making a personal appearance!" I hugged him, too.

"Congratulations, Alex!" Valerie screamed. "We fast-forward through the show every night to see you!"

"That's the only way to watch it!" I exclaimed into her ear. The unmistakable beat of that high school hymn "You Spin Me Round (Like A Record)" was emerging like a dance-mix phoenix from the ashes of the previous song. Our eyebrows all shot up simultaneously and we started pushing toward the dance floor.

Sara put her hand on my shoulder and her mouth up to my ear. "What the hell happened?" Her eyes held a craving for positive dish.

I gave my head a "mmm-mmm-mmm girl" shake. We were almost to the dance floor. I collided with a rippled, tank-topped back and killer buns encased in 501s. Their gorgeous Hispanic owner swiveled around.

"Sorry," I called, as Sara pulled me past him. He winked. Valerie and Chuck were already working it hard on the floor. I put my arm around Sara and yelled, "It was incredible! He kissed me and I kissed him and we just about *made love in his office!*"

She gaped at me, not knowing what to believe. *"Are you kidding?!"*

"No!" I screamed, hugging her. It was time to dance. I put my glass down, amazed it was already empty. Sara took my hand and we got into the groove. Book of Love, New Order, Eurythmics—the eighties lived forever at Oilcan Harry's. I had polished off my drink way too fast, or maybe just fast enough, and the tension that had been coiled inside me since I first heard Nick's voice on my answering machine in L.A. was melting into technopop-fueled euphoria. I was a lava lamp, joyously recreating myself a hundred times over on the dance floor, not even tempted by the college crowd of handsome homos beginning to pack the place. *Nick wanted me.* What a wonderful, deep-heating thought.

A crummy song finally came on and the four of us slithered over to the bar. I ordered us a round of drinks. We toasted "success and romance" and retreated to the rows of theater seats that faced the dance floor. A spike-haired male blonde in a cut-up UT sweatshirt started to French and dry-hump a skinny male teen with a skull earring two seats away from Chuck. He put on a great mock-shocked expression, then continued telling me about the house he and Valerie were buying. He was a real sport when it came to queers. Valerie checked Sara's watch and groaned.

"I have to be at work in six hours," she said, holding up the corresponding number of fingers as a visual aid. Then the Go-Go's kicked in and I grabbed her and Chuck and insisted on one more dance.

After they left, promising to visit me in L.A. "and eat all your white meat," Sara and I retired to the patio, where, in fresh air and moonlight, I spilled my guts about my dinner-plus with Nick.

"Jesus Christ," she said. "This thing is never going to be over."

"No, it never will. Not until he does what's right for him."

"I don't know what to tell you, Alex." She put her hand on my shoulder. "I hope it works out."

"You're skeptical."

"Aren't *you*? I don't want you to be crushed if this isn't going to amount to anything."

I sighed, boosting myself up onto a drink rail, not caring if I got wet. I cupped my face in my hands and watched through my fingers my legs swinging in the breeze. She was right, as usual. Nick hadn't said anything to indicate he was planning on running away with me. Still . . .

"Sara, if you could have felt the way he held me . . . that kiss . . . it was like he was starving."

"He never was very good at resisting you. Remember? You were gone a long time and he missed you and now you're here and you're incredibly successful and attractive and I'm sure the chemistry sparked and that was that." I could tell from her sad, compassionate eyes that she knew I was shriveling up inside. "Alex, please. You know how happy I'd be to finally see the two of you together. I love Nick. But he'd have to uproot himself from this tar pit of a situation here and neither one of us can make him do it."

"I'd do it for him," I practically whispered.

She nodded. She knew. "Fuck this," she said, tossing back the rest of her drink. "Let's have fun. What the hell are you even here for?" She pulled me down from the rail. "Listen." I did. It was the Pet Shop Boys' fabulous affront to easy listening, "Always On My Mind." At some point during the song, I swiveled around and she was gone. I spotted her on the sidelines conducting an animated chat with a couple of guys I vaguely recognized from *The Daily Texan*, the infamous UT newspaper Sara had been a staple at throughout our college careers. Senior year she'd been Entertainment Editor and had run weekly contests like "Wilson Phillips: The Satanic Verses."

I watched myself dance in the mirrored wall. I was starting to sweat a little. Okay, a lot. My hair had compressed into a damp, bangs-impaired skullcap, my face was shiny, my shirt a limp, silk nicotine filter. It was the ideal moment for the fan attention that had eluded me since I arrived.

"Excuse me!" a denim-vested crew-cut kid hollered, whacking his hand against my arm. "You're on *Hearts Crossing*, aren't you?" He scrutinized me quizzically, as if he suddenly thought he was wrong.

"Yeah!" I yelled back.

"I told my friend it was you!" he barked into my ear, breathing beer on me. I looked up and saw his friend was the gorgeous Mexican guy in the tank top I'd accidentally goosed earlier. He smiled radiantly. Gosh.

I extended my hand. "I'm Alex Young!" The friend shook it. His name was Paul Gonzalez. The other one was called Chester. They wanted to buy me a drink. We had rum and Cokes and I told them I'd gone to UT. Paul said he went to Southwest Texas, in San Marcos.

"But he's on scholastic dismissal this semester," Chester bitchily informed me.

My tolerance to alcohol was almost as weak as my resistance to Latino sex gods. Two drinks was my absolute limit—oblivion was setting in. It was accompanied by the insistent pressure of Paul's thigh against mine. He kept yammering away about getting his new car totaled by an uninsured driver while I half glanced around for Sara and half stared at the dark, pointy outline of his nipples through the fabric of his tank top, stretched taut from pectoral overdevelopment. Where was his little friend Chester? Chesty and Chester. What a cute pair. This struck me as hilarious and I started grinning. Paul mistook this for encouragement and moved in closer, putting his hand on my waist. My buzz had plunged the entire club into a languid undersea torpor—even my dick was getting hard in slow-motion. Paul was asking me if I'd "done" any of the guys on the show. Please . . . I haven't even had *lunch* with any of them, I thought wildly. His relentless, steely thigh cozied up to my crotch and he leaned in to kiss me, Eternity zapping one of my nostrils, Aussie hair products the other. I looked over his shoulder— where the hell was Chester?— and saw Trevor Renado walk by. It couldn't be. I practically fell over trying to catch another glimpse of him before he vanished into the mass of tightly compressed bodies. There was no way. Still . . . I started to drift through the throng, Paul and his brazenness already a blurred memory.

"I thought you were being molested somewhere," Sara said, latching onto my arm.

"Trevor's here! I just saw him!" Words were gooey caramel nuggets I could barely spit out.

"That slut from L.A.?!" she shouted dubiously. "How much have you had to drink?"

I tried to protest while continuing to scan the crowd. Paul was back over by the bar, Chester sucking on his neck like one of the Lost Boys.

"Come on, Alex, let's go!" Sara started to guide me to the exit. I needed help. Before we got to the exit, I turned to survey the floor. I saw him. Dancing, in black shorts, an art-deco crucifix whipping against his sculpted shirtless chest. I had a perfect strobe-lit view for five seconds, then he was swallowed up by a hundred sweaty, pumping, gyrating queers. I backed into a wall and would have gladly slid right down it if Sara hadn't yanked me away. We scurried out of the club and into the October night which still sighed the warm breath of summer.

April 1990

"For God's sake, don't call him," Sara said. We were in direct violation of her apartment complex's pool rules (eating tortilla chips) while lounging under a killer sun two days after I'd first kissed Nick. "It was bad enough you made plans before he walked out the door," she said lightly, flicking a piece of tomato stalk out of Valerie's home-blended salsa.

"I know, I know," I snapped. My burnt-orange *Psycho Beach* skin looked oh-so-lovely next to my blue Speedo. I wondered what the introduction of actual sunlight would do to my complexion. Whatever it was, it wouldn't be more screwed-up than my state of mind.

When Nick had walked out the door with a promise to day-trip to Houston with me the next week, I had tried to remain calm by doing some Spanish homework and taking a long, hot shower, but had ended up masturbating twice and staring at an infomercial with Meredith Baxter and Lisa Hartman for forty-five minutes. It had been too late to call Sara, and of course phoning Barney with my big news was tragically out of the question. Somehow I'd made it through the preceding thirty-six hours, including two perfs of *Psycho Beach Party* and a long, leisurely lunch with my parents, who'd driven into town for the afternoon. ("Doing that play is really great for you, honey," my mother said. "You're practically glowing." Well, actually, Mom, it's 'cause I just went down on the man of my dreams. Please pass the pepper.)

If I'd been a mess worshipping Nick from afar, I was now a complete shambles. Had I worked six grueling months to get close to him for a fifteen-minute payoff that would make it impossible for him to face me again, much less fall in love with me? Before he left, he'd hugged me and said not to be afraid. "You're not scaring me away," he almost sang, softly, in my ear. What did that mean? How could our friendship continue if I could never touch him again?

Any time I wasn't concentrating on something immediate and specific, my brain would lapse into a slide show of magic moments from That Night. I constructed an elaborate fantasy based on the knowledge that Nick and Dogface's lease was up in July; it ended with a euphoric cohabitational montage of me making the two of us breakfast, landscaping our yard and bringing Nick to unimagined heights of sexual conquest whenever I could get him out of his clothes.

In the real world, Nick *was* nailed down as far as the trip to Houston went, but I had no idea how to proceed once this romantic idyll was underway. "How do I make the physical part happen again?" I asked Sara.

"If you try to *make* anything happen, the whole thing will probably explode in your face. No pun intended." She reached into the ice chest and dug out a couple of non-diet Dr Peppers. She had something against NutraSweet. Not that a few tablespoonsful of sugar mattered one way or the other. I was already as jittery as I was ever likely to get.

"It's just that I've always had to be the aggressive one, and I doubt he's ready to start initiating things even though he'd probably be receptive if *I* did." I was rationalizing in a mad attempt to get Sara's approval to jump Nick's bones on Monday.

"This situation is so dysfunctional," she lamented. "You probably *will* need to make the next move." Goody. "But it's dangerous."

"How?"

She slathered suntan lotion on her arms and drum-taut stomach. "Your relationship is changing. It's at its most delicate right now. Before you get frisky, you have to be absolutely sure it feels perfectly relaxed and okay. If you force it, I can't be responsible for the consequences."

"I'll be careful," I promised. I strolled over to the pool and jumped in. When I came up, shaking water out of my ears, Sara was talking to me.

"Huh?" I hoisted myself out of the water on carefully toned triceps, flicking my eyes down to make sure the swimsuit wasn't dipping below the close-cropped pubic timberline.

"I said you don't seem too concerned about your Shake-speare audition."

I wasn't. It was hard to muster up enthusiasm for a summer doing six Shakespeare plays in sweaty, Ridley Scott-ish Houston, even though auditioning for the goddamn festival was the whole purpose of the Nick trip. If I was cast, I'd probably tell them no. They were bound to put the company up in some commu-nity college gymnasium, so conjugal visits from Nick would be out of the question. We went inside and I explained this to Sara while she packed for a quick run to San Antonio. After a couple more warnings about keeping my lust and insecurities in check, she took off.

I was playing Edie Brickell loud and cleaning my apartment the next day after my matinee and didn't even hear the phone ring till my machine beeped. "Confess at the sound of the tone," I quipped on tape just before Nick started talking. Hands foamy with Softscrub, I ripped it off the hook, causing piercing feed-back whine.

"Nick! I'm home," I blurted.

"How's your weekend going, Mr. Young?" Nick asked, the voice of Texas friendliness.

"Great," I insisted. Thank God you called. Please don't tell me it's over. Jesus. Please. "We still on for tomorrow?" It sounded pretty flip considering I was digging my nails into my palm hard enough to raise welts.

An eternity, then: "Sure. I'll come by around ten. You playing hooky?"

"Sort of." I love you so much. Eyes closed, I affectionately stroked my cheek with the receiver. "My acting teachers know I'm auditioning. I can afford to miss Spanish." *Mi corazon es tuyo. Vamos muy lejos de aqui, Guapo.*

"Stay out of trouble till then, okay?"

"Okay."

We hung up. I threw on a T-shirt and drove around till I found an open car wash. Then I hit the grocery store for road snacks to fill the ice chest I'd borrowed from Sara. I bought Cokes and a bag of the miniature Peppermint Patties Nick loved. I considered going whole hog and making us submarine sandwiches to stick in extra-large Zip-Loc bags, but decided that would be too *Good Housekeeping*. I passed the condom display. If only.

I had a hot shower before I went to bed and looked at myself naked in the mirror after toweling off. I shoved my face in close to the glass and discovered a blackhead which I promptly eliminated. Then I stepped back and surveyed the whole package. Nick could do a hell of a lot worse. Christ, he had been for years. But of course there was more to life than defined pecs, a cute little puss and a good-sized pipi. "I love you," I practiced saying to the mirror. I cocked my head slightly to the right, displaying my best profile. I looked deep into my eyes. "I love you, Nick." There was no way he would have agreed to this trip if he didn't want to see me anymore. I went to bed and tried to dream about him.

He knocked punctually the next morning and I opened the door, jazzed to the point of breathlessness, and I knew everything had changed.

"Hi," he said, with a smile about one-tenth as big as it should have been. He stood in the doorway, shoulders rigid, hands stuffed into the pockets of his shorts. The same red shorts

I had gone exploring under several days ago, I noted with a fluttery twinge.

No kiss. No whispered "How y'doin', Alex?" while he embraced me and laid his head on my shoulder. No nothing.

As I grabbed my backpack and the ice chest and set the air conditioning to seventy, I thought for a brief but lucidly crystal moment about calling the whole trip off. Oh, no. I went bravely and stupidly down to my car with Nick and drove us to fucking Houston.

As each dull prairie mile of the nearly three-hour ride unfurled, I became more confused and uneasy. Nick had never been this quiet and withdrawn. I had to fill up the tomblike climate-controlled space by randomly babbling about any neutral subject I could latch onto: my family, the Student Association elections at school, rayon versus one-hundred-percent cotton. Nick maintained the most very minimal level of chattiness.

I thought of a dozen ways to start a conversation about what had transpired between us and what it meant to the direction of my life. Any of them would have been deadly.

Things went from weird and tense to embarrassing and infuriating when I took the wrong exit for the University of Houston and we ended up fifteen minutes late for the audition. Nick went to the bookstore while I ran to the drama department, found a bathroom, toweled the sweat off my face, then was told by a weasel-faced beret-head signing people in outside the auditorium that I'd missed my appointment and would have to wait an hour. While I deliberated about going to the bookstore, a white woman with dreadlocks came out and asked who I was and ordered me into the auditorium. After chastising me for being late, she made me sit backstage. "We'll see you in a minute," she snapped.

I tried a few quiet warm-up exercises as some hopeful's bombastic monologue echoed through the building. It was no use. Alone in the dark, the reality of the situation with Nick set upon me like a flock of evil birds. How could things have gone from the tender, erotic revelation of our most private and special feelings to the impenetrable malaise of today? How could I ever find the Nicholas I had become close to and nurtured and made able to trust me, and how could I bring him back from whatever icy tower of guilt he'd exiled himself to?

When the lords of the Houston Shakespeare festival finally summoned me, my performance was mediocre at best, but it was a hell of a lot better than the quiet, strained dinner Nick and I underwent at the intimate Italian restaurant I had carefully selected from Valerie's Houston guidebook. Depending on how the day went, I had planned on suggesting a movie at the River Oaks Theater. Needless to say, we headed for Austin as soon as we ate. Conversation was spotty and superficial. About forty-five minutes into the drive, Nick fell asleep. I initially thought he could have been faking it to avoid further interaction, but occasional glances (every three seconds or so) showed him to be genuinely relaxed. Head tilted gently onto his left shoulder, legs spread, hand unclenched and resting at his side. After twenty minutes of vicious deliberation, I reached over and carefully closed my hand around his.

He started to stir a little when we were about a half hour outside Austin and I let him go, blackly thinking I'd touched him for the last time. At my building, I got my backpack and the chest containing a couple quarts of melted ice and the uneaten mints out of the backseat. Nick surprised me by wordlessly following me upstairs. It was almost dark. Nick excused himself to the little boys' room. I had just gotten a CD player—the only disc I owned was *Tusk*. I put it on. Nick came out and sat a respectful distance from me on the couch. We talked a little about my plans for the summer (zilch) and his upcoming Bar Review course and job hunt. Then he yawned and said, "Sorry I'm so tired. Guess I'm worn out."

Terrified, I slid in closer and started to massage his neck. He drooped his head forward. Everything was okay. I let out a quiet, shuddering sigh of relief. Then with the first chords of Fleetwood Mac's "Sara" softly filling the room, I stopped kneading Nick's tense neck muscles and kissed him. As I did it, I heard Sara screaming, "No! No! Big mistake!"

"Alex," he said, pulling away sharply, "we can't." I put my hands on his shoulders and kissed him again. "We can't."

"Why not?" I whispered.

The sea of love, where everyone would love to drown, Stevie Nicks chanted.

I tried to kiss him one more time, praying that his defenses would crumble in the wake of our muscular, chest-to-chest contact. This ploy worked like shit.

Nick stood up. "I know this is what you want, Alex, it's what you need, but I can't enter into that kind of relationship right now."

It was such a lawyerly thing to say. What it meant was that everything I'd worked so hard for since that open backpack at the library had been blown to bits because I couldn't take a fucking day-long hint and give him his space and play it cool and keep my goddamn paws off him. I started to cry.

In the weeks to come, I replayed the revised, corrected version of this scene in a torturous, endless brain-loop. Instead of mouth-to-mouth contact, I continue with his neck, bringing both hands into play. His head rests on my chest while I work his shoulders with rhythmic firmness. He relaxes and is still and I hear his breathing even into sleep. I barely kiss his cheek. I luxuriate in the closeness, the warmth, the delicious smell. He sleeps.

Nick put his hand on my back and sat beside me. He held my hand, fingers interlocking with mine. Everything was out of my control. I wiped my tears away, hating myself, hating the day. "I can't help the way I feel," I managed to choke out. Brilliant.

"I know," he said. "It's painful. But you'll find somebody—"

"Don't say that!" I hissed. Then I looked him in the eye and broke another sensible romance rule: "What about the other night?"

He shook his head. "A moment of weakness . . ." What poisonous, awful bullshit.

"You're not weak, Nick. Please stay. I won't—"

"I gotta go home," he said. He stood up, fumbling for his keys. I didn't hear the door slam because I was sobbing.

Dear Alexander,

I just had to tell you what happened at my job! See, every day me and my girlfriends on the floor watch <u>Hearts Crossing</u> during our lunch hour.

So yesterday, our supervisor Mr. Hyde (uh-huh, that's his name, child) toted his big white ass into the break room and planted himself right smack in front of my favorite and only soap to tell us we gotta be takin half-hour lunches for the rest of the month!

I said, "Uh-uh, child, you gotta be joking, when Phalita is about to discover that diary's a big old nasty fake? Now you're telling <u>me</u> to move my onion outa here? Look here, sucker, you can just go find yourself another g.d. nurse, 'cause I ain't <u>even</u> missing my Simon, not for one lousy episode! I gotta put up with needles and enema bags and pap smears all day and you're trying to eliminate my one hour of happiness? Excuse me, I don't think so!"

And don't you know he marched outa there pronto and not one more word was said about it? He knows I'll file a g.d. lawsuit in about nineteen seconds if he starts messing with my soap.

Anyway, honey, you are cute as pie and bad to the bone and we all cannot get enough of you.

Sincerely,

LeRoi-Jacques Fortenberry III, R.N.

Atlanta, GA

My mother was right. The fat blonde in the QVC Fashion Channel sequined sweater had been following us around the mall since we left Crabtree & Evelyn. I'd seen her at the pet shop, browsing scratching posts while I admired the iguanas. Then she just happened to be coming down the escalator when we were exiting Dillard's. Now, at the food court, we watched her carry her Corny Dog tray over to a nearby table and sit down with three other gals, all positioned for an unobstructed view of our politically incorrect Chick-Fil-A luncheon.

"They must watch the show," my mom said, careful not to make eye contact with them.

I started in on my second sandwich. "They're not sure it's me because I don't look as good in person."

"Honey, that's ridiculous. You're very, very handsome."

"Thanks, Mom."

It was the day after my Austin adventure. I'd woken up very late, thinking about Trevor for some reason, bars of noon sunshine striping my lovingly preserved high school bedroom. It took a few seconds for me to remember what had taken place the night before, as it always does when something great or really shitty has just happened, so that every time you awaken you re-experience the thrill/devastation afresh.

Dedicating my morning erection to Nick, I embraced one of my massive, April-fresh pillows, and buried my face in it, reliving the delicious pressure of his lean, hard body on top of mine, simultaneously soothing and ferociously exciting.

Then my mom knocked softly and I cleaned up my act and told her I'd love to go shopping with her. So here we were.

One of the women from the QVC blonde's table was walking this way. Sauntering was more accurate, since she obviously was trying to avoid the faux pas (or fox pass, as they said at Texas A&M) of slowing her pace dramatically only upon passing us. I unbuttoned the top of my shirt and tossed my head poutily, knowing she wasn't looking at me yet. My mom was not amused.

"Alex!" she gasped. "Don't!" I knocked it off and Mom and I looked directly at each other and mumbled phony conversation while we tried not to crack up and I saw the woman out of the corner of my eye cruise by and brazenly check me out before stopping at the pizza counter and making quite a production of pulling red-and-white checkered napkins out of a dispenser. She was wearing too-tight acid-washed jeans and a T-shirt that read, MY OTHER HUSBAND IS A GORGEOUS MILLIONAIRE.

"You know how proud I am of you, honey, but that kind of rudeness"—she jerked her head toward the woman, who was actually taking the long way back to her friends—"really pisses me off."

I laughed a little and pilfered some of her waffle fries. "Do you want to go home?" she asked, still worried about me.

"No," I said. "I'm having a great time. It's nice, just the two of us hanging out."

"Yes, it is."

I kissed her cheek. "Let's go to Structure." As we left the food court, a quick backward glance revealed the gals hastily gathering their bags and, hopefully, disposing of their litter and stacking their trays in a neat, orderly manner.

Structure was Nick's favorite store. It was also, I observed, entering with my mom and making a beeline for some choice relaxed-fit jeans, the gayest national retail chain. From Greek columns framing the doorway and a Ken Haak book on the glass-topped waiting-area coffee table to a staff composed entirely of buffed and hairless eighteen-year-old boys, it was like a little islet of West Hollywood smack-dab in the middle of San Antonio.

I picked out a few items for myself, then came across a sweater the exact color of Nick's eyes. A wistful sigh was halfway out of my lungs when I realized I was allowed to give him presents again! I charged the whole wad and hoped there'd be appropriate wrapping paper at home.

My mom bought us each a Strawberry Julius and we decided to go home. First, though, she had to use the rest room. "Let's go to Penney's," she said. "I haven't used those mall bathrooms since I walked into the ladies' room last Christmas and somebody had taken a crap in the sink." I forced her to elaborate on this vile experience while we drifted toward Penney's.

I told her I'd meet her in the electronics department. I'd reached the point in my life when it was time to start pricing a second TV set. Thirty identical detergent commercials played on thirty screens. I sat down on a piece of modular furniture and watched the riveting minidrama of how a husband's b.o.-soaked work clothes almost ruined a healthy marriage. Then a familiar logo popped onto each set. "We now return to *Hearts Crossing*." And there I was times thirty. Neat.

Simon had dropped by Sean Nortonsen's house ostensibly to offer support in the wake of Cyrinda's mysterious coma. "Was there anything Cyrinda was working on for the paper that might have put her in some kind of danger?" I called to Sean, who was in the kitchen getting us some iced tea. As I waited for his answer, I carefully slid open his desk drawer and planted a fatally incriminating letter that would seal my frame attempt.

"Why would you ask that?" Sean (Rick Brewer) came in and set two glasses down in front of us. When he went over to close the window, I switched them, just in case he was on to me.

"It just seems that would be the next direction for the police to take. Wanda told me they haven't been able to come up with a single lead." I sipped Sean's tea.

"There's something rotten about all this, Simon," the troubled former ski instructor confided. Babs Flanagan, the tipsy daytime dowager who played Wanda Blake, had confided to me off-camera that Rick had shortened his name from Breuerstein and lived in mortal fear that the public would get wind of his "five figure nose job, the silly boy. All I can say is it's a good thing circumcision isn't just a Jew thing these days, because that wang's been seen by more women than *Bull Durham*." I'd been working on the show less than four hours at that point.

As they cut to my sphinxlike countenance, the scene's last shot, I heard, "Oh God, it *is* him!" I looked to my left. Standing on the stairs was the lunch bunch, still stalking. Thirty TV sets had just proven their hunch right. I was dead meat.

"Simon!" Gorgeous Millionaire bellowed. I got up and started to walk in the other direction, out of the store, brisk yet controlled. I looked over my shoulder. They were spilling off the staircase, pointing wildly and chattering at whomever would listen. I spun a glance around for my mom—nowhere—then began to run.

I looked back as soon as I cleared the Penney's entrance. Seven or eight women were stampeding toward me. "It's Simon from *Hearts Crossing!*" they shrieked at stunned mall-goers.

Of course, I'd been left with all our purchases and so now tried to dodge baby carriages, oldsters, and four movie ticket lines while toting half a dozen well-stuffed shopping bags. Where was security, for Christ's sake? I'd heard tales of soap actors losing glasses, rings and locks of hair to rampaging fans. I envisioned myself lying senseless on a bed of pennies and nickels in the mall's wishing well, clothing shredded, getting kicked by irate viewers unable to separate the evil Simon from the real, lovable me.

I bounded up the first stairs I came to and saw the approaching horde numbered about twenty, and now included men and kids. The group was well aware of my route, and a faction broke off and hit the escalator, intending to cut me off on the second level. I put on speed and scanned the upstairs for refuge. There was a security guard, but, horrifyingly, the escalator mob was going to reach him before I could. Okay—a clear path to Victoria's Secret. I took it.

"Hi, what can I do for you today?" the pretty customer service representative asked.

"Please help me," I panted.

"Oh, my—you're . . ." her eyes widened with recognition. I couldn't believe this. It was just like *Rosemary's Baby*. Without waiting, I careened to the fitting cubicles, banging into an adorably dressed display table and sending a basket of bras 'n' potpourri flying into the air. I heard my pursuers invade the store as I locked the flimsy half door behind me.

I peeked through the slats and saw wall-to-wall people. "Over here!" The QVC blonde was on the floor looking right at me through the foot-high space below the door. "He's in here!" I backed up against the mirror. She tried to squeeze into the dressing room with me but was too fat.

The rest of the mob surged to the door, pushing against it and the trapped obnoxious blond woman alarmingly. "Crystal! I'm stuck! Shit!" QVC howled.

Faces bobbed up over the top of the door. "Jason Priestley's in there!" some idiot screamed. *Crack!* The top hinge tore off, leaving a jagged splinter I could easily imagine plunging into my eyeball when the rest of the door went in about eight seconds.

"All right, clear it out! Security! Clear the area!" Angry, disappointed complaints.

Someone unstuck the blonde. "Simon!" she called. Her bubblegum-colored fingernails clawed the carpet as she was dragged away, still groping for a handful of celebrity.

Two black rent-a-cops peered into the cubicle. "What the

hell's going on, man?" one asked. They escorted me to the security office and paged my mother. We left through a back exit.

I couldn't resist tuning in the ten o'clock news that night, and sure enough, they'd sent someone to Victoria's Secret, "the site of a near-riot this afternoon over the alleged appearance of soap star Alexander Young of *Hearts Crossing*. Young grew up in Windcrest and graduated from Theodore Roosevelt High School, but neither he nor his family could be reached for comment."

Actually, two reporters had called while we were eating dinner to verify if I was in town. My dad had told them to "piss off."

My parents went to bed and I stayed up daydreaming in the dark about my life in L.A. with Nick. He'd give thirty days notice at that ungrateful law firm and tell Barney he needed to spend some time apart. He'd load his things into a U-Haul and I'd fly back and drive it to California with him. In the meantime, I'd have rented a beautiful Spanish house in the Fairfax neighborhood, with a turret and hardwood floors and a two-car garage and a little yard for To-Bel. Nick would volunteer his time at the gay community center's legal clinic and AIDS Project Los Angeles while studying for the state bar. He'd meet me for lunch at the studio and we'd spend days off frolicking on the hunkiest beaches and I'd buy him a forest-green Jaguar XJS for his birthday and he'd start a law practice on San Vicente Boulevard and we'd have searing, unprotected monogamous sex every single night (five times on weekends) on bedding purchased at Bullock's.

I took out the picture of him I always kept in my wallet. I propped it up next to the lamp on the nightstand and left it there while I wrapped the sweater I'd bought him and phoned a hotel on the river and made a reservation for Monday night under the name Alex Miller. It was still there when the call came in late Sunday morning.

"Honey, it's for you," my mom said. "Nick." I zipped upstairs like a roadrunner, flopped down on my bed and picked up.

"Hello?"

"Hi, there, Alex." He sounded great. "Whatcha been up to?"

"Just hanging around . . . looking forward to talking to you again."

"It was nice catching up the other night." *Catching up?* What was he going to call his divorce from Barney? A little schedule change?

"Listen, Nick, I was thinking about Monday, and I guess the easiest thing would be for you to meet me here and we can go downtown for dinner."

"That sounds fine, Alex . . ." Then why that tragic note in his voice? Oh, no. Oh, fuck. "And I wish I could do that. But I don't think I can."

"Why not?" For a few seconds I thought I really might get through it this time without crying.

"I just can't leave. All this."

"But you're not happy. You said so," I whispered. A tear splashed onto the receiver then dripped to the comforter.

"It's more complicated than that," Nick began.

"I know what it is, Nick. I know exactly what it is." I cried softly. Nothing ever changes.

"My job in Austin—"

"You can quit that tomorrow. I make three thousand a week now. That's plenty for both of us. You can do the kind of work you really want to."

"Alex, I can't leave Barney."

"Why? Why?"

"Because I love him." But you're not *in love* with him, are you, Nick? How many years has it been since you could say that? And how many more will it be before you escape a barren relationship with that thankless deadbeat? I wanted to ask him those things. Instead . . .

"What about me, Nick?"

"Oh, Alex, you know how special you are to me."

"No, Nick, I guess I really don't. I thought I did Thursday night . . ." My voice broke in an embarrassing, childish sob.

"But it doesn't matter what we do or what I say or how easy it would be for you to come with me. I can't make you."

"Alex, please try to understand . . ." I thought I heard him choke back a sob.

"No," I said. "I love you." Then I hung up.

Thirty seconds later the phone rang. It was Nick, telling me he loved me, too. That we could work it out. I snatched it up. "Hello?"

"Alex, it's Juliana."

"Who?"

"Juliana Butts. From Roosevelt?"

"Oh, hi." Jesus, not now.

"You didn't tell me you were making a personal appearance at the mall," she accused.

"I was just shopping with my mother. It wasn't an appearance. Look, Juliana, this isn't the best time for me."

"Anyway, you told me to call today. About lunch."

I sighed. My eyes found Nick's picture on the nightstand. Juliana babbled on. "I hope you still want to go. I can pick you up as soon as I change out of my church clothes. I think we should go casual, don't you?"

"Juliana, I can't go to lunch. I'm sorry. Maybe next time I'm in town. Definitely, okay?"

"Alex, you promised!"

"No I didn't, Juliana. I'm having a really bad day, so please—"

"I don't understand why you just can't give me an hour or two. Maybe you can tell me what's upsetting you."

That was rich. I came close to emitting a few peals of hysterical laughter. "No, okay?"

"You can't treat people this way. This 'star attitude' I keep hearing about. I guess it's totally true. You're not going to have any friends if—"

"Fuck off, Juliana!" I slammed down the phone. I had to admit: I was a tiny fraction less miserable.

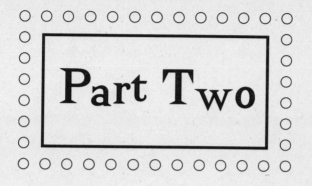

Part Two

The stage manager cued me and I pivoted into the breeze of an electric fan (as opposed to the nonelectric ones who squealed and swooned around the studio entrance after getting a glimpse of us while they were in line for game show tapings of *Cash Crazed* and *Date Bait*). I aimed my malevolent yet seductive grin at the camera and purred, "Cross over to danger."

"Cut," the on-air promo producer intercommed from the booth, adding this familiar, inexplicable directorial couplet: "That was perfect, Alex. Now let's do it again."

I repeated my performance, wondering if the voice in the booth was the one who'd conceptualized the snazzy "Cross Over" campaign. I was happy to have been chosen to participate, even if it did mean two extra hours hanging around this semitacky limbo set complete with a wooden footbridge and bloody orange lighting that evoked prom night in Hell. I felt like the new kid in the class who'd just gotten invited out for pizza and a chocolate malted with the way-coolest, Most Popular people in school. The only others on hand to tape mini-commercials for the show were Brent Bingham ("Cross over to passion"), perky teen Nori Ann Marshall ("Cross over to romance"), and token negress Phalita Renee ("Cross over to excitement"). Brent was required to doff his shirt for his spot—apparently he and his Lord Jesus Christ didn't have a problem with above-the-waist nudity—and his yummy manly chest was very reminiscent of a certain Texan attorney.

We taped a couple of duo and group spots (with Brent tragically shirted), then they released us. I was itching to scrub off the makeup I'd had on since 9:00 a.m. but was stopped en route to my regular assigned dressing room when Phalita started handing out invitations to her housewarming party. They had been color-Xeroxed and featured a photo of En Vogue with all four heads replaced with Phalita's sassy noggin. After the date and time, invitees were discreetly advised to "Call Phalita For Address." Keeping the location of her new digs a secret would be no easy task for the same reason her party would be an E-ticket above and beyond the soap opera set: She was shacking up with a sitcom star who'd just left his wife of fifteen years, the last six months of which had been devoted to a torrid affair with our own Miss Renee. To make things juicier, he was white. The scandal officially broke in Hawaii during the shooting of a special two-part episode of loverboy's show, although everyone at *Hearts Crossing* had been a tad suspicious since a soon-to-be ex-intern from Cal State Fullerton had barged in on Phalita smoking the pole several months ago. I told Phalita I'd love to go. I was hardly in a position to condemn adultery.

Or enjoy it. I'd heard from Nick exactly twice since I returned to Hollywood last fall. 1. A phone message in November: "Just wanted to see how fame and fortune was treatin' you. I'll call you back." He didn't. 2. When I got home from Christmas, thankfully spent far from Texas at my grandparents' Palm Beach condominium, there was a Rockshots card simply and ironically signed "Love, Nick."

The only positive note was that I was able to use my sense

memory of the Xmas card incident (Uta Hagen, take note) to cry convincingly in a *Hearts Crossing* scene in which Simon confides with utter insincerity to love interest–patsy Jane Parkins, who happens to be the Crossing Hospital chemist assigned to the comatose Cyrinda's case, how torn up he is over the rift between him and half-sister Natalie. A rift naturally caused by my insistence on blackmailing the girl with nude photographs in order to get access to our late, demented father's scientific journals which Natalie had inherited and wanted sealed forever.

The show kept me occupied. I'd worked an average of four days a week since going under contract, which meant lots of money and not much time to indulge my loneliness. I'd broken down and called Trevor two weeks after I returned from San Antonio, but he was leaving the next day to shoot a horror movie in Israel that made *Teenage Brides of Christ* sound like *How Green Was My Valley*. I did see him frequently in a current national beer commercial in which he danced a Texas two-step with a l'il filly almost purtier than he was. During an exclusive interview with *Soap Opera Weekly*, I was able to truthfully chirp, "Nobody but Simon," when asked if there was "anyone special" in my life. I was simply "too busy" to date. You know how it is.

My new best friend was my TV agent, Connie, a chain-smoking tough gal somewhere between thirty-five and seventy who represented six other daytime stars. Agents love it when you're on a soap. Those checks come in week in and week out and they don't have to submit you for anything else. Plus, compared to prime time and movie stars, you're real low-maintenance. Connie visited all her "people" on the set once every three weeks, because "a month is too long, but any more often . . . please . . . I get home at night and I'm a dead woman." When my second thirteen-week option cycle began, she sent me a bottle of champagne with a card: "Congratulations on officially not blowing it. All my very, very best."

A few weeks ago Connie and I turned down an infomercial I was offered five thousand dollars plus twenty-five cents a minute a call to participate in. It was for a prominent female recording artist's psychic hotline, a 1-900 number that anyone over eighteen could dial, twenty-four hours a day, and receive a reading from a live "psychic friend" for only $3.99 per minute, which made it considerably more expensive than psychotherapy. Two other stars (from cheesy New York soaps) had already sold their asses to the project, but I just couldn't stomach sitting in some hideous simulation of my living room being interviewed by Missy Famous Singer (my mom owned several of her albums) about my uncanniest psychic experiences and why I thought that a psychic hotline was the most practical, convenient and exciting spiritual development since Parker Brothers started marketing Ouija boards. After all, I had to draw the line somewhere. Fortunately this line lay to the right of the Fiesta Soap Cruise— twenty-five daytime actors and a couple of hundred disposably incomed fans floating from San Diego to tropical Mexican ports on a frolicsome three-day weekend that would be paying me three thousand dollars plus all expenses.

I told Phalita about it during the party in the two-acre kitchen of her new Beverly Hills lovenest. "I did a few of those," she said, donning a Laura Ashley oven mitt and shooing away a caterer before removing a piping hot tray of miniature quiches from the broiler. "They are *fan*tastic. I mean, those tiny rooms suck, but the buffets are straight out of Oprah's wet dreams, baby. Of course, I'm too big to go on a cruise like that now. Those fans would just clobber me for three days straight. But you're gonna have a blast, Alex. Women are going to be serving themselves to you naked on a silver platter." I smiled politely. Phalita's boyfriend wandered in and said hi. When he put his full champagne glass down to rummage through the refrigerator, Phalita picked it up and finished it off. "And there's some cute-ass cabin boys on them ships, too, honey." She winked, then sashayed out to circulate. The sitcom star emerged from the fridge with half an apple pie and a wedge of cheddar cheese. Imagine: a hundred and seventy-five thousand dollars an episode and he likes the same dessert as my grandpa.

"Great party," I told him. It was. Phalita had given a few of us a tour of the house, pointing out the room in which she hoped a Barbara Walters interview would soon take place, as well as the heart-shaped tub and swimming pool that the previous owner, a sentimental sheik, had installed. The food was rich, the music fabulous obscure hits of the sixties, and how about that crowd? The Bob Sagets, Martha Quinn, Katey Sagal, James L. Brooks, Sammi Davis-Voss, Vanilla Ice, Shelley Long, soap giants Eileen Davidson, Jon Lindstrom, Michael and Hunter Tylo, Karen Moncrieff and Victoria Rowell, Corey Parker, the Roseanne Arnolds, Jerry Van Dyke, Debbie Allen, Dana Ashbrook, Lee Grant, Trevor Renado.

I encountered the last over a tureen of spinach dip as we simultaneously inserted cucumber spears. "Alex! Hi!" he exclaimed. His hair was quite a bit longer than the last time I'd seen him. As usual, he sported perfectly burnished tan skin, and lots of it. He wore a brightly colored paisley vest with no shirt and black pants that were baggy everywhere but the ass. Somehow he had become even more muscular.

I quickly chomped my cucumber. "How's it going?" I asked casually.

"Just the best."

"Excuse me, boys," Charlotte Rae trilled, en route to the grilled swordfish.

"Oh, my God!" Trevor gasped. "Mrs. Garrett!" He launched into a theme-song rendition as we stepped over to the fireplace. "Wow. I feel so stupid. Of *course* you would be here. You're the real star of that show."

"Thanks. Who are you with?"

"Just myself. I used to know Phalita's personal trainer."

Ah. "You used to *know* him?" I smiled sweetly.

"Actually, I used to fuck him," Trevor said. His huge brown eyes danced merrily. "But that was a long time ago. How are you?"

"Fine."

"Good Christmas?"

"Wonderful. We all went to my grandparents' in Florida." He was sitting very close to me. "I keep seeing your Bud Dry ad."

"I thank my plastic Joseph and Mary nativity figurines every night for that job. It was so wild. At two I'm doing hanging sit-ups in my apartment and get the call. At three I'm meeting the casting director and at six I'm on a plane and the next morning I'm shooting."

A minor chain of microbits clicked together in my brain. "In Austin, Texas?" I asked.

"Yes . . ." Trevor said, the tiniest shade on-guard.

"And did you go out dancing by any chance? At a club called Oilcan Harry's?"

"Yeah . . . why?" He smiled mischievously, as if he were famous enough to have engendered some gossip that had somehow made its way back to L.A.

"Because I saw you there. Remember? I went to Texas, too? You dropped me at the airport?"

He made a retarded face. "No duh, Alex. How come you didn't talk to me?"

"I was being dragged out the door and really, really buzzed at the time. Nothing personal, of course."

"Of course." One flap of the vest was askew, revealing, if memory served, a notoriously sensitive nipple. "I make it a point to never drink when I'm out alone in a strange town. Ever since that time in Benidorm when I woke up in skivvies in the garden of a Catholic boys' school."

Before I could quiz him about this, Nori Ann Marshall, with Bardot hair and matching Eurotrash boyfriend, was there, kissing my cheek and asking me who my friend was. I introduced them and got to meet Silvio, who was "getting into music management."

Nori handed me an uneaten quesadilla. "Finish this, Alex. I'm bloated. God, this is like being at work. Only with celebrities. I mean, *everybody* from the show is here. Well, except Megan." Megan DuBois was taking advantage of her character's vegetable state to star in a TV movie that told the true story of a housewife involved in a murderous love trapezoid with her twin daughters and a sadomasochistic gymnastics coach.

"Did Brent show you his new Mercedes?" I asked her.

"God, he made us drive around the block in it. He actually had one of those cardboard Jesus air fresheners hanging from the rearview mirror," she moaned. Silvio shook his head sardonically. Those tacky Americans. "Were you there when he spazzed out Thursday?"

"No, but I heard," I said.

"What happened?" Trevor wanted to know.

"He had a tantrum on the set over some stupid line of dialogue," she said, "and wouldn't finish the scene! And I'm waiting on the other side of the door to *come in* and so finally I just entered and said my first line and they'd taken an engineering five and I felt so damn dumb!" She giggled over it. "Brent has just been so difficult since Rhonda left the show—" She suddenly stopped dishing.

"Hi, kids!" said Jerry Reynolds, our co-executive producer. He was in his early thirties, painfully and obviously closeted, a terribly nice former nerd. *Hearts Crossing* was his entire life. He usually sat up in the production office furiously writing scripts, but every so often he'd observe onstage and excitedly offer the kind of creative input our exec producer was too rushed and disinterested to provide from his perennial seat in the tech booth. "We beat *All My Children* last week, you guys!" He sat down next to me and put a skinny arm over my shoulders.

"That's great, Jerry!" Nori gushed, reverting to her sugary ingenue character from the show.

"What's great is having a cast like all of you. I meant to tell you how much I loved that scene of yours, Alex, from a couple of days ago. Where you stood up to Rutherford at the newspaper office? The subtext about your father and the secret formula was really strong."

"Thanks, Jerry. It was well written."

"Aw, thanks. I did sort of whip that one up myself." He noticed Trevor sitting on my other side and self-consciously withdrew his arm.

I sat back so they could get a better look at each other. "Jerry, this is my friend, Trevor Renado. Trevor, Jerry Reynolds, a top-ranking producer on my wonderful show."

"You look so familiar, Trevor," Jerry said, rather googly-eyed.

Trevor rattled off an abbreviated resume. "And he does a lot of work for International Male and Undergear," I added, figuring those catalogs were probably Jerry's favorite beat-off material. Bingo. Jerry became flustered and excused himself to chat with Phalita.

"He's nice," Trevor told me. He flashed a naughty, intimate grin. I felt, then visually confirmed, that his big hand had alighted on my knee. One second later, it was gone.

"I'm going to find the dessert tray," Trevor said. "See you in a bit."

I picked up a glass of champagne and wandered around, trying to mingle, wondering if I'd ever have my own mansion and who the hell would live in it besides me and my iguanas. Sound-bites from conversations blew back and forth like cumulus cotton speech bubbles.

". . . I'd call it more of a support group than therapy. She's helping me relax into my power . . ."

". . . they're so fucking cheap it has to be a pilot *presentation* . . ."

". . . Deborah Aquila loves me . . ."

". . . looking so hot I hardly recognized you. Can I just say something, and don't . . ."

". . . I'm in bed with Lorimar and Amblin and Kiefer Sutherland's attached . . ."

". . . MTV Music Awards she had the silicone taken *out* . . ."

I spotted my co-star Anna Ford—she played Jane Parkins, unwittingly being used by Simon to recreate his father's dangerous sexual potency drug—making out with a member of an all-boy bubble-gum pop group. I had to kiss her next week on-screen, so observed a moment to know what to expect. Lots o' tongue and her hand between my buttocks obviously.

"There you are!" Trevor had been looking for me. "There's a gross of Mrs. Fields' chocolate chip cookies behind the layer cake. I wish I had pockets." He handed me a cookie. "Wanna go do something?"

"Like what?" I bit into the cookie, way more interested than I was afraid to let on. Trevor shrugged. "Okay. Let me find the bathroom first."

"While you're doing that, I'll introduce myself to Roseanne." He slithered toward her, a compliment already poised on his carefully moisturized lips. I ducked into a handy powder room, displacing a joint-smoking series regular. I closed the door and marveled at how the Liquid Vanish offset the pale pink commode. The medicine cabinet contained Lady Schicks, dental floss and Extra-Strength Tylenol. I opted for number three— two caplets washed down with a handful of tap water in anticipation of the tension I could already feel massing at the back of my head. I steadied myself against the pale pink sink. Trevor wasn't worth this much worry. He simply was not. The problem was that I still considered him the only semi-significant non-Nick romantic relationship of my life, which was stupid. Thinking of Nick and Trevor in the same terms was pointless. It was like comparing the *Santa Maria* to a jet-ski. Still, I couldn't help wondering what the jet-ski would look like emerging from the clear, warm waters of the pale pink bathtub I was now focusing on as I rubbed my temples. There was a rap on the door.

"Come in," I said.

It was Trevor. "Ready?"

"Absolutely. Let's say goodbye to Phalita." We found her at the piano singing a duet of "Success Has Made a Failure of Our Home" with Richard Mulligan. After the applause died down, we said our goodnights.

Trevor played with the zippers on his biker jacket as we waited for the valets to finish their game of chicken or whatever with our cars somewhere down the hill. I noticed a shiny black car with the license plate BING parked in a corner of the driveway and elbowed Trevor. "There's Brent's Mercedes."

"It's only an E," he snipped.

We were just about to check out the air freshener when our cars pulled up. "How do you want to do this?" I asked him.

"Follow me back to my place and we'll take it from there." He reached into his car and pulled out a parking permit. "I'll wait outside for you."

Trevor lived in West Hollywood, just north of Santa Monica Boulevard, conveniently midway between the disco dinosaur Rage and Pavilions, the cruisiest upscale grocery store west of Aruba. I had to assume Trevor was only teasing with phrases like "follow me home"; he lived at the hub of Boystown and could have had any number of hang-out activities in mind—dance clubs, after-hours cafés, live sex shows. The possibilities were endless. But they most definitely did include going up to his apartment. (To watch a video, perhaps.) Under any circumstances, I had to maintain my dignity and willpower. If I was going to use Trevor like the mouthwatering hard-bodied Palm Springs guest-house toy that he was, *he* was going to damn well insist on it.

We turned left on Santa Monica from Doheny into bumper-to-bumper midnight traffic. Ten minutes later we'd traversed the block and a half to his house and I had to suffer the shame of trying to parallel park under pressure. Wheel all the way to the left, then reverse, then all the way to the right. Wasn't that it? Shit. I squinted through the steamy windows to see if anyone was making fun of me. Two cars ahead of me I noticed glowing red taillights. Someone was pulling out in front of Trevor's building. Thank Christ, I thought, backing out of my abortion of a parking job and casually sliding into the vacant spot, nicely adjacent to but not impinging upon a hydrant. I slipped the parking permit around the rearview mirror as Trevor opened my door for me. "Get out of the car, Alex. I'm freezing. Let's go warm up." I looked involuntarily toward his apartment. "Come on," Trevor urged, tugging me in the opposite direction. What the hell was going on? I made certain to keep a poker face as I followed him down to the Boulevard. That tart.

"Hey, Simon!" a tipsy reveler leered, swiping at me as we paraded up the street with the rest of the Saturday night party boy squad. I waved. As always, I marveled at the sheer volume of great-looking, bright-eyed men making the same old rounds —from Micky's to Rage to Studio One and back again, with optional pit stops at Revolver, Motherlode or A Different Light, like gerbils running through a neon Habitrail. Okay, hamsters. In one block, I counted nine faces handsome enough to kiss with little or no personality-intelligence data available. Couldn't one of them be Mr. Right, lonely, bored, sick of smoky clubs and their empty-hearted poseurs, not to mention terrible house music? How could you ever know?

"What have you been up to?" I asked Trevor after I'd been recognized a third time and he'd pretended not to notice.

"I had a pilot callback yesterday. And I'm recurring on *The Bold and Beautiful* Monday."

"That's great. How many times have you been on?"

"This'll be four. I play a Spectra model. Just something else for my tape. Did you see my *Step By Step*?"

"No," I said, not feeling guilty about my tiny smirk. "When was this?"

"It was on last month. And it's not funny, Alex." Before I could reply to that, he growled, "It's a charming show. My little niece in Pennsylvania loves it. Suzanne Somers has been one of my idols for years, so meeting her was like . . . yeeeowww! She even autographed her poetry collections, which I'm proud to own. 'To Trevor, My Sexiest Co-Star Since Joyce DeWitt.' "

"Bull," I countered.

"No, it's true! They're at home. I'll show you. Don't let me forget." So he *was* planning on taking me back to his place. A tremor of excitement rippled my nerves.

Just as I expected, our destination was Little Frida's, a hip, dykey coffee house nestled within a mock-French Quarter shopping plaza directly across from The Sports Connection, where the finest in nineties health-club facilities meet the sleaziest in seventies steam-room action. Trevor owed his lucrative physique to six stamina-stretching workouts a week there. I preferred to keep firm, fresh and fun to look at at the Powerhouse on Beverly, a cozier, scaled-down, less meaty exercise experience.

We ordered mocha lattes and Trevor scanned the room for Madonna. Darn the luck. At our tiny corner table, he said, "You never told me how your trip to Texas went."

"You never told me how yours went, either."

"Fine. Fun. It was only three days."

"Mine was interesting. I went back to my old high school, alternated between my mom's cooking and all my favorite restaurants, spent a lot of time with my friend Sara, caused a minor riot at the mall."

He laughed at that, thinking I was kidding. I decided not

to explain. He had something else in mind, anyway. "How do things stand with Nick?"

Feel free to get right to the point. "We had dinner when I was in Austin. The night I saw you, as a matter of fact."

He took a sip of his mocha latte and licked foam off his upper lip. "How'd it go?" Was that concern and vulnerability darkening his fine features?

"Okay, I guess. Nothing's changed as far as the Barney situation. Nick's really stuck in a rut, but that's not my problem, right?"

Trevor shook his head. "So it's really over?"

"Yeah." Now he was going to tell me he was madly in love with someone he'd met rollerblading.

"That's good to know," was all he said.

Okay, enough. I plunged in. "How's your love life?"

He narrowed his massive peepers and raised one eyebrow simultaneously. "If you must know, I've been celibate for six months."

I laughed out loud. "And I'm Colonel Sanders."

"I'm not kidding, Alex!" He challenged me with a grave look.

"What brought this on?"

He shrugged. "I had an HIV test last summer and it came back negative, thank God, and I thought, okay, great, let's pull in the reins. What's the point of screwing around with guys I don't give a damn about when I can masturbate and get the same results without the risk or the aggravation?" He paused for more coffee. He was a real P.O.W. (or piece of work, as my agent dubbed many in show business). "No one knows what feels good to me better than I do, right? I picked up some great lotions at Bath and Bodyworks, a few mags, treated myself to some new pillowcases . . . I've been very happy ever since." Performance piece played, he smiled gorgeously. The image of him jacking off was a tad hard to shake.

"And there haven't been any slipups?" I inquired.

"No," he said, then had to look away, smirking, caught in a lie.

I nodded condescendingly. "I see."

"Okay, it was only one time, right after Christmas. And it almost doesn't count, because it was just, you know—" He cupped his hand around an air penis and stroked it for two seconds. "I was sitting in the sauna at the gym, absolutely innocent, wearing a towel which covered everything, just relaxing, alone, when the door opened and this *guy* walked in, totally strapping, perfect bodybuilder physique. I didn't want to stare. I mean, I did, but I couldn't, or else . . . so I closed my eyes for a little while and tried to remember the cast of *Mayberry RFD*, but when I opened them for a second"—he leaned forward confidentially—"his dick was as big as a baby's arm and he was sliding the foreskin back and forth and staring at me and we ended up whacking off together." Our faces were about two inches apart. "He was from Sweden and spoke three words of English so I didn't even get his name."

I shook my head. "So bittersweet."

"Alex, don't you ever do anything trashy?"

"Just my show. Did you see it last week at all? There was a great scene where Gwen was seducing this stud in front of Ollie—they're trying anything to help him get it up—and she started flashing back to her rape on the yacht and freaked out. Plus Sean got beaten up in jail and I tried to kill Cyrinda again in the hospital."

"How do you keep track?"

"I only worked one day last week so I watched it at home. It was great. I slept in, heated up Trader Joe's frozen entrees, talked to *Soap Opera Digest* on the phone."

"You have such a dream life."

"Stop. You're killing me."

"All I want is a series, Alex. A soap, some sleazy late-night detective show, a nuclear holocaust sitcom, a pilot. One pilot. It doesn't even have to air. I just need to have 'series regular' on my resume. It's the next step if I want my career to go anywhere."

"Well, it is pilot season. Have you been out a lot?"

He sighed petulantly. "Some. The callback I had was for this hideous sitcom pilot. Elayne Teitelbaum and Karyn Wulbrun are casting."

"I love them. What's the show?"

"*Dino and Muffin.*"

"You'd be playing, Dino, I hope."

He giggled spasmodically. "No, Ky. That's K-Y. As in jelly. Dino will be played by Corey Haim."

"No."

"Yeah, he's set! I can't wait to tell him how much I loved *License to Drive*. Both Coreys were in that, you know. Corey Haim and Corey Feldman. It was a Coreyfest, just like *The Lost Boys*."

"*That* was a great one."

"Anyway, you have to read this pilot script. I'll show it to you when we get back to my house"—Yes!—"because it's just atrocious. Muffin is this adorable black tot who's adopted by— okay, ready?—a fraternity. I'd play Corey's zany, fun-loving roommate. I'll never get it, though."

"Why not?"

"I'm just totally wrong for it. You don't think I'm too *effy* to get a series, do you?" He sat back in his chair and folded his arms over his flexed chest in a pseudo-unconsciously butch manner.

"Oh, no, Trevor. Don't ever think that." I saw no reason not to lie.

He kicked me lightly under the table. "Do you have to get up early tomorrow?" he asked.

"Well, it's Sunday and there is my paper route."

"Skip it. Let's have a film festival. I rented *Two Moon Junction* and *Make Them Die Slowly*."

Trevor had moved to his apartment from Venice about a year ago, but I'd never been inside. It was a Victorian affair—high ceilings, hardwood floors, a fireplace in which he'd cleverly installed a TV set. Trevor gracefully snatched clothes off the plush scarlet sofa. "Have a seat!" He disappeared into the bedroom.

I couldn't help noticing Trevor's modeling portfolio, displayed as it was on the coffee table like someone normal would have *France's Wine Country* or *A Norman Rockwell Christmas*. I picked it up. Page One: Our host on a crunch machine, tummy rippling, shorts riding up buttery, hairless thighs. Page Two: A tuxedo shot beneath the full moon. Page Three: Back to the program with the cover of *Undergear*, featuring Trevor and all his two thousand parts laced into a hi-tech jockstrap. Page Four: Wait. Let's go back to Page Three. Jesus. I made a mental note to order something from *Undergear* tomorrow and reactivate my position on the mailing list.

"Sorry, Alex." Trevor slid out of his room in stockinged feet. "Let me just check my messages." He turned on his answering machine. I quickly and carefully put the portfolio back on the table.

"Bon soir, Trevor. It's Marcel. I got the how do you say contact sheets, and I want to shoot another roll, somewhere nice like maybe the tar pit. Ring me back." *Beep.* "Hi, it's Larry. . . . Guess you're not home. . . . Anyway, it's Saturday so tomorrow's Sunday. . . . um, I kind of wanted to drive down to La Jolla tomorrow. . . . Give me a call, dude." *Click.*

"Who was that?" I asked pertly.

Trevor rewound the tape and sat down beside me. "Larry. This dumb blonde I met at the grocery store."

"At least this one speaks English."

"Barely. We had lunch a couple of weeks ago and all he talked about was what kind of tattoo he should get. It was a nightmare."

I'm sure it was more of a nightmare for the young blond hopeful who had every reason to think Trevor would be getting into his pants and vice versa. That was if I was to believe that celibacy crap. And what if it were true? Did I want to be the reason Trevor fell off the meat wagon?

"Do you want to watch a movie?" he asked.

"Do you?"

"I don't know. . . . Why don't I give you the tour?"

"Lead the way."

Highlights included his autograph from Suzanne Somers, the refrigerator (empty except for a bottle of Calistoga and chocolate-covered espresso beans), and the stone-and-glass patio table he was mistakenly charged $19.95 for at Cost Plus. We ended up in his room, which had been mysteriously candle-lit.

Cherubs and angels were the dominant motif—plaster ones seated on his nightstand and dresser, ornately carved ones fluttering around the frame of the obligatory full-length mirror, painted Renaissance ones gazing down from a huge picture hanging over his bed.

We sat down. The cozy aroma of melting wax scented with jasmine was suddenly very prevalent. "It's a great apartment, Trevor. And you haven't even shown me your CD-changer yet." He smiled and tentatively reached one of his big hands to my face and brushed my hair behind my ear. I kept my eyes on the hastily made bed for a few seconds, then looked at him.

"I hope this is okay," he said, still smiling. His hand came to rest on my shoulder.

I undid his single button and the vest fell open. I laid my hand on his bulging pectoral. His skin was feverishly warm. ("Metabolism," he'd explained long ago.) My thumb brushed against his semi-hard nipple and he inhaled sharply. Then his arms were wrapping around me, pulling us together. I smelled Paul Mitchell gel and something smoky and decadent—sandalwood?

After several sizzling make-out minutes, Trevor started to undress. The vest sailed across the room, followed by his socks. He stood up and I unsnapped his pants then lowered the zipper, feeling irresistible pressure from within. I reached around his waist and pulled them down, my fingers trailing over his perfect buns (no underwear, as usual).

"What about celibacy?" I just had to ask.

"It really sucks," he said, slithering on top of me and starting to pull off my clothes while I grabbed handfuls of hot muscle with my eyes closed and didn't fantasize that it was Nick until I felt Trevor's lips riding the nerve-ending railway up the back of my neck.

August 1990

I hadn't dreaded a school year so much since the fourth grade, when I'd had advance information that my homeroom teacher was going to be megabitch Miss Cookstone, who, it had been widely reported, had gotten into a screaming, wrestling altercation with her Weight Watchers counselor the previous Christmas vacation. UT started on the last Wednesday in August, so I drove up Tuesday night. My apartment, unoccupied for the summer, was dusty but intact. I turned on the TV, dialed Sara's number and started rummaging through the grocery bags my mom had packed for me. Sara's machine kicked on.

"Hello, gorgeous," I said after the beep. "Be the first and only person to welcome me back to sultry Austin. Same number. Bye." I hung up and started flinging clothes out of my suitcase, trying to dig out my phone and address book for Sara's number at *The Daily Texan*. She'd stayed in town the whole summer to work on the paper and moved across the river to a studio apartment in the overpriced, heavily Greek West Campus area.

I found the book and flipped to the Rs, pausing briefly on the M page. Nicholas Miller—address scratched out. New phone number inked in. Apparently, he'd moved right on schedule at the end of July. I'd called from Maine a few weeks ago, jumping out of bed (after tearfully listening to both sides of a special tape of depressing songs I'd recorded) and creaking down the stairs as my grandparents slept. I punched in Nick's number, knowing damn well that whatever the outcome, it had to be shitty. If Barney answered, I'd hang up. If Nick answered, ditto. Hearing his voice after three months, even just saying "Hello" would undoubtedly let loose a Pavlovian spurt of lust and misery. The final option—listening to some recording stutter out the new number—meant Nick didn't care if I had his new phone and address or not. Okay, so I'd been away all summer, but there's no reason he couldn't call Sara—*dee-doo-deep*! "The number you have reached . . ." I scrawled it on a napkin. Now go to bed. But I still don't—enough! All you can possibly find out is that Barney's still with him. There's *no way* to prove that Barney's *not* there. I dialed the new number. One ring. Three rings. Then: "Hello?" It was definitely Barney. Becoming more impatient: "He*llo*?" I hung up hard. So the saga continued. Had he wavered for even a second before leasing himself to another year with Dogface? Not that it even mattered. The end result was the same as if I'd never met Nick. I wondered if it was too late to transfer to executive secretarial college.

I did one-handed push-ups and dialed Sara's work number. "Entertainment," some guy drawled.

"Sara Richardson, please."

"Who's calling?"

"Her albino love slave. Tell her it's way-urgent."

Endless hold as I barely cranked out eighteen push-ups, weakened from a month of fried clams and rhubarb pie at my grandmother's salty Downeast retreat. Then: "Alex?"

"Hi!"

"You son of a bitch. School only starts tomorrow."

"I don't have class till twelve. I got back from Maine thirty-six hours ago. I swear."

"Then get down here right now. We'll go to happy hour and I'll tell you my good news."

"The twins *aren't* brain-damaged?"

"No. Wait a sec." She whispered: "It's completely unofficial for at least a week, but they're making me Entertainment Editor."

"That's fantastic! A celebration is definitely obligatory."

"A Chuy's margarita and a buttload of nachos sound mighty appealing. I've been trapped in this rat hole since nine a.m., trying to compose a Fall TV Preview for the kids. Thank Christ you make me watch *Twin Peaks*. Hurry, Alex. It's already ten-thirty."

" 'Kay. Bye."

"Oh, wait. Did you hear from Nick?"

"No! Did you?"

"Yeah, he called me about three weeks ago, with his new phone number and address."

"Did he mention Barney?"

"Uh-uh. He asked all about you, though. I said you'd be back from your tremendously busy and exciting summer in time for classes."

I hopped up and looked for the box containing my answering machine. "Did he leave any message for you to relay?"

"No, honey. Look, just get down here before I have to eat one of my nubile young assistants." A few spirited whoops from the boys at that one.

"Thanks! See you in no more than five minutes." I clicked off, set up the machine, recorded the perfect greeting and left the apartment in no more than twelve minutes.

All I could think of as Sinead and I sped down Duval Street was, "He's going to call. He misses me. He's going to call." Sara apologized for not tracking me down in Maine after she talked to Nick, "but I didn't want you obsessing and freaking out some place, lovely as it is, where they can't even pick up the Fox Network."

As we enjoyed one of the best student dining values in Austin, $2.50 for a frozen drink and unlimited visits to the nacho bar, I was careful not to monopolize the conversation, although I did feel it was fair to structure my half around various declarative and interrogative versions of "He's going to call. He misses me."

I scurried up the stairs to my apartment at 12:45, anxious to rinse the fiesta taste out with a hit of Listermint then crash, hoping my dreams would follow the "He's going to call. He misses me" theme. The machine said I had one message. He misses me. He called. No, it has to be someone else. He had called. "Glad you're back, Mr. Alex. Why don't you give me a ring at the office tomorrow and we'll see about grabbing a bite of dinner this week. Might be easier now that I'm not preoccupied with the damn Bar exam. Talk to you soon." Preoccupied with the Bar exam? And all this time I thought he never wanted to see me again. Mustn't be sarcastic, I scolded myself as I slapped sheets onto my bed. I loved him too much to be anything but thrilled. I slept naked with the air conditioner at sixty-five degrees just to celebrate.

The next morning I looked up Nick's work number (which I'd uncharacteristically not memorized) and called him, extremely careful to keep any giddiness under control. We could only talk for about twenty seconds, because "some a-hole" needed him in his office. He sounded great. He wanted to have dinner. I suggested Thursday, because it would give me all of tonight to rearrange my living room. I didn't want our next scene together here to have anything in common with our last one, including stage design. We decided he'd pick me up in front of the Co-Op bookstore at 5:30.

My last class Thursday was Advanced Acting, taught by a visiting professor whose major credit was a supporting role in *The China Syndrome*. There were a few kids I liked in the class, most of them riddled with anxiety that they would graduate with their Bachelor of Fine Arts degrees next May without ever having been cast in a University production. I stuck around briefly to chat, then walked across campus to the Texas Union, where I extracted new clothes and beauty aids from my backpack and transformed myself into what I hoped was a vision of boyish charm. I cut an imposing figure in the bookstore, nimbly dodging sweaty, disoriented shoppers and efficiently snagging used copies of all required texts. I checked out and assumed my post by the falafel stand at exactly 5:27.

And like magic, there he was. He rolled down the passenger-side window of the Mitsubishi and deadpanned, "Hey, little boy. Is ten bucks enough?"

I opened the door and hopped in. "I'd pay twenty."

We went to Kerbey Lane Café. I had chicken fajitas and absolutely no idea what was going on. Was this a date? He was warm, friendly, adorable, hot. He made me tell him all about my summer—which had begun, I didn't remind him, with him devastatingly rejecting me after the Houston fiasco. He told me he was hopeful about the Bar exam and would know in November if he passed. I told him my LSAT results—ninety-sixth national percentile—and let him get excited. I listened to every word and searched his awesome blue eyes for some clue that things were different. He didn't mention Barney, but every time he talked about the little house he'd rented east of the Mopac Expressway, I winced. After almost two hours, I was unsure of anything except that Nick was driving me home and that I really should carry a pack of gum in my bag at all times.

I asked him up, he said sure, we went in, I broke out a couple of York Peppermint Patties. Nick munched his and surveyed the living room. "Is this the same apartment? I mean, did you move over one or something?"

"No, it's the same." I sat down on the sofa, respectably close to the edge. "It's just that I'm a *senior* now, so everything looks cooler."

"Ah." He joined me. Just to show how relaxed and nonthreatening and unseductive I could be, I zapped on the TV and we flipped through the channels for twenty minutes or so, just hanging out. Then a *Twin Peaks* promo gave me a real good idea.

"I just bought an album I think you'd really like. Wanna hear it?" I quickly muted that bitchy nun on the Catholic Channel, my heart leaping a little for the first time since initially reacquainting myself with his Mel Gibson's-little-brother gorgeousness in front of the Co-Op.

"Let's do it," he said. I went to my CD shelf and found what I wanted between Tracy Chapman and Culture Club—*Floating Into The Night* by Julee Cruise. It was the ultimate romantic record for fans of the ethereal. I started it up, walked back to the couch, turned off the TV and sat down next to Nick.

"Mmmmm," he hummed. His eyes were closed. We sat together, touching but not touching, and listened. When the second song started, he kicked off his Topsiders. I was breathing very deeply. I continued to do so as I gently laid my hand on his bare thigh and lightly kneaded it. Experiencing zero resistance, I unbuttoned his white cotton shirt from the bottom and stroked his stomach. If he had touched my basket, my cock would have bruised him. I was careful to keep my own paws away from his khaki crotch.

I felt his hand on the back of my neck and almost cried out. "This is real sweet music, Alex." I looked at him and mouthed a kiss. He took me in his arms and I pressed my face against his deliciously hairy chest, running my lips over his right nipple but not licking or biting. I hugged him to me, really, truly content just to be curled up next to him in the dark.

Agonizingly soon, the disc was over. He sighed and patted my shoulder. "I really should be heading out," he whispered.

"Okay," I whispered back. And it was.

"Let me rinse off first, if you don't mind."

I wasn't sure if I should be offended, but conspiring to deceive Barney had definite appeal. "I'll help you," I told him.

We went into the bathroom and I soaked a washcloth in hot water, then squirted a stream of Softsoap onto it and lathered it up. Nick hung his white shirt on the door handle and stood before me while I scrubbed lingering traces of Grey Flannel off him. There had been no nudity, but tonight had been somehow infinitely more erotic than that first little round of Hide-the-Salami last May. Little did I know how young the night actually was.

I gave Nick's back and shoulders a couple of perfunctory swipes with the washcloth, then hung it over the tub to dry. He was hunched over, hands on the side of the sink. He didn't move. I put my hand on his shoulder. "What is it?" I asked.

"I guess I'm just waiting for you to rub my back."

Whoa. "Sure, but . . . I thought you had to go," I stammered quietly.

He turned around and we were chest to chest. He leaned in close to my ear and said, "We got time."

I took him by the hand and we went into my room. He lay down on his stomach with no coaching from me. I picked up his hand and kissed it. "I'll be right back." I loped into the living room. First—turn off the phone. I set the machine to mute pickup. Second—a candle. My grandmother had sent me one from Maine last Christmas. Got it. Matches were with the incense by the CDs. I scraped three to shreds trying to light the Christless thing, as Grandma would say. Finally, ignition. I'd taken three steps back toward the boudoir when I remembered the music. One flick of a switch and Julee was crooning again. I raised the volume to compensate for distance. Then I went back in.

I doffed my shirt and straddled my dream date, massaging his neck and shoulders and back, firmly, tirelessly. Unbelievably, he seemed to be enjoying it more than I was. "You've got real strong fingers," he sort of mumbled into the pillow. I slid my thumbs under the waistband of his khaki shorts.

"If you took these off, I could do your lower back." Three seconds later, he raised his hips, reached down and unlocked everything. I didn't hesitate. Down came the khakis and the white briefs. I tossed them onto a chair.

As promised, I gave his lower back a tension-liquidating workout, my professionalism undeterred by the presence of his adorable manly buttocks beneath my wrists. Of course, those buttocks needed a thorough, lengthy workout of their own. This wasn't a problem for me. Or Nick, if his sighs and appreciative groans were any indication, and they were. His feet. His calves. His thighs. His inner thighs. I spread his legs and sank my fingers into the erogenous zone.

It was time for him to roll over. He did. The view was stunning. I worked on his legs and chest and arms for a few minutes before he said: "Why don't you massage this muscle?"

And with that, he reached down and lifted his stiff, smooth, eight-inch penis from his stomach. I had entered Fantasyland. This was Ed McMahon knocking on my door with a camera crew and the American Family Sweepstakes check.

"I'd love to," I told Nick, and grabbed his cock. I stroked it up and down to maximum rigidity, then gripped it at the base and went down like a sub. Whether by instinct or multiple video screenings of *The Young and the Hung*, I seemed to have a talent for this. To such an extent that Nick sat up, groaning, "You're gonna make me scream." His hand dropped to my button fly. Pop pop pop. "But it feels too good to stop," he added. I stripped off my pants and he pulled me down into bed underneath him. The kissing was so rapturous—God, those lips—I was barely conscious of him jacking me off. He was rubbing his dick against my stomach, nibbling around my ear, whispering something. I stopped thrashing my head to listen.

"Alex . . . can I please fuck you in the mouth?"

Oh, why not.

Afterward, under my comforter, Nick lay tranquil in my arms and I plotted to make this a nightly occurrence. My immediate options—hysterical confessions to Barney, suicide attempts—seemed trite. I tried hard to make right now be enough—the intimacy, the fulfillment of almost a year's worth of dreaming and longing. I wondered if I was still a virgin. How did queers tell? Obviously, if you boned somebody up the butt, you weren't. Same if you were the bonee. But that left the vast world of the blow job fuzzy and gray. I didn't think getting sucked off counted as losing your gay virginity. It was just such a basically noninteractive event. Giving head was another matter. In my limited experience, it seemed to have a certain level of intensity and commitment that put it in a more prominent position on the deflowering scale. I decided sustained, deep-throat penetration by or of someone you loved constituted losing it. Due to current medical knowledge and conditions, swallowing did not figure into the equation.

My first nonvirginal semester was hardly the nightmare I'd dreaded all summer. (Of course, I *was* a virgin then.) I was immediately given the lead in a departmental production directed by a string bean Cuban grad student named Alfredo. It was a revisionist version of Shirley Jackson's *The Lottery* from a Latin American revolutionary perspective. At the play's climax, the audience, innovatively seated all over the stage, was encouraged to throw papier-mâché stones at the heroine along with the rest of the cast, several members of which seriously considered slipping a few real rocks into the pile to fling at the twatly prima donna.

Sara was busy with the newspaper most of the time, so I actually started hanging around my drama friends a little. We'd get together and watch tapes of that week's *Twin Peaks* episode. (Someone suggested regularly eating cherry pie and drinking "joe" during the shows, but that was just too geeky and obnoxious.) They bemoaned the rotten studio scenes they were in and the neurotic people they had to act with and how they could never reserve rehearsal space. They debated acting graduate programs at the University of Delaware at Wilmington and Louisiana State. I told my parents I'd be applying for law school at UT. They were so excited we went out to dinner and they insisted on buying me new Reeboks.

Nick was on my mind at least once every ten minutes of every waking hour. We were Having an Affair and I was The Other Man. Innocent little me. All my notions of propriety had been spun around, twisted and hung out to dry. Surely it was wrong to try to bust up a couple's relationship. But then again, why shouldn't I get a shot at Nick? Barney had gotten there first, but was there some sacred covenant that kept Nick a prisoner when the relationship went stale? Wasn't my happiness just as important as Barney's? It was more important, goddamnit. I put myself in Barney's place. Constantly. And the conclusion I kept drawing was that if I *were* in his place—in Nick's house, at his breakfast table, on his couch, in his kitchen, in his bed— Nick would never, ever have to go anywhere else for the attention, appreciation and sexual prowess *I* knew he deserved. Wasn't it completely possible to meet the soulmate of your life at an incredibly inconvenient time? The chances of meeting such a person were slim enough to begin with—expecting things to work out neat and tidy right away was really pushing it.

We saw each other once or twice a week, usually at my

apartment for dinner. I became proficient at about seven different dishes, which I served on a rotating basis, as well as massage therapy and hot, penis-pleasin' action. It was impossible to tell what Nick thought of the situation. I knew he liked me and the food and how I made him feel, but where did he see our relationship going? We didn't discuss it. But he called me a lot and accepted my invitations and didn't tell me to stop when I put my hands under his shirt. He'd made my dreams come at least partially true and I loved him for that and wasn't going to fuck it up by asking questions he probably didn't know the answers to.

"You're being very mature about this," Sara said. "I don't think I could handle it. He's a great guy and everything, but I couldn't stand it."

"What?" I squawked.

"Y'know . . . sharing him."

"Yeah, but I hope it won't always be like that. Anyway, I didn't tell you my excellent news. He's coming to San Antonio for Thanksgiving."

"Holy shit. How did you manage that?"

"Barney always goes to his parents' house alone, right? They hate Nick because they think he turned their little baby into a fag. They ought to be thanking their paint-by-numbers Bible pictures a treasure like Nick took that deadbeat off their hands."

"Anyway . . ."

"Okay, last year I knew he was alone doing nothing on Thanksgiving, so I asked my mom if I could bring a friend down and she said yes and it'll probably only be one night, but I don't think I've ever been happier."

"It's pretty major, Alex. Home to meet the family. I'll be down, too, so maybe we can all go out, show Nick around, stop by the Bonham for a drink."

"That'd be great."

"Okay, I gotta run. One of the staff reporters wrote a rave review of this album I can't stand and I have to make sure there's no room to run it."

"You power-mad dominatrix."

Nick was hired by a highbrow law firm in mid-October. He and Barney celebrated with a lavish dinner at The County Line, Austin's swankiest restaurant. He and I celebrated with pasta at my place, where I gave him an office-warming present, a sterling silver tarantula paperweight.

"I'll call it Mr. Young," he said, smiling.

"Thanks a lot," I replied.

He hugged me from behind so I couldn't get hold of him. I felt his five o'clock shadow nuzzling my nape and quaked. "You spent way too much money on me." I shook my head violently. "You know, I really appreciate you takin' such good care of me."

"Any time."

The next Sunday I decided to fill out the law school application that had been sitting on my dry bar for almost a month. It was basically a formality—with my test score and UT GPA, I'd be an auto-admit. Still, it was a good excuse to see Nick. Maybe if we completed the app together it would forge some Olympian romantic bond that would stretch through my legal education and deposit us in love and as one at the Sunflower graduation ceremony three years from now, I thought spacily as I crossed Lamar for an utterly uncharacteristic rendezvous at Nick's house.

Barney was off boring his cousins in Lockhart for the day and Nick was "on call"—he'd already worked six days that week on a big case at his new job but had to be prepared to make it seven. "So far so good," he grinned, cocking a thumb at the phone as I made my entrance, hair still damp from the gym.

It was only the second time I'd been to their house and it felt weird. There wasn't much physical evidence of Barney's existence—a tiresomely kitschy collection of Warner Brothers cartoon figurines, a stray *Playguy* subscription card sticking out of a pile of debris on the desk, clothing from Mervyn's that Nick wouldn't be caught dead in—but this was Barney's domain, all of it, and I was hyperaware of that as Nick ran down the list of home projects he'd accomplished that day and I followed him around the place, looking at the new window frames through which Barney peered at sweat-sheened UT students jogging by and the garbage disposal Barney would forget to empty his dirty dishes into and the toilet in which Barney took his daily dump. I felt a perverse, powerful desire to be alone in the house, to pry into every inch of it, every drawer, every closet, every file stashed away in every box, just to learn what secret kept Nick and Barney together. Was it psychotic of me to think like this, or just to admit that I did?

We sat down next to each other on the couch—I could almost feel the permanent crevice left by Barney's TV-addicted buttocks—and Nick and I started roughing out the brief essay on the application, inserting phrases like "destiny of this nation will be fought for and won in the courtroom" and "First Amendment activism and my artistic background."

"You might wanna mention how your dream is to never work one day outside the state of Texas. And that you promise not to out any of the gay professors. How 'bout a Coke?" Nick put his hand over mine and I popped one. Way to go—real mature.

"Yes, please," I said, a well-behaved choirboy. We went to the kitchen, where he busied himself with ice and glasses and where To-Bel uninhibitedly frotted herself all over our legs. She knew who her *real* parents were. Barney was merely a wicked stepuncle. We hit the couch again, a little closer together and continued for a few minutes until the phone rang. Nick went into the bedroom while I listened carefully. "Hello . . . well, hi. . . . How's it going down there?" He appeared at the door carrying the phone and waved me in.

I brought the app and Cokes with me and went into the room. Nick sat on the bed, his back against the wall. "I've got those rental grosses on file in the computer," he told whoever had called. "But let me just read 'em to you." He took a folder out of his briefcase. I stretched out on the bed (*their* bed) facing away from Nick, my right leg loosely hooked around his. "You know I'll come right over if you need me. . . ." He laughed. I started nudging his crotch with my stockinged foot. "Okay, ready? . . . January through March, $187,904. April through June, $184,567." I isolated his penis and increased both pressure and rhythm. "Yeah, I think there's an excellent chance they'll make that motion. . . ." He patted my thigh, suggesting I stop.

But I was not to be deterred. And three minutes of mountingly cryptic legalese later, Nick was just happy to see me. So happy the naughty first-year associate had to unsnap his shorts as he wound up the conversation. "I'll be here. . . . See you tomorrow. . . . Bye." *Click.* "You're just incorrigible."

"Who? Me?"

I rolled over. He was yanking his pants and underwear off. He was climbing on top of me. He was pushing my shirt up and cupping my freshly exerted pecs. He was kissing me.

He was jerking his head up, frozen, listening to something. Something that sounded bloodcurdlingly like a key unlocking the front door.

"What is it?" I whispered.

"Barney. Oh, fuck." He leapt off me and the bed and shut the door. " 'Late tonight,' he said. Alex, shit!"

"What do you want me to do?"

"Get under the bed."

"Really?"

"Yes!"

I got on the floor and flattened out, getting a Russ Meyer shot of a naked Nick pulling the sheets down and hopping into bed. "I'm sorry," he said.

"It's okay," I insisted. I slid under the bed, my heart pounding against the sheaf of law school papers I held on top of my chest. I'd been fantasizing about observing the two of them alone together forever. I just never thought it would happen, much less as a scenario from a *Laverne and Shirley* episode. What if Nick was a basket case and Barney became suspicious? What if the appearance of normalcy was preserved? How long would I have to stay under here? My car was parked in front of the next house. What if he recognized it? Would Nick rationalize this misadventure as some kind of spectral omen that we shouldn't see each other anymore?

The bedroom door opened. I looked down the length of my body. The bedspread hung to within half an inch of the floor. I turned my head to the left. I had an unobstructed view of everything to that side of the bed, but I was far enough underneath so that I couldn't be seen by anyone unless they were on the floor, too. "Are you asleep?" Barney asked at a volume that basically said, if you are, wake up now.

The bedsprings heaved above me as I imagined Nick sitting up. "Just taking a little nap. Hey, you're home kinda early, aren't you?"

Barney's grungy sneakers clopped into my strip of vision. "They all decided to go tubing on the river."

"That sounds like a good time."

"You know I hate getting too much sun."

I experienced a scratchy tickle at the back of my throat and suppressed a surging need to cough. I let my mouth water and swallowed, hoping to wash the irritation away. It worked. But now To-Bel had discovered something strange under the bed and was crawling toward me.

"Hey, I got an idea," Nick said. "Why don't we go grab a bite at Taco Cabana?"

"I thought you were on call today."

"Well, yeah. But it'd only take about twenty minutes or so. We can get the stuff to go." Good thinking, Nick.

But no. "I don't feel like it."

"Where would you like to go? Martin Brothers?"

"We had ice-cream sundaes for lunch. I'm tired." With that, I felt him splat onto the bed. The springs shook as the entire contraption sagged into me. As if this wasn't Edgar Allan Poe enough, To-Bel became alarmed and sank her claws into and through the sleeve of my University of South Beach sweatshirt.

"Why are you naked?" Barney asked.

"Just tryin' to get comfortable," Nick explained.

Silence. What was going on? What if Barney was *touching* him? If they had sex on top of me, I might as well institutionalize myself. The springs announced a shift above. I had a sickening image of Barney gobbling Nick's rod, cluelessly nipping at it with plaque-stained teeth. To-Bel curled up next to my head and licked my ear. Claustrophobia came calling.

Seconds later, Nick's hairy leg swung down and he got off the bed. Thank God. He recovered his pants and began to dress. Barney got up, too, and dragged himself into the living room.

Nick peeked under the bed. "What are you doing down there, little kitten?" He extended an arm and clasped my hand. "How we doin' there . . . To-Bel?"

"Okay," I whispered.

"I'll figure somethin' out soon," he whispered back. "Come on, cutie," he said to To-Bel, removing her from my side. "Barney, want to go to a movie?" I heard a newspaper rattle. "*Raising Arizona*'s at the Hogg Auditorium in half an hour. We haven't seen that since it came out."

"Nah."

"What about *Last Exit to Brooklyn* at the Dobie?" No! Nick and I were supposed to see that together this week. I guess this *was* an emergency.

"Pete said it was homophobic." Oh, Christ. What the hell did Barney's friend Pete the Musicland manager know? If I remembered correctly, his favorite film was *Shock Treatment*.

"A play might be kind of interesting. That Joe Orton thing, *Loot*, is at school tonight. Sound fun?"

"It's too expensive."

"I think it's only five or six bucks with a student ID. I don't mind paying."

"Don't you have to stay here in case they call you?"

"I think if I don't hear from them by around five I'm off the hook. I can always give 'em a ring now and—"

"I don't feel like going out." I heard the TV zap on.

What better moment than now to give Barney the axe?

"And I don't feel like putting up with one more minute of your lazy fucking apathy!" Nick could shout. "You don't give a frog's fat ass about my feelings or this relationship! I've had it. I've found someone who makes me happy to be alive, someone who thinks I'm worth gettin' off the goddamn couch for. Alex, get in here!"

I'd pop out from under the bed, a stole of dust bunnies fluttering from my shoulders, and stand beside Nick as Barney's flat eyes twinkled and bulged with newfound horror. "Why you shitty little—" he'd sputter.

"Shut up, Barney," I'd command. "You blew it. Now I'm taking my new boyfriend to Whole Foods. Then I'm going to

cook him a fabulous dinner before we scale peaks of sexual ecstasy on no atlas *you'll* ever peruse. So why not trundle over to
the drama department and get a real choice seat before the curtain goes up—my treat?"

This dreamy extrapolation was shattered by a ringing
phone. Barney stampeded into the bedroom to answer it. Probably thought it was me. Ha! "Hello? . . . Who's calling? . . .
Hold on, please. It's for you, Nick." I noticed how he screened
the call without revealing the info to Nick. The prick.

"This is Nick. . . . Hi, there. . . . No problem. . . . See ya."
He hung up. "They need me down at the office for a couple of
hours."

"I told you it was stupid to go anywhere." Oh, go get a job.
If Nick said anything back, I couldn't hear it. He came into the
bedroom and briskly changed clothes. Then a piece of paper
drifted to the floor next to the bed and Nick kicked it toward
me with a loafered foot. I twisted my forearm backward and
pinched the note between two fingers. It was becoming quite
dark under there but I made out Nick's heavy pencil strokes—
"Give me about 20 mins." I guess he wasn't waiting for a response
from me, since I heard him tell Dogface goodbye and walk out
the front door. Leaving us alone together. The absurdity of the
situation struck me for the first time, and I had to bite back
laughter. If Barney found me in here and considered me an in-
truder (and who could be more intrusive?), he probably had the
right under Texas law to shoot me.

On the TV in the living room, Ginger was trying to break
up an argument between Mr. and Mrs. Howell. "I won't have
it, Thurston!" Lovey bawled. "You can just keep your silly old
coconuts!" Flip to thirty seconds of a Roxette video, then Richard Simmons screaming over a grade-D rendition of "Please Mr.
Postman." "The sooner we lose those *tummies*, the better!" Fade
to more Richard: "I'm here with Yolanda of Springfield, Ohio.
Yolanda, this picture was taken eighteen months ago. How much
did you weigh then?"

"Three hundred nineteen pounds."

"And what did it feel like? To wake up every morning in a
fat body?"

"Oh, Richard, I was a prisoner. Completely powerless over food. I worked at The Cookie Company in the mall, and I would actually damage-out rolls of frozen chocolate-chip cookie dough and eat a whole one whenever I worked a solo shift. I was like a heroin addict with an endless supply of free syringes."

"And now look at you . . . one hundred sixty-eight pounds . . . you're beautiful, Yolanda. Say it with me. You are a beautiful person."

"I—oh, it's just so hard, but . . ."

"Say it, honey. Come on . . ."

"I *am* a beautiful person! I couldn't have done it without Deal-A-Meal. . . ." Barney was moving around the living room. Had I inadvertently made a telltale noise? I heard what sounded like a tape being inserted into the VCR. Silence for a bit, then cheesy generic synth-pop blared forth. It reminded me of porno.

Silence again, as if he were fast-forwarding to the good part. Then this emanated from the TV: "No, man! That's way too big! I'll choke on it!"

"Then bend the fuck over, dude!" It was stupefying—he'd had Nick's buffet of sensitive manhood laid out before him in bed half an hour ago. And instead . . . luckily, the cranked-up music layered over "Man, that's a tight hole!" and "Fuck me with your hot surfer cock!" obscured the monkey-spanking noises I absolutely did not want to hear Barney make. "Awww! Uhhh! Ohhh shit man I'm cumming!"

"Blow that creamy load!"

"Yeah yeah *YEAH!*"

Silence. Five seconds later: "Ohhh shit man I'm cumming!" etc. He had rewound to watch the wet shots again. That's not funny, that's sick. Finally, the ring I'd been waiting for.

"Damnit," Barney mumbled. He picked up the phone, which Nick had cleverly left in the living room. "Hello?" The TV went mute. "What? . . . Yeah, I see it." Weary sigh. "All right . . . I'll leave now." He hung up, stomped across the room, presumably grabbed something and left.

I made myself wait through a count of thirty before emerging and making a mad dash to piss like a racehorse. I ascertained I had what I came with and headed for the front door, pausing only the briefest of moments to press the record switch on the VCR, instigating total erasure of *Laguna Beach Boy-B-Que*. How careless of Barney to have hit the wrong button on that remote. He'd really be kicking himself later.

When I got home, one of my messages was from Nick: "If you're listening to this, it means you made it home. I hope you're not too mad to see *Last Exit to Brooklyn* this week. Give me a call and tell me what day's good for you. And thanks."

I'd been afraid the close call, not to mention the unflatteringly accurate glimpse into Barneyville, would embarrass and frighten Nick away for good. But was it possible that the day's high jinx had brought us closer together? Yes, I thought, as I dropped off my law school application in person after classes a few days later and bought Nick a Peppermint Pattie to eat at the 5:15 *Last Exit*.

A splendid month came to an end with a Halloween bash at Valerie and Chuck's. The host and hostess appeared as a priest and a pregnant schoolgirl, respectively. I resisted pressure from family and friends to dress as Christina Crawford and went as Billy Idol. Sara was Cruella de Vil. Nick was Elvis.

We got back to my house a little after midnight. We sat in the Mitsubishi in a discreet corner of the parking lot and he closed his eyes while I massaged his right hand, anticipating his imminent departure. "That was a wild party. You've got real nice friends," he said.

"They all think you're terrific, too. Not just me."

Silence for a little while. Then I heard him say: "Wanna go upstairs?"

I clenched my teeth to keep my jaw from hitting the floorboard. "What for?" I picked up his hand and flirtatiously slid a slender finger into my mouth.

"I dunno," he shrugged, averting his eyes self-consciously. "I guess it's kind of late . . ."

"Come on," I said, hopping out of the car. We went up. He went in before me and stood in the entryway. I put my leather jacket on a hook and asked, "Would you like a Coke?" He shook his head. "I think there's a couple brownies left, if you're hungry." He shook his head again, luscious lips almost spreading into a smile. He put his hands on my waist.

"Maybe what you want is in the bedroom," I said, mock-tentative. He nodded, then slowly led the way to my room.

I lifted the plastic lei over his head—he was the Hawaiian concert Elvis. I unzipped his skintight white jumpsuit and started to peel it off. Presently he was naked except for a few chains and medallions and, of course, sideburns. With surprising agility, I swabbed my throat with his mammoth dick while shucking off my costume (except for the studded bracelets). My hands were all over him, relishing every texture. I stroked down the length of his brawny arms and interlaced all ten fingers with his. He tightened his fists and hoisted me up off the floor. We hit the bed in an indecent tangle. When the dust cleared, I found myself on my back with Nick stretched over me à la 69, thrusting between my tongue and hard palate while he gripped my big business in his right hand and licked it up and down. This was fun but too much like trying to watch two incredibly entertaining movies at the same time.

I carefully emptied my mouth and squeezed Nick's penis rhythmically in one hand. He groaned.

"Nick?"

"Huh?"

"Why don't you fuck me?" He had never had anal sex with anyone, including Barney, but had told me he was "pretty curious" during an intimate chat several weeks ago.

He twisted around and sat up beside me. "It's too dangerous," he murmured.

"You know I'm safe and I know you are."

"We can't be absolutely certain. . . ." His fingers danced lightly over my chest.

My right hand cradled his semi-erection. I pulled open a drawer in my nightstand with my left and fumbled out a gold-foil Trojan packet and a container of Astroglide, making sure the dildo I'd been practicing with didn't bounce onto the floor. That was one little secret even Sara wasn't going to find out about. I daubed some Astroglide onto my palm and rubbed it vigorously against one side of his dickhead. Then the other. Back and forth. Again and again. When every one of his muscles was squirming under the delicious frictionless sizzle I had orchestrated, I stopped, then began to slide my palm over the tip of his penis.

He gasped, moving back, then picked the gold packet off my stomach. I was faint from disbelief and fabulous, forbidden excitement. I gave his cock a generous dollop of Astroglide and spread it evenly down the shaft as he tore open the packet and fitted the condom onto his dick. I remembered to pinch the Trojan's reservoir tip before tossing my legs back, as seen on TV. He slathered on enough Astroglide to lube a frathouse for two weeks, then . . .

It was a little painful going in, but he went slowly and made it fun for me by moaning a lot. "Tell me if I'm hurting you," he whispered.

"I'm fine," I panted. "How do you feel?"

"Fantastic."

We kissed and I kept my eyes closed. I opened them to the glorious sight of Nick hammering me, his face contorted into a near-rictus of pleasure. I thought it was going to be the end, but he was only slowing it down, breathing deeply and growling like the world's most sensuous bear: "I wanna see you jack off."

This I needed *no* practice at. I waited until he was just as close as I was, then made quite a spectacle cumming all over myself. "Jesus Christ!" Nick cried, pressing every muscle against me as he flooded the reservoir. I held him like that for a long time afterward, gently massaging his neck and shoulders while he rested and made sweet little noises at the back of his throat. It would have been the perfect time for me to say I love you, but that was Not Allowed. Sara had been quite specific on that. Nick had to say it first, after which we'd share a warm, wet kiss and only then would I express reciprocal sentiments. Instead, Nick fulfilled a lesser if more macho fantasy by telling me I was "incredible." We showered together and he went home. I unsnapped the studded bracelet and went to sleep, promising myself not to use any Elvis puns when recounting the torrid interlude to Sara.

The pressures of the next two weeks were exacerbated by an ominous absence of Nick. He showed up at the second of the two performances of *La Loteria* wearing his three-piece lawyer suit and gave me a quick peck on the mouth backstage before rushing back to the office at 9:30 p.m. to put in two or three more hours. I had three atrocious midterms clustered together right after the play finished and had to spend the next few nights hunched over annoying, prehighlighted textbooks and my disinterested class notes, not to mention a heavy load of Colonial prose and poetry, the castor oil of American literature. I waited to hear from Nick, sprinting for the phone at each infrequent ring and telling myself he would definitely call if I just got through one more practice quiz/subchapter/Anne Bradstreet poem.

The day of my art history and English exams, I went home and crashed as soon as possible. When I woke up it was dark and someone was rapping on my front door. I got out of bed quietly, in my underwear, intending to ignore the pest after a routine peephole check. I mean, you never knew. It was Sara. I opened the door wide. "Come on in."

She stifled a fake squeal at my outfit. Then her eyes widened and she whispered, "Is Nick here?"

"I wish. I was taking a nap."

"So much for the study marathon," she said, coming in. She gestured toward the door. "Don't you care who sees you like that?"

I made a muscle and snapped my waistband at her. "No. And my other test is in mass communications and it's a Scantron." I went to my room and put something on. "Two more hours prep, minimum. I was planning on settling back with a bowl of popcorn, turning on public access and knocking myself out. What's up?"

She put a stack of what looked like magazines on my table and collapsed onto the couch. "I was coming back from Valerie's—Chuck laserprinted my resume—and I missed my exit so here I am. I hope you don't mind if I do all my grad school applications here."

"I hope one of them's for UT, 'cause I'll probably be here, too."

"One is." She sat up. "I want you to know I'm sick of going to school and don't give a shit about a master's degree in journalism. I just don't know what else to do."

"Join the club."

"I take it back. I do know what to do. Graduate and just move the hell away and start freelancing. It's the same with acting. Why don't we go to New York together?"

"New York?" I groaned, dropping beside her and kneading her shoulders. "There's no work there. And I can't sing a note, so Broadway looks bleak. I'd have to be on some lousy soap opera."

"Mmmmm," she said. "You really are good at this."

"So I hear."

"Has he called?"

"No."

"I wouldn't be too worried. You two passed a sexual milestone the other night. A little lower, please. Ohhhh, perfect. He needs time to deal with that."

"I guess. I just hope he's not boffing Barney now."

"I doubt it. Thanks, Alex. I was really tense."

"How's Evan?" They had broken up amicably at the beginning of the summer, he had moved to Corpus Christi to start a surf shop that bombed, and now was back getting a second degree.

"Being a pain in the ass about the grad thing. He thinks I should stay here and take classes and write for *The Chronicle* or God forbid, *The Statesman*. Men are such idiots. Straight men. Except Chuck. Ow, easy."

"Maybe you can work out a time-share agreement with Valerie."

"Don't even joke about that."

"Have you thought about working for *Texas Monthly*? You had a great internship, they liked you. . . ."

"That one editor liked to look up my skirt. Working there was cool, but it's a little dry. I'm not that wild about a career profiling Odessa football scandals."

"True. Something will work out, Sara. You're a wonderful writer."

"I know. Thanks. Hey . . . those apps would be a helluva lot more appetizing over pepperoni pizza and unlimited beverage refills. What do you say? I'll even buy."

"Mr. Gatti's?"

"Buffet till eleven. Come on. Study later."

"Twist my arm. Hey! Ow! That hurts!"

I spent the weekend in San Antonio, away from it all, listening to my dad complain about his assault case. It was finally going to court in six weeks and everyone was pissed that the company that had placed the asshole who had beaten Dad in rehab wasn't agreeing to a settlement. Since the incident, Dad kept a gun in his desk drawer and had even hired a couple of strapping young male nurses, whom I'd had the pleasure of occasionally peeing next to during my lightweight summer employment at the clinic.

When I got back to Austin late Sunday night, there was a message from Nick that had come in at one that afternoon. He was "hoping to get together Monday or Tuesday."

He came over Monday after work. I could tell something was bothering him. Don't panic—remain normal. I gave him a hug and kissed his neck. "Hi, handsome!"

"Hey there." He sat down while I got us a couple of Cokes with lemon.

"What's up?" I asked. I joined him on the couch, making sure not to crowd him.

He closed his eyes and shook his head. "I just don't have any time anymore. I had to cancel the last two times I was supposed to man the switchboard at the GLSC. And now . . . Barney's not real happy with me."

"Oh." What he'd just said reminded me of the verbal section of those standardized tests you take in middle school—the part where you're given a paragraph with huge gaps in it and have to fill in the correct series of phrases for it to make sense.

Nick put his hand over mine. "I'm afraid I'm gonna have to bow out of Thanksgiving."

My heart was sinking fast, but I forced myself to take a deep breath and hold it. Keep it together, baby. You knew it was too good to be true. Getting him out of town for a romantic, fun Barneyless holiday would have been too much of a goddamn coup. "How come?" See how easy that was? My voice hadn't quavered an instant.

"Barney's parents want us both to come over to dinner at their house. To sort of celebrate my new job and all. It's the first time in five years, so I can't really get out of it." His tone was gentle and soothing and he was caressing my sensitive interdigital area with his fingertips in a way that would normally have driven me crazy. Now I barely felt it.

This was truly gross—Barney's parents treating Nick like the Antichrist just until he coincidentally lands a position at a prestigious law firm. Now was he a suitable husband for their dorky Little Precious? I felt tears of indignant rage (and plenty of jealousy) well up and shut my eyes against them. No weeping. None.

"We're going to have to see a little less of each other for a while," I heard Nick say in the same cradle-rocking voice. Keep those punches coming, Nick. There's got to be one more in there to completely finish me off. I know—tell me our Halloween lovemaking was a "terrible mistake."

Amazingly, my tears were under control. I decided being wet-eyed was okay. I looked at him and asked, "Is that what you want?"

He stared at the slumbering TV for a while, then dropped his head toward his chest. Melting ice cubes clinked loudly in his Coke glass. "I'm not trying to blow you off, Alex. Honestly. I'm just very confused right now."

I leaned closer, interested. Confused was different. Confused indicated turmoil and activity in heretofore sedentary areas of the brain. Confused was good. I laid my hand on his shoulder and moved in close to his ear. I could smell him and it was heavenly. "For the record," I whispered, "there's nothing I wouldn't do for you."

I sat back and watched him. He opened his eyes and smiled wearily, patting me on the leg. "Can you—no, I shouldn't. It's not fair to you." He stared into the entertainment components again while I fought simultaneous impulses to roll my eyes and throw myself prostrate at his feet.

"What?" I asked. "Can I what?"

He sighed and directed the all-powerful blaze of his blue eyes into mine. "Will you just hold me for a little while?"

"That's it?" I couldn't help blurting.

He nodded and I knew it was the truth.

"I need some more time, that's all, Alex. I don't know what else to say."

"You don't have to say anything. C'mere."

Dear Alex,

I just had to write again to let you know how very happy and thrilled I am to hear you are staying on the show. I can't tell you how happy I am.

If I may be honest, I think you are a nice gorgeous guy, but your character seems so sad. You never get to smile any. But I love "Simon" anyway. I don't think I have ever saw you smile on the show.

I have seen you on Anything For Love and Quantum Leap and enjoyed every one, especially the scene with Mimi Rogers where you laughed and you danced and laughed. I can't wait to see what they have in store for "Simon." I hope it is real nice. I would love to see "Simon" happy for once on the show.

Just remember you have one fan out here who is on your side, good or bad. Wasn't for the villains, wouldn't be any show. I wish they would let you be in a scene where you get to smile. I can't wait to see that b-tch Cyrinda in a coffin.

Much love & God Bless,

Rhonda Matthews

Tulsa, OK

P.S. Smile!!

"Worst childhood trauma?"

I chuckled politely, thinking the reporter was kidding. But she just twirled the pen between her fingers and kept her eyes on her steno pad, so I had to ask, "Really?"

She looked up, phony PR smile hastily tacked on. "Sure. You don't have to answer it, though." Her name was Heidi and she was on the set covering the gala 2500th episode of *Hearts Crossing* for *Soap Opera Magazine*. She had coerced me into my dressing room to do a "star profile." These were special boxes in the magazine that featured a glossy color photo of you flanked by a list of essential personal data, such as favorite movie (Andy Warhol's *Bad*), favorite snack (Benita's Frites), and favorite pals on the set (Phalita Renee and Allison Slater Lang). It reminded me of those slam books we used to fill out in sixth grade, except that Heidi wouldn't dare ask who was cuter, Ponch or Jon. Not that I would have answered *that* question back then, either. A simple "NC" (no comment) scrawled next to my sign-on number would have had to suffice. After all, I was a boy.

I decided to tell the truth. "My worst childhood trauma happened on Easter when I was eleven. The night before, I'd left out a plate of carrots for the Easter Bunny and the next morning I came down and next to my basket of chocolate and candy was the plate with just the carrot tops left on it. Every year the same thing happened and it always left me thrilled that magic really existed in the world. I'd sort of eased into the knowledge that Santa wasn't real a couple years before, but I'd held onto the Easter Bunny. I don't know why. Maybe because I liked rabbits." Heidi was scribbling this down, shaking her head like she was loving it. I went on: "Anyway, I was getting myself a glass of milk and in an obscure corner of the fridge I discovered a bunch of carrots with the tops cut off. I took them out and just started crying. My mom was rushing around cooking Easter dinner and she saw me and gave me this embarrassed, sympathetic look I'll never forget. Although I think she must have been relieved. I *was* going on twelve."

"What a great story, Alex!" Heidi gushed.

This is what it looked like in print: "Worst Childhood Trauma—No Easter Bunny."

Life was good. I was on the cover of *Soap Opera Update* ("HC's Simon's Wicked, Wicked Ways") and the TV insert of the Sunday Newark *Star-Ledger*. The fan mail was pouring in, mostly love-to-hate-you-type adoration, with a few screwballs sprinkled in. Not a peep from Juliana, though. *Soap Opera Digest* named me Best Psycho in their colorful and informative Daytime Villains Guide. When my *Soap Opera Weekly* interview hit the checkout stands, my castmates started asking who my press agent was. "I just do a little self-promotion," I told them, trying to be diplomatic. (Actually, I did zilch.) They smiled and nodded, insanely jealous.

My mother came out for a week and I got her extra work on *Hearts Crossing*, a beauty parlor scene with phabulous Phalita. I naughtily neglected to tell her until we arrived at the studio that morning, but her initial shock and terror faded to simple jitters by the time they slapped her with makeup and propped her under a hair dryer, and she ended up having the time of her life. We ate in a different restaurant every night and had a long-overdue chat about the whole Nick situation. She told me she thought it was hopeless. The day before she left, I introduced her to Trevor at his most charming and hilarious.

We had been dating six weeks, and he was shaping up to be an all-right boyfriend (although, considering my history, at this point anyone I could call at home would have qualified as "all right"). What wasn't to like? Flawless body (except for the chest hair shortage), great sense of humor, exceptionally perverted mind. One afternoon, the day after I mentioned my recurring junior high doctor's office fantasy, I went to his apartment after work and discovered a note that said, "Please step into the examining room and undress. Dr. Renado will be with you shortly." An arrow pointed toward his bedroom. Intrigued, I went on in. The bed sported a starchy paper cover like the kind they use on the examining table to ensure you aren't planted on the traces of someone else's bare butt. The nightstand had been covered with a smaller square of the same paper. Neatly arranged on it were a tongue depressor, a big thermometer, a tube of K-Y and a small plastic specimen bottle. Hoping Trevor hadn't just screwed a doctor to get all this, I took off my T-shirt, sneakers, socks and jeans and sat down on the crinkly paper. The bathroom door immediately opened and Trevor came out, wearing one of those headbands with a silver disk over the forehead, an unbuttoned white smock, Calvin Klein jockeys and nothing else.

I grinned as he strode to the bedside. "Please shuck off those shorts," he ordered blandly. I giggled. Trevor would sooner shop at the LaBrea Bargain Circus than refer to underwear as "shorts." He stared at me. "I'm not sure why you find this amusing." He was really in character. I was impressed. "Remove them at once."

Starting to get turned on, I did. By the time he took my temperature the hard way, my penis was pointing straight up like some celestial weathervane. He didn't touch it until the hernia check, which involved lubricating his large index finger with K-Y and running it along my scrotum. Ohhh, fuck. I got one last glimpse of Trevor's tented briefs before he fell to his knees, my balls still cupped in his palm. "Tsk, tsk. I'm afraid I must take a semen sample." Getting it all in that little bottle was no mean feat, let me tell you.

Except for the mutual nervous need we both felt to constantly entertain the other, our relationship was virtually stress-free. He was there for me to wake up next to three or four days a week, and hoot at Home Shopping Club's Bargathon with late at night and to go on drives with the top down on Pacific Coast Highway, singing along with KROQ. I insisted to myself that he had changed and matured for the better since our first brief but memorable go-round almost two years before, but I couldn't help wondering if his egomania was simply being balanced by my quasi-fame. If that was the case, what would happen now that he had been cast in *Dino & Muffin* and could be a household name and *Tiger Beat* mini-poster in a few short months?

We spent many enjoyable hours ridiculing the insipid pilot script after he got the part. I ran lines with him, playing every single role but his. Apparently, the producers were banking on reeling in the entire Nielsen family from Grandma and the little ones to horny teens. My favorite moment was Dino (the "really nice" Corey Haim) and his bimbette girlfriend discovering six-year-old Muffin in his bed—Oops! Cancel that nookie! My other favorite moment occurred when Muffin lovably asks the shirtless, pectorally gifted Ky (Trevor), "How come you got boobies and I don't?"

Trevor hated his young co-star, whom he shockingly dubbed "that spoiled rotten little pickaninny." But he valiantly endured countless photo shoots with her and was actually observed openly cuddling the precocious moppet during the taping, which I attended, to my horror. The audience was "one hundred percent real people" according to the show's braying, big-schnozzed executive producer, who had made damn sure that the studio crowd, with few exceptions like myself, consisted entirely of clueless tourists who thought waiting eight hours to see a sitcom taped live was a privilege on a par with dinner at the Hard Rock Cafe.

They of course were wild about *Dino & Muffin*, providing thunderous applause and squeals of delight during such comic high points as Muffin turning Dino's jockstrap into a knapsack. "She won't be carrying much around in that," the stern but beneficent Irish housemother comments.

"That's okay. Neither does Dino," Trevor cracks.

By the end of the episode, when Dino and his frat brothers convince the cold-hearted social worker (Special Guest Star Linda Gray) that they can be a real family to Muffin, there wasn't a dry nose in the house. Afterward, we stayed for a wrap party catered by Numero Uno. I ended up interrogated by someone's fourteen-year-old sister, who happened to be a *Hearts Crossing* fanatic, while Trevor worked the room and the star child actress threw pizza toppings, screamed at her mother, then ran around the stage until she threw up. "She'll be earning forty grand a show if we get picked up," Trevor marveled.

The network loved the pilot, immediately slated it as a summer replacement, and ordered six additional episodes. Trevor was now an honest-to-God series regular.

About ten days after the joyous announcement, I woke up at six a.m. for an early call, took a shower, ran a brush through my wet hair and drove to the studio with my face buried in my script. Somehow I was in nine scenes, mostly with Allison and

Megan, but after lunch I was opposite Anna Ford, my onscreen pseudo-girlfriend, who usually copped the attitude that she was doing me a favor acting with me.

I hit the hair room at 7:00 sharp, expecting the usual coffee-fueled dish from Tommie, our gray-ponytailed morning makeup man. Megan was in the chair, getting her blond perm sprayed stiff and squirting what was undoubtedly Tab into her mouth from one of those forty-four-ounce sports bottles available at finer convenience stores. "Hi, sweetie!" she chirped. Her character Cyrinda had just awakened from a four-month coma and apparently had no memory of Simon's deviltry. I went over and chatted for a minute. She had the reputation of being a manipulation-mad pill, but I'd never had a problem with her. We'd sort of hit it off at my series test when she said, with an ambiguous degree of seriousness, "You better hire him or I'll quit," in front of all the producers and a network rep right after we played our scene.

I entered the adjacent makeup room. Tommie sat on the ratty vinyl love seat with a cherry danish hanging limply from one bejeweled hand, staring into space. "Hi," I said.

He jumped. "Oh. Alex." Something was definitely amiss. He focused on me and assumed a miserable expression that reminded me of Dana Plato on *Diff'rent Strokes* when she was told she wouldn't be allowed to move to Paris to become a model. Tommie closed the door (also weird) and started to slap on my base. Finally, he said, "How is everything, Alex?"

"Just great."

"No problems?"

"My car needs a new water pump."

"Are you happy with all the, uh, press you've been getting?"

"Oh, yeah. A lot of scrapbook material for the folks back home."

He bit his lip. What the hell was wrong with him? I hadn't been in a conversation this stilted since my audition for that Joel Schumacher film. He reached for the eyeliner, then stopped, unable to continue.

"Christ, honey. I didn't want to be the one to have to show this to you." He pulled a tabloid out of his jacket and shook it open. The cover depicted an extremely prominent country music queen with a black eye and a huge bandage over her nose. The headlines shrieked that she'd left her "cheating, beating hubby for good!"

"Is she a friend of yours?" I asked Tommie, more than a tad befuddled.

"Huh?" he bleated, then glanced at the cover. "No, no, no! *Here!*" He pointed and moaned to himself as I read one of the little blurbs on the bottom of the front page: "Gay soap tryst!" He had flipped to the middle of the issue before I could begin to process anything. It was the "Gossip Hound" column, and under its trademark logo of a dog in sunglasses and pearls yakking on a cordless phone was a quarter-page photo of Trevor and me kissing in his car. I read the caption, stunned: "Sexy soap star Alexander Young, super-baddie Simon Arable on *Hearts Crossing,* is out at first base with an unidentified hunk at LAX International Airport." Next to it was a picture of me getting out of the car, to clear up any doubt that, yes, kids, it was definitely me. The issue was dated next week. I looked at Tommie, not having any idea what to say.

"It came in the mail yesterday," he explained. "It'll probably be on the stands tomorrow. I subscribe to a few of them. They call me sometimes for dirt, you know, but I'd never blab." He gestured distractedly to the wall, which was adorned with autographed pix of the luminaries he'd prettied up over the years.

"I don't get it," I stammered. My mouth was dry. I tapped the Sparkletts cooler for a cup of water. "That . . . happened in October. Why—now?"

"You're a lot bigger now, hon. Try to relax. Take a seat." Now that the cat was out of the bag, Tommie obviously felt much better. He finished my face then handed me the paper. "You better hold on to this. By the way, who *is* that guy, Alex? He is drop-dead gorgeous."

I headed for Trevor's after being released into premium 5:15 rush hour traffic. It felt like I'd been awake for three days straight. Make that three days in a row. I'd spent my time off-camera hiding in my dressing room. I wanted to call my mom and warn her and I wanted to call my agent and see how the fuck she suggested I handle this little bombshell, but every time I looked at the phone, I froze up. I felt stiff and awkward on the set, but nobody noticed because Simon was supposed to be nervous and agitated throughout the episode. For the first time in my life, I relied on cue cards.

It was raining and it took me forty-five minutes to get to West Hollywood. The Miata wasn't in Trevor's space, so I used my key to let myself in. He'd left a note on the sofa: "Dear A. STOP Be back soon STOP Commercial audition STOP Do telegrams really exist in our world today STOP Trevor." Whenever he signed his name it was achingly neat and formal and looked like the insignia on the back of a china plate. I untaped the note and absently folded it into eighths. I went into his room and lay down on the unmade bed. The pillow smelled like jasmine body lotion. I closed my eyes and was suddenly asleep.

I heard metal striking the floor and there was Trevor stepping out of his Girbauds. His knee-length underwear glowed a preternatural white in the dark room.

"Hi," I said. He dove into bed and enveloped me in smooth, hot muscle. He started grazing around my neck and slid his fingers under my sweatshirt and walked them up my spine. I held him close for a moment, taking comfort until an evil insectoid Simon-voice whispered, "Hope you're enjoying this, bud, because it's going to cost you your career." We both stiffened, him inside the Calvins, me all over. When he started to kiss me, I had to intervene.

"Trevor . . ."

"Hmmm?" He started pestering my crotch.

"Something really shitty happened today," I began. He encircled both of my wrists in one big hand and yanked them over my head, lowering himself on top of me at the same time.

"Did Anna Ford try to upstage you again?"

"Trevor, I'm serious." I sat up and plinked on the lamp. The rolled-up tabloid was wedged in my bag next to the bed. I pulled it out and passed it to Trevor. He looked at me, horrified, then flipped to the cover, then back to The Page. "Can you tell that it's me?" were the first words out of his mouth.

"I don't think so," I said, watching him squint at the picture like it was a hide-a-word puzzle. His erection still bulged through his underwear but, I suspected, was softening rapidly. "My face is in front of yours and you've got sunglasses on." Concern for *my* public exposure could be exhibited anytime now, Trev.

"I can't fuckin' believe this," he said. He hopped out of bed and stomped to the living room. "How'd you find out about it?"

"The makeup man at the show brought it in for me."

He returned carrying his portfolio. "Those sleazy assholes. I'll sue. I will sue." He began comparing each shot of himself in his book to the picture. I'd pretty much had it.

"*You'll* sue? I'm the focus here, in case you missed the phrase 'Sexy soap star Alexander Young.' Nobody knows that's you, Trevor. I'm the one that's going to have to answer for this!"

He stared at me open-mouthed and petulant. "You expect me to take this lightly?"

"Taking it—"

He cut me off. "This could ruin everything for me. I have a series about to go on the air. A national primetime *family* series."

"And what do you think I do for a living, dinner theater?"

"It's different, Alex. Daytime is different. You're not in the public eye as much."

Typical. "Bullshit. Who do you think reads these rags?" I tossed the paper off the bed. "I'd say the cross-section of soap opera fans is on the huge side."

He snatched the tabloid off the floor and continued to try to match it with one of his modeling pix. Which reminded me. "I can't believe someone who posed naked for the centerfold of *Beatoff Buddies* is obsessing over *those* pictures!" I told him.

"That was a long time ago."

"Yeah, but I'm sure everyone who bought it still has it."

His mouth popped open to reply to that backhanded insult but said nothing. I brushed my hair and picked up my bag. "Where are you going?" he asked.

"I want to be alone." It was a lie but he really left me no choice. "Thanks for your support, though." I left before he could say anything, but I was still sorry he didn't.

On the drive home I thought about how Nick would have reacted if it had been him. I could hear him: "They should have asked for my name. I'da spelled it for 'em." Or maybe I was just flattering myself. In any case, Nick would undoubtedly see the picture and feel sorry for the persecution I might face as a result, while simultaneously feeling better about abandoning me since I obviously had no trouble attracting unidentified hunks.

I dreaded what might be on the answering machine, but when I got to my apartment, there were no messages. Before relief set in too comfortably, I reminded myself that the issue was not yet available at the nation's Winn-Dixie checkout stands. I ordered Italian food and pulled out some recent fan mail forwarded to me by my agency. I answered a few letters, reflecting that now at least a Rachel Finster would tell everyone in Fort Wayne, Indiana, that I was a *nice* faggot. It was getting late but I decided to call Connie at home. What was I paying her ten percent for, anyway, if not stroking at a time like this? I explained the situation and she told me to relax, to not discuss my private life with anyone, and to meet her for lunch on Friday. I went to bed still thinking Trevor would call, but he didn't.

Of course, it took no time at all for every damn person at the studio to find out all about it. When I got to my dressing room at ten the next morning, I'd no sooner taken my subtle all-black outfit for the day off the hanger when a staccato knock on the door preceded the immediate entrance of Megan DuBois.

"Oh, sweetie," she mewed, scurrying over and encircling me with tiny arms that were surprisingly strong. "I just saw it. I'm so, so sorry." She sat down on the cigarette-smoke-soaked sofa and carefully removed a tear from the corner of her eye with one lacquered fingernail. "Believe me, I know what it feels like. I still see red when I think of how those bastards dragged me through the mud over that fertility clinic nightmare." She popped open a can of Tab and took a long swig.

"But that whole thing was a fabrication. Wasn't it?"

She nodded vehemently. "But it still hurt, Alex. Some fan of mine had used my name when she checked in and that rag couldn't wait to report that I was being impregnated with an African prince's semen." She drained the remainder of the soda and checked her lipstick in my mirror. "You learn how to be tough, sweetie. That's what stardom is really about. Survival. You're going to be just fine. I know it." Another hug and she was gone, flitting away like a Donna Karan sprite.

During rehearsal, I was sensitive to any new and unusual treatment from the cast and crew. Was the cue card guy smiling more than necessary? I was being ridiculous. "Nobody cares," Allison Slater Lang assured me after our scene. "On this show? Two gay directors, Reggie Van Wyck"—the septuagenarian bachelor who played Cyrinda's father, newspaper magnate Rutherford Blake—"the prop lesbos, hair and makeup, Will DeSisto—"

"No way," I exclaimed. Will was a megahot teen stud who'd recently quit the show to star in a Meg Ryan movie.

"Oh, yes. He used to bring his tricks here to visit. Do you still use that word, 'trick'? It's so *Boys in the Band. . . .*" I gave her a look. "Not to mention Jerry Reynolds, that poor thing. I bet Brent Bingham could even be one. He *is* a Scientologist, isn't he?"

"Assembly of God, actually, I think," I laughed.

"Whatever. Anyway, it's hardly a big deal. The Phalita scandal was much juicier."

As for Phalita, if she recognized Trevor in the photo, she never said so. Her only comment on the outing was to proclaim, "When they have to run a picture of two cute-lookin' guys kissing in L.A., it's a sorry-ass day for gossip. And baby, I ought to know."

I went upstairs to the production office to pick up scripts for next week and ran into executive producer Linda Rabiner. "Hello, Alex," she said, giving me the kind of close-mouthed smile one would usually reserve for plucky amputees determined to wheel themselves across the country in a human-interest news segment. She leaned in closer and rested a hand on my shoulder. "I just want you to know that any calls we've gotten or may be getting concerning . . . gossip items are told that the show has absolutely no comment on anything related to your personal life." The smile remained and I wondered if she was picturing me getting it up the ass.

"Thanks, Linda," I said, resisting a perverse urge to apologize.

"Keep up the good work," she actually said before vanishing into her office.

When I got home, I found a manila envelope that had been slid under the door. It was ominously stamped "confidential" in red and double-sealed with clear packing tape. Expecting either a death threat or photos of me purchasing Erasure albums, I slit it open and withdrew a pasted-up creation that could only be the work of one man.

The entire note was constructed of cut-outs from the tabloid in question. Across the top: "Eye-catching buttocks instantly!" Then The Picture itself, across which had been glued letters that spelled out, "This is stupid." Then the fragment, "I'm sorry" and strung-together: "Tonight no cameras. Promise." He'd "signed" it with a photo of his mesh-encased ass clipped from the International Male catalog. Trevor got points for effort, anyway.

I went to the phone to call him and saw that I had four messages. The *Hearts Crossing* p.a. with dialogue changes for tomorrow. A titillation-heavy local gay paper requesting an interview. My mother, sounding worried, asking me to call her back. The tape climaxed with a guy saying, "Alexander . . . I wanna suck your dick . . . (*grunt*)"—whack whack—"I want that big bad dick going in and out of my butt . . . (*sigh, groan*)"—whack whack—"Lick my cock . . . (*grunt, grunt*) . . . yeah, lick—" *Click*. I played it back but couldn't recognize the voice. I'd have to get a new unpublished number (although the big bad dick part was sort of flattering), despite the fact that actors' phone numbers were notoriously easy to obtain by anyone peripherally associated with show business. Anyone walking through my agency or the *Hearts Crossing* office could flip it out of a Rolodex. Not to mention the Rolodex of every casting director who'd ever hired me, and everyone knew casting directors tended to employ an endlessly revolving list of often unstable and dishy assistants.

I stretched out and dialed 5 to speed-call my parents. My mother answered on the first ring. "Hi, Mom."

"Oh, honey. It's so good to hear your voice." A few seconds passed before she said, "I suppose you've seen it."

"Yeah. I guess you must have, too."

"Someone put a copy in the mailbox last night. It's Trevor, isn't it?"

"Yup. . . . How's Dad taking it?" My dad knew about me but avoided the subject as a rule.

"He's fine. Angry. At the paper, I mean. The important thing is, how are *you*?"

"Terrific. Really, Mom. It was a shitty, low blow, but it's not going to have any far-reaching effects. Gay actors aren't exactly rare."

"I had to go to the grocery store today and it seemed like there were hundreds of those damn things. I just wanted to rip them down and set them on fire. How dare they—violate your privacy like that? It sucks."

She was the best. "Please don't worry about it, Mom. Or me. I'm still making the big bucks. Trevor was freaked out at first, but he's okay now." Nick smiled down at me from the wall. I know Trevor didn't like me having that picture up, but every time I thought about taking it down, I'd see Nick giving it to me before I left for L.A., handing it over like he was embarrassed about doing something terribly immodest.

"So you won't forget *all* about me," he'd quipped. I was of course bawling by this point and couldn't do anything but shake my head.

"Honey," my mother said, and I heard her draw in a long breath. "Your grandparents saw the thing."

"Oh, Christ." That particular consequence had somehow escaped the flow of my anxiety.

"One of their so-called friends had to run right up and stick it in their faces, you know. Anyway, they don't believe it. Grandpa thinks the photo's a fake and we thought it'd be best if we let them believe that. Dad told them you couldn't take any legal action because it would just bring more attention to the whole thing."

"I'm sorry." I felt worse than I had in months. To think of my seventy-five-year-old grandparents in their little condo by the beach devastated by that piece of shit tabloid was too much. If the "gossip editor" had been there I would have gladly pried out his or her heart with a tire iron and shoved the gory, pulsating mass down their weaselly little throat.

"You have to live your life, Alex. They're old and they can't understand. . . . That's not your fault, honey."

"Mom, can you hold on a sec?" I clicked over and Trevor said, "I'm sorry, okay?"

"Yes. I was about to call you. I'm talking to my mother."

"I'm downstairs."

"Come on up." I buzzed him in and switched back to Mom. "Mom, Trevor's on his way up."

"I'm glad. I don't want you to be alone."

"I really appreciate everything, Mom. I hope you and Dad don't have to go through a ton of crap over this."

"Hey. That's what happens when you've got a famous kid."

"I love you."

"We love you, too. Sleep tight."

"Bye." I hung up just as Trevor started pounding a tribal rhythm on the door. I opened it and he fell into my arms, wisely bracing himself with one hand on the doorframe so I wouldn't drop him.

"Please, Simon, your evil secrets are safe with me," he panted. "Why kill me when you can . . . have your way with me?" He closed his eyes and tossed back his head. I debated whether to go for his bronzed neck or the hard ridge of stomach visible between his cut-off sweats and Fendi T-shirt. The neck was the better choice, strategically speaking. We ended up on the floor anyway.

"I brought you something," he said when his mouth was free. He passed me an envelope he'd been holding. In it was an 8-by-10 color photo of Muffin inscribed by the star in a precious childish scrawl "To Alex."

"You *really* shouldn't have," I told him. "I'll have to send her one of mine." We caught each other's eyes as I realized he'd want to downplay his association with me as much as possible where *Dino & Muffin* was concerned. "Or not," I added, producing a quick smile to let him know I "understood."

He went into the kitchen. "Can I have a Perrier?"

"Sure. How'd it go today?" It had been the start of *Dino & Muffin*'s second episode.

"Awful. We had a table reading and everyone was *wincing*. It makes me want to write sitcoms. How hard can it be? I already have an idea: Muffin pulls one of Ky's extra-large lubricated Trojans over her head and when she runs out of the frat house, suffocating, the sorority next door thinks she's a space alien. Hilarity ensues. What do you think?"

"That you probably shouldn't work with children."

He flounced onto the couch beside me. "That little bitch racked me in the nuts today. I'm seriously considering sedating her frozen yogurt from now on."

The note he'd assembled for me was lying on the floor. He reached over and collected it, then settled against me and looked it over, obviously pleased with himself.

"Doesn't it scare you?" he asked a minute later.

"What?"

"Having everyone know."

"What do you mean? Like . . . scared of getting bashed?"

"That's part of it."

"Whenever I hear about violence like that poor Navy guy getting stomped to death in Japan, I never think, Wow, that could have been me. I guess doing what I do in L.A. makes me feel safe."

He sat up a little and put his arm around my shoulders. "I know. Me, too. What scares me is just knowing how few places there are for me. I *can't* live with my parents in Wilkes-Barre, Pennsylvania, and be myself. It's dangerous for me to mingle with the general American population. We're like exiles."

"I don't know about you, Trev, but I don't want to be anywhere but here. We're *not* like everybody else. Our lives are what ninety-nine percent of the population can only dream about. And I don't know if we can attribute that to being gay, but I think it's involved somehow. And if it also makes a lot of things harder and I have to be a little more careful walking around, that's the way it is."

"Honestly. Do you think this is going to affect your job on the soap?"

"No."

"It's nobody's business." He folded the note and deposited it on my tile-topped granite coffee table. Then he said it again: "It's nobody's business." He got up. "I'm tired. Why don't we watch TV in your room?"

"Okay." He took my hand and pulled me off the couch.

In my bedroom, he kicked off his hightops and dropped the sweats. I turned on the TV as his bubble butt vanished under the sheets. No sooner had I modestly stripped to my underwear and joined him the phone rang.

"Machine, machine," he commanded, throwing an arm over me to restrain any answering attempts. I poked my index finger into his lightly haired armpit and grabbed the phone when he spasmodically jerked back, ticklish.

"Hello?"

"Well, hi."

Oh, my God. Nick. "Hi," I said, striking the perfect tone between nonchalance and tender reverence.

"I stopped by Seven-Eleven for a Coke Slurpee and saw something pretty interesting in the *National Inquisitor* or whatever the heck they call it."

"It was quite a shock all right."

"You doin' okay?"

"Yeah. I'm sure it'll blow over." I hadn't spoken to him since I was at my parents' house last fall. The fact that it took something this vulgar to put us in contact was an apt signifier of the distance between us (his choice), but as always, with the warm, hickory-smoked tones of his voice, hope cascaded out of places that had long since run dry. Of course I couldn't explain the crucial point that nothing had been going on between me and the "unidentified hunk" with whom I was liplocked at the time of said liplock because I happened to be in bed with him at the moment. To add to my torment, Trevor had crawled to the foot of the bed on his stomach to better hear the TV, his balls playing peek-a-boo beneath the cleft of his sublime, globed buttocks. I looked away and tried to concentrate on Nick.

"If there's anything I can do to help, you let me know." Okay. Sue their yellow asses off for me. Then with your share of the settlement, rent a villa on the outskirts of Florence and ensconce yourself in the master bedroom while I take a humpy hiatus from show business.

I screwed my eyes shut and said, "Okay." I could see him perched on the edge of his futon couch in jeans and a white shirt, the house dark except maybe for a light in the kitchen, and quiet since Barney was obviously not around, which meant the TV had a chance of being off. My words sounded robotic and brittle—Trevor would definitely pick up on the stress. "How's everything? The same?" I hoped Nick would translate this to, Are you still chained to that soulsucker?

He must have, because several seconds elapsed during which I thought I heard a slow, quiet sigh. "Yeah, Alex, it is."

Okay. Fine. Great. "That's what I need to know."

"I just—" The rest caught in his throat. I couldn't or wouldn't help him out of his frustration. I inhaled as deeply and quietly as possible. Trevor seemed to be engrossed in the Farrah-era *Charlie's Angels* rerun where they go to prison and are abused by Mary Woronov, but I was sure one ear was cocked toward my conversation, laconic as it was.

"I should really go. I've got company."

"The unidentified hunk?" he asked, a slight bitter trace in his voice shocking me as much as if the phone had suddenly turned to ice.

"Thanks for calling," I said. "I mean it." Was that supposed to sound sincere? *I mean it.* What a stupid thing to say. Before I could chastise myself further he said bye and hung up.

"Who was that?" Trevor asked immediately, muting Kate Jackson.

"Chuck."

"Are you mad at him?"

I wanted to slap his ass and could have so easily. "No. It's hard for me to talk about it with my friends back home."

Good answer.

I had been to my agency exactly three times before. The initial meeting had been set up by the director of the psycho-cop hit. After they agreed to rep me, I went in to sign the papers and was served croissants and "cappuccino" I suspected was actually a General Foods instant creation that eerily turned out to be a key *Hearts Crossing* sponsor. My third visit involved dropping off the new headshots I'd splurged on after a guest lead on *Quantum Leap*. Two months later, I booked the recurring role on the soap and they'd been happily commissioning every paycheck since.

The agency was in a monolithic office building in Century City, West L.A.'s answer to midtown Manhattan. Luckily they validated for parking. One epic elevator ride later, I was being greeted by Tiki, the atomic-permed receptionist who interrupted her perpetual rosary of "Will they know what it's in reference to—Please hold—Will they know what it's in reference to—" to buzz Connie and announce "Alexander Young is here" while smiling at me so perkily I immediately became suspicious. This is how Jessica Hahn must have felt every day for years.

"Come here, Doll," I heard Connie call, as she paradoxically trotted to my side with tiny, rapid steps. She was wearing a *League of Their Own* sweatshirt over a wine-colored silk skirt and white sneakers. She initiated a hug which was actually a maneuver to get her arm around me and propel me back into the silver-carpeted recesses of the agency.

"We're meeting with Bernie Solomon, the head of TV. Remember him?" Vaguely. "He has a tendency to blow hard, so bear with me." She paused before a closed door and knocked once before cracking it. "Bernie, it's us."

"There's no goddamn way I'm sending anyone in without reading a fucking script," Bernie was telling someone. "No. Thank *you*." He hit another line. "Dana? Sorry, baby. . . . No, of course I'm not mad. . . . I dunno. . . . If you skip the appointment, do you still have to pay for it? . . . Look, I can't talk about this now. . . . Leave her out of this! . . . Fine fine fine goodbye." He hung up. "Jesus. Come in, come in. Great to see you, Alex." He leaned forward in his seat and sort of waved at me.

Now I remembered him: By turns loud and faux-intimate, decked out in Armani Exchange, looking in the glow of his desktop halogen lamp from Z Gallerie exactly like the kind of guy who thought he was real class because he put *five*-dollar bills into the stripper's G-string.

"Tiki, hold the calls, okay?" Bernie commanded, via speakerphone. He tucked a paper towel into the collar around his just-so-slightly fleshy neck as Connie unpacked lunch from the Stage Deli. I tried to fit my mouth around one of those ridiculous sandwiches that consisted of three inches of sliced turkey between two slabs of dry, unmayoed bread. Meanwhile, Bernie was anally arranging potato chips and a kosher dill around his pastrami on rye.

"You understand that nobody here is *judging* your private life or preferences or whatever," Bernie said to me, after discovering a chip much darker than the others and flicking it into his wastebasket. "We're only interested in your career."

"And that you're happy," Connie added as soon as she swallowed her macaroni salad.

Bernie pointed to a mini-fridge in the corner of his office. "Connie, can you hand me a Canfield's?" She complied. "Now, Alex, ordinarily these piece-of-shit tabloids are pretty harmless —rumors, gossip, blah blah blah—but when they start taking pictures is when you have to maybe start worrying. Am I right, Connie?"

"What I think he means, dahling, is that photos are pretty tough to dismiss compared to some randomly printed dish items."

"Like I said, we don't care if you're bi or gay or in or out or anything," Bernie went on. How cool of you. I nodded agreeably at the condescending prick. "And neither does anybody in Hollywood. The problem is the rest of the country."

"We're not publicists, Alex, and it would be presumptuous of us to act like we are—" Connie was cut off by Bernie, who gestured with his half-eaten pickle for emphasis.

"*But*, we've got you started on a very nice career"—how silly of me to think my career started with the three movies and four TV guest spots I did before signing here, Bern—"and it'd be a real crime to ruin it over something like this. So we need to do a little damage control." His voice sounded like the giant wasp in *Sinbad and the Eye of the Tiger*.

"I'm not exactly sure what the damage is." I directed this at Connie to sound less confrontational.

Bernie answered. "Look, Alex, let's cut to the chase. America is not ready for openly gay series regulars. Especially the housecoat and Bisquick America that watches soap operas." This was exactly what I had told Trevor, but coming from a cocky hetero pig like Bernard M. Solomon, it sounded moronically simplistic and irritating. He wasn't finished. "We represent a very young lesbian actress . . ." I thought I knew what was coming and couldn't believe it. But before he could finish, the phone beeped.

"Bernie?" Tiki queried.

"I said hold the calls." His tone was the same as if he'd discovered she'd put sugar in the gas tank of his Porsche 911.

"It's Bob Harbin from Fox on line six. He says it's urgent."

"Ah fuck . . . Hello, Bob. I haven't heard from her yet. . . . Don't bust my balls, Bobby. We don't have to close yet. . . . I will. Bye. As I was saying before that rude interruption, Alex, there's a cute gay actress we handle and I was thinking of setting you two up." I looked at Connie, already shaking my head.

"We didn't talk about this, Bernie," she began.

"Hear me out! Hear me out! I'm not talking about a marriage and adopting a fuckin' baby, for God's sake. A couple of parties, premieres, maybe something on E. Be good for both of you."

"No, thanks," I said. I wanted to tell him asshole shams like that were a big reason why Velveeta-eaters across the nation were still shocked by a picture of two men kissing. "I think I can avoid sucking dick in public without a female escort to rein me in."

"Oh, God," I heard Connie mumble. She quickly began to

stuff the lunch debris back into the bag. Bernie's upper lip curled like he was a mastiff ready to spring. I kept my lovely blue eyes unblinkingly fixed on his beady, crow-footed gaze.

"Fine," he said, royally pissed. "Connie, do you have anything to add?" Beep. "Goddamnit, Tiki! I said hold the fucking calls!"

"It's Kimba, not Tiki."

"Didn't she tell you we were in a meeting?" he hissed.

"No. She's at lunch."

Bernie threw up his hands helplessly.

"Alex," Connie said. "I've gotten a few calls from the gay press. And *Hard Copy*. Wanting to talk to you, cover the whole thing."

"Yeah, *Edge* called me at home," I told her.

"Doesn't he have an unlisted number?" Bernie squawked at Connie. We ignored him.

"I don't think it's a good idea to talk about it with anyone," Connie said. "You obviously don't want to deny it—I mean, those pictures—and beyond that, there's nothing to discuss. Otherwise you're just asking for a label that's going to be impossible to scrub off."

Bernie snorted. "A gay activist soap star! You'd be about as marketable as Lucie Arnaz." The intercom buzzed again.

"Connie?" Kimba said. Bernie shook his head in amazement, pointing at the phone and looking at me as if expecting me to empathetically call Kimba a stupid cunt.

"What, honey?" Connie responded.

"Arlene from Consolidated Amusements on two."

"Okay. Come on, Alex. I'll take it in my office. Bye, Bernie." He waved dismissingly, already on the phone.

I skimmed *Variety* while Connie argued briefly with Arlene. She hung up. "That was the Fiesta Soap company. They're dropping you from the cruise, Alex."

"Did they give you a reason? Not that we don't know what it is." I took mild solace in the fact that we weren't still with Bernie.

"She said they were overbooked. Fuck 'em. You get a five-hundred-dollar cancellation fee. I'm sorry, Alex. I'm also sorry about Shit-For-Brains Solomon. I honestly didn't know he was going to suggest that dating scam."

"I hope I didn't embarrass you too much."

"You gotta be kidding, Doll. I haven't been embarrassed since *Can't Stop the Music*."

"What did you have to do with—" I began.

"Never mind. Now beat it, Hon. Lunch on the set next week?"

"Sure."

"Everything's going to be great, Alex. Trust me."

The first fan mail to reflect a change in the public's perception of me consisted of four letters: one begging me to turn from a life of sin and "sodommy" and embrace my saviour Jesus Christ ("like Brent Bingham"), along with a request for an autographed photo; two supportive notes basically insisting I was the victim of a cruel hoax but uneasily requesting confirmation; and my favorite, a long, deliriously gushy love letter from a twenty-year-old Myrtle Beach health-club attendant named Trip. "Finding out that you're homosexual was so incredibly ballistic I could barely concentrate on the show today. Is that your boyfriend in the picture? You are so evil and sexy at the same time. Please do more scenes topless because you have a beautiful chest. Needless to say, if you're ever down here, come by the gym for a free workout." I wondered what the prim, silver-haired fan mail lady at the studio thought of this one.

Trevor's show was taking a short break while they fired all the writers and assembled a new staff. He decided, surprisingly, to use the opportunity to fly home to Pennsylvania instead of modeling the Tear-Away Bikini for International Male in Las Hadas, prompting a hysterical call from his print agent. "You can act and model at the same time! Look at Brooke Shields!"

"Yeah, look at her," Trevor snapped, hanging up.

I called Sara and invited her out for the weekend. "Three days' notice Alex? Have any idea how expensive dilettante airfares are?"

"I'm paying," I told her.

"See you Friday night."

I picked her up in Burbank at 7:30 and we headed straight for Spago. Phalita had gotten me reservations. Over pumpkin ravioli, we had a celebrity thrill-sighting. "Oh, my God! Is that Aidan Quinn?" Sara whispered. "I'm going to wet myself."

"*You* are," I said.

"This is a long way from Mr. Gatti's all-you-can-eat on the Drag," she observed, as I divvied up a duck sausage pizza. "Remember when you first moved here and we used to smuggle muffins and chocolate chip cookies out of Soup Exchange? You probably still do that, though . . . Richard asked me to marry him."

"And how long ago was this?" I sputtered indignantly through my grin.

"Yesterday, dork."

"This calls for champagne." I signaled our Bridget Fonda look-alike waitress.

"Hey. I said no."

"But I thought you were crazy about him."

"I guess I am. But we've only known each other eight months. And I'm just not ready. For that. But I did agree to move in with him next month."

"Aha!" I barked. The waitress appeared. "A bottle of your cheapest champagne, please." She chuckled convincingly and was gone. "You're moving into his house?" I asked Sara.

"No. He's coming to my place. He lives in a garret. There's no way. Shacking up is really an ideal compromise. If we got married, he'd have to change his name to Richard Richardson. Isn't that Sophie Hawkins over there?"

"I think so. That's such a great album. Especially that last song. I bet she's a really good kisser." Sara raised her eyebrows. "If you like that sort of thing. What does your mother have to say about your new roommate?"

"The notion doesn't exactly thrill her, but what does, besides those Shih Tzus she breeds?"

"As long as you're happy."

"I am. How about you?"

"I'm okay." Bridget arrived with the champagne. We toasted Sara and Richard and freedom of the press. "I think I'll survive being outed." She put her hand over mine and gave it a squeeze. "It's weird because I always really resented celebrities who had it all then couldn't resist acting like total out-of-control slobs in public and ending up in *The Enquirer*. Now here I am."

"Bull. This is different."

"Yeah, kind of. It seems ridiculous. I wasn't trying to hide it. So why should I care at all?"

"Because they took something natural and personal and treated it like it's some grotesque character flaw."

"Sounds good to me."

"And Trevor's fine about the whole thing?"

"Yeah, now. He's realized it's not going to have any effect on his budding superstardom. He's been okay. I still can't believe we've been *dating* this long. He's . . . fun."

"Do you love him?"

I thought for a second, sipping champagne and looking down at the Strip, realizing momentarily that we were the only people from our high school class who would ever be sitting here. "Does lust plus affection equal love?"

She considered this. "No. You of all people know what love feels like." She gave me a little whack on the arm.

"It doesn't feel like that," I admitted.

"He called me twice this week."

"Nick?"

She nodded. "He's worried about you. Said he called you and you sounded 'odd.' "

"I was in bed with Trevor."

More eyebrow action. "I told him I knew that guy in the photo and that he was just a friend."

"You did?"

"Well, he was at the time."

"What else did Nick say?"

"That he wanted to come out here and see how you were doing. Look, Alex, maybe I shouldn't have said so, but I told him unless he was ready to commit to you, he shouldn't try to see you."

"No, Sara. That's exactly right."

"You know, I try to get him to talk about his . . . situation and Barney and everything. But he won't."

"He told me things were the same."

"Of course they are. I doubt Barney got a personality transplant. Oh—Valerie saw Barney at Highland Mall recently and she said he was really getting fat."

"No!" I leered, delighted.

"Thought you'd appreciate that."

"Can I get you anything else?" the waitress asked, eager to assign our table to a more extravagant, heavier drinking couple.

We skipped dessert and got the check. Sara snagged it. "I'll write this off as an expense. I'm going to interview you for *Paseo del Rio* tomorrow."

We had talked about this a couple of months ago, but I'd assumed that in the wake of the "scandal" it wouldn't happen anytime soon. "Are you going to cover the outing angle?"

She adopted her most professional demeanor. "It's irrelevant to your success. I didn't quiz Robert Rodriguez about his sexual tastes, did I?"

"Not on the record," I said.

She tried to look offended, but just then Warren and Annette walked by.

March 1991

The whole apartment smelled like chicken soup because it had been slow-cooking the entire day. I'd assembled all the ingredients the night before and turned the crock-pot on before I left for class at 8:30. It was cooking when Nick called at 11:17, simmering freshly chopped carrots and potatoes to a melt-in-your-mouth consistency as it sealed a delicate blend of herbs and spices into succulent chunks of high-grade white meat while my machine recorded the message that he would be unable to make it for dinner. When I burst in the door at quarter to six with cookies and a baguette from Texas French Bread, the soup was bubbling industriously under the glass cover, unaware that it was all for naught.

I turned it off and put it in the fridge. The dinner had been short-notice, but I still felt betrayed. My acceptance letter from the University of Texas School of Law, the reason for tonight, was propped up on the dinette. I left it there. Would I be feeling these same outrageous highs and lows for *the next three years* if I sent in my tuition deposit and sentenced myself to law school in this apartment and this town? Or was the extra time here the crucial factor I needed to wrest Nick away? I had told no one of the letter—I wanted Nick to be the first. Now who knew when that would be.

I immersed myself in homework—made especially irrelevant by my new official pre-law status—with background scoring by Peter Murphy and The Indigo Girls. At 10:38 the phone rang.

"Hello?"

"Are you havin' an okay night?"

"Nick. Hi. What happened?"

"This and that." Rueful, resigned, maddening. "Still want some company?"

"Sure." The elation nearly knocked me to the floor.

"I'll see ya in just a minute."

"Okay. Bye." I leaped off my bed and stripped away my T-shirt and gym sweats. In my underpants, I hastily straightened the bedroom before selecting a stonewashed cotton shirt from Banana Republic and a pair of Levi's shorts. I was in the bathroom reaching for my brush and wondering what the hell was going on when the knock came. I had literally hung up less than three minutes ago. He must have called from the Stop'n'Go on the corner. I threw open the door and there he was.

We didn't say anything at first. His unearthly blue eyes seemed softer, somehow tarnished. I realized he'd been crying. I took a step forward. He swung the door shut behind him and I took him in my arms. His body went limp, his face resting just above my clavicle, his arms loosely encircling me. I held him, gently caressing the back of his neck with my palm.

"Sorry I'm late," he said gently.

"I got into law school here," I told him.

He looked at me. "Aw, that's fantastic, Mr. Young. I knew you wouldn't have trouble." I was having trouble resisting flinging him onto the couch and feasting on him. I asked if he was hungry. "I didn't eat. Wanna call for a pizza?"

"No need," I said. "Fresh chicken soup will be served shortly."

He assumed a supremely cute gesture of tender surprise. "You made dinner?" I nodded. "I'm sorry, Alex." He hugged me again, harder. I grazed his ear with my lips and he kissed me. This would have been the ideal time for me to find out what had kept him, but I just couldn't ask.

We ate next to each other, his right leg bent at the knee and resting on my lap, my left hand under his short sleeve, taking his shoulder into protective custody. He praised the dinner and the dessert, semi-instant chocolate mousse pie in a crushed Oreo crust. Together we cleared the table. I ran a sinkful of suds while he examined the letter from the School of Law. "This is great, Alex."

I dried my hands. "Thanks for your help."

"I didn't do nothin'." Our eyes met and stayed, making me feel as if I'd cracked open an arcane treasure chest and the secrets it contained could actually evolve me to a higher level of existence as long as I could keep the light and heat generated from within from liquidating my soul. He closed his eyes, my signal to attack him. I hooked a finger into the waist of his jeans and undid the three buttons of his collar. I kissed the hairy northern region of his chest until he tilted my head upward and pressed his bee-stung lips to mine. I put my hands on his ass and pulled our bodies together. I'd never had this much fun in a kitchen before. He whispered, "Would you mind if I spent the night?"

I'd been waiting sixteen months to hear that question. If only I'd known he was going to ask it tonight. Think of the misery I could have avoided. It just proved what an idiotic waste of time feeling sorry for myself and fretting about the future was. Every day should be lived ecstatically in the knowledge that your dreams *will* come true as long as you never give up.

"Please stay," I said to him, after mentally jettisoning such clichés as Oh, God, do you even have to ask? What did this mean? Obviously he'd had some falling out with Barney, major enough to warrant a drastic move like this. Was it over me? Had they broken up? Would I come home tomorrow to find his suitcase at the front door, chock-full of the items he'd need until Barney had moved from their house to an efficiency over his parents' garage?

I looked at the clock. 11:55. Which meant seven hours of bed together. I vowed not to waste another second. He went down to his car for tomorrow's suit and an overnight bag (what a ring that phrase had) and met me in my room. I brushed my teeth and watched him take off his clothes in the mirror. When I walked in the room, he was tucked into bed. My bed. For the night. I stopped to drink in the scene. I could talk with him, massage him, kiss him, play with his big penis. In any order. For as long as we wanted. Then finally drift off into sleep, knowing that no one in the universe was closer to him than I was and that when I woke up he'd be there and maybe tell me he loved me.

It was the happiest day of my life so far. Easy.

Dearest Alex,

I knew it. I knew you were just like me. It is Fate. More than ever, I need to see you. To touch you in the flesh. Let me describe myself. I'm 5'9½", dark hair and eyes, slender build, generously endowed. I have a pierced nipple but do not have to wear my rings if that's not your taste. You're on TV right now, taking your blue shirt off. The producers of your show know how to display you.

Enclosed is an original erotic charcoal rubbing and an Aleister Crowley poem. I am an artist as well as a wizard. Soon we shall meet. Forgive me if I admit I want to suck you dry.
"Astaroth"

"This is brilliant, Jane," I told Anna Ford. I looked up from the graph-paper notebook the art department had scribbled arrows, equations and chemical symbols all over. "No one else has seen this, have they?"

Anna was wearing a forest-green sweater that offset her bobbed chestnut hair and a black miniskirt with matching tights, although she wisely kept her chicken legs curled up beneath her on-camera. I didn't know what the writers were planning to do once Jane completed the first lot of Simon's father's sexual potency drug (which she'd been told was a cure for leukemia). But right now I had to make her believe I was planning on unveiling her as the Madame Curie of Harts Crossing. And that I was falling in love with her.

I couldn't stand Anna. A former teen star of a notoriously mediocre early-eighties family drama, she'd been on *Hearts Crossing* six years but had never really achieved big-time soap prominence. She had delusions of being a serious thespian and was constantly invoking the acting teacher in whose class she studied with Sharon Stone; two years before she'd written and produced a play in which she played three roles opposite Glenn Scarpelli at some Equity-waiver theater in Los Feliz. She'd been pissy to me from Day One. I figured she resented our mutual storyline: before I arrived she'd been involved in a passionate triangle with Gwen's younger brother (Italian teen sex pistol Cary Rietta) and Debbie Kringle (Nori Ann Marshall) and had been taken on a ten-day location shoot to Key West.

"Oh, no, Simon, I've had complete privacy in the lab," she assured me.

"Sounds cozy," I observed flirtatiously, sliding down the chintz sofa toward her. I put my arms around her, per script and rehearsal. It was like embracing fiberboard. I held back, waiting for her line, "You've given me so many reasons to be excited." It didn't come.

"Sorry," Anna called. I was only too happy to release her. This was the third take and she couldn't stop fucking up.

"Engineering five," the technical director intercommed from the booth. The crew dispersed for a five-minute break, although Tommie was conscientious enough to touch up my face before retiring to the open-air deck to smoke.

"How's it going, sugar?" he asked.

"I've had better moments."

"She's being a real little c-word today. You know I don't tell tales out of school, but Miss Anny-Fanny was in the hair room pitching *a bitch* about the scene you just didn't finish. Specifically, the kiss."

"She doesn't want to kiss me?" I was outraged. I had kissed Anna exactly twice before. And both times my breath had been so minty fresh I practically had a Scope mustache. There was only one explanation. And it stank to high heaven.

"Look out. Here comes trouble." Tommie ducked around the back wall of the Jane's apartment set just as Anna appeared with exec producer Reese Jacobs, who waved to me.

"C'mere a sec, you two," Reese said, leading us to Jane's couch. "The scene's not working. Something's off."

"Should I be doing something differently?" I asked, the picture of cooperative innocence.

"No, Alex, you're fine. What we're going to do is end it earlier." He unfolded a piece of yellow legal paper. "After 'This is brilliant, Jane,' she'll say, 'Thank you, Simon. I'm so glad you chose me for this project,' then she'll go behind the couch and put her hand on your shoulder and we'll end with a two-shot of her all happy and you giving us one of those evil looks you do, Alex. Okay?"

"Great," I said. We did it and the next take was a buy. Thank God it was my last scene with her.

It had been about a month since the outing. I was in the second week of my latest option cycle and had started to think that no upheavals were going to threaten my status as a daytime regular. Now this. Right in front of the entire crew, not to mention Babs Flanagan's coed niece and her sorority sisters, who happened to be visiting the set. I cringed at the gossip that would arise, undoubtedly speculating that I had AIDS. Could that stupid bitch have lived in Hollywood for fifteen years and still think you can get it from kissing? I channeled my hateful feelings for Anna into my remaining scenes, all the while mentally composing a blistering rebuttal I intended to lambaste her with. But by the time I was in my dressing room slathering on the cold cream, I realized going off on her, delicious or not, would be counterproductive. Making waves at the studio was severely ill-advised. I grabbed my bag and walked out, secure in my maturity, but as I passed Anna's door, a suitable compromise came to me. I knocked. She answered, hair wet, in a gaudy Picasso-esque shift that probably cost three hundred dollars. "Hi," she said blankly, very surprised to see me, I'm sure.

"I'm HIV negative," I told her. "But if I were you, I'd still get the test." She looked like she'd walked in on some cousin she had a crush on masturbating. I savored her discomfort for only two seconds before wordlessly exiting. I had to walk by a studio audience waiting in a carefully cordoned line for the late taping of *Cash Crazed*, a game show that recently attained notoriety for persuading a librarian to strip down to her bra and panties in the middle of the Beverly Center for a way-too-generous $18,000. I said hi to the page guarding the crowd and headed for my car. Wait a second—did someone in line just call me a faggot? I could have sworn that's what I heard. I realized I'd stopped walking so made a deliberate show of fishing out my keys. I was just paranoid. There was no way tourists would be that rude. The Anna Ford incident had upset me, that's all. I popped The Shirelles' greatest hits into my tape deck and practiced deep breathing techniques. I told myself everything was going to be fine. The dirty phone calls and that persistent guy from *Edge* had ceased plaguing me since I changed my number. The gay-issue fan letters had also slowed to a trickle. So I had to act with Anna and she was an asshole. I was up to the challenge. And I had eleven weeks to be professional and accomodating before they'd have the option to fire me.

It would have been nice to talk about the situation with Trevor, but since homosexuality was a sore spot with my gay boyfriend, I planned on keeping the Anna story to myself. I'd basically been living at his apartment the past couple of weeks. It was just more convenient, since our white-hot careers left us little time to spend together. And it wasn't just sex. The water pressure at Trevor's was better, too.

He was out doing the gym and getting a facial when I got there. The place was immaculate—Dora the maid had been in. I checked the fridge, hoping she'd made a batch of enchiladas verdes. Nada. I extracted a Fresca, then called my answering machine, which picked up on the first ring, indicating messages. I'd just punched in my "secret" code, the unoriginal 666, when Trevor's call-waiting beeped in my ear. I hung up frustrated. His phone started to ring. As always, I let his machine pick up. It was the discreet thing to do. Trevor's overly friendly greeting, a beep, then this: "Hi, Trevor, it's Vidal from the *Advocate* editorial office. I've got a message I maybe should give you from a guy who says he knows you and *urgently* needs to get in touch with you. He's called twice today. His name's Barney Gagnon. . . ." As Vidal rattled off a Santa Monica phone number, I felt unreality cascade around me. There's no way, there's just no way, an inner voice kept babbling. I couldn't replay the message because then the machine's memo readout would reset to zero. But I really had no doubt. He had said "Barney Gagnon." And the chances that there was another Barney Gagnon in the world who just so happened to know the current boyfriend of the guy the other Barney's husband had had a torrid relationship with were about the same as Tipper Gore's going on tour with Shakespear's Sister. And he was in town—today.

I called my machine and Nick was on it. "Hey, TV star. I called you at the show and they said you were gone already. But it might have been a security measure, I guess. Anyhow, I finally made it to L.A. So call me. . . ." He left a number. It was the same one on Trevor's message. They were here together. Next to a contract role on *Big Brother Jake*, this was my worst nightmare.

Before I could formulate a plan, I heard Trevor's key in the door. He pranced in, pumped up and exfoliated. "Hi!" He dumped his gym bag on the sofa and wandered over to the kitchen. "No enchiladas." Then singing: " 'Damn . . . I wish I was your lover . . . I'd rock you till the daylight comes . . . make sure you were smiling and warm . . . I am everything—' they're having me sing on the show this week."

"Trevor, you've got a message."

"I'll listen to it later."

"I think you should play it now."

He came out, already sweatshirtless. "What's going on?" he asked, troubled, and a mite annoyed that I was ordering him around. He hit play on the machine without waiting for an an-

swer from me. We listened to Vidal's message without looking
at each other. When it was over, he turned to me, a paler shade
of tan. "Alex, I can explain . . ."

"Go ahead." I was actually more curious than upset.

"Remember when I was in Texas?"

"Yeah."

"The night you saw me at the club?" I nodded. "Okay, I'll
start at the beginning. Since we first met, you always talked
about Nick and how you couldn't believe he'd stay with somebody that ugly and dorky and I thought you were exaggerating
out of jealousy. So I was in Austin and had some time and
wanted to see for myself."

This was downright intriguing. I waited for him to go on.

"So anyway, I looked him up in the phone book and called
and asked for Nick. He said he was at work and then asked who
I was. Real curious. So I said, 'Is this Barney?' and he said yes
and I said I'd call back and hung up. Then I went down and
borrowed a bike from the hotel and rode over to their house.
Austin's so easy to get around in. I really liked it. And I was
wearing my cycling shorts and this string tank, but when I got
near the house, I took off the top and stuck it in my pocket.
Then I got some grease from the bike chain and kind of smeared
it right here." He stroked a zigzag just east of his right nipple.

"I tossed the bike down under a bush next door and then
rang their bell. God, Alex, you weren't kidding. He was a complete geek. Homely, baggy, rumpled clothes, stupid haircut that
hung in his face."

"What did you say to him?"

"That my bike chain broke and I needed to make a call.
But while I was pretending to use the phone, he was just, like,
staring at me like he'd never seen a good-looking guy before.
Which I knew wasn't the case," he added hurriedly. "And this
wicked part of me kept telling me to push it. To see what he'd
do."

"Oh, God, Trevor. You *didn't* . . ."

He sat down next to me and kept touching my arm as he
continued, occasionally breaking into a disarming, self-conscious
smile. "So I ask if I can use the bathroom. To clean up. And he

sort of mumbles yes and shows it to me and he's kind of loitering by the door and I start the shower and take off my shoes and socks and am about to lose my pants and I look over at him and he darts back into the hall, so I get in the shower and start lathering up and then I call him. 'Barney, can you come in here a minute?'

"Listen to this. I hear the front door slam shut. Then he's in the hall saying, 'Uhhh, what is it?' So I pull back the shower curtain, naked, soaking wet and I say, 'I think I pulled a muscle trying to fix my bike. Can you help me wash my back?' It was just like a William Higgins film."

"Trevor, if this is some elaborate, mischievous little improv, stop right now, okay?"

"It's all true."

I sighed. "So what happened?"

"He came up to the tub with this stupid look on his face, half terrified, half I don't know what, trying to be sexy or raunchy or something. And he started fondling my back and touched my butt just for a second and I thought I'd start laughing, so I turned around and put my hands on him and got his clothes wet. And it was the strangest thing, because I found myself getting *really* turned on and it was, like, in *spite* of him because he was such a mutt. I guess it was the power, the fact that he was totally under my domination and would never have anything like this happen to him again, ever, without paying someone, I mean."

"Did you kiss him?"

"Please. I eat with these lips." Ouch. "He started to blow me. Very incompetently, I might add. So I started ordering him to do things. Like, 'take off your pants.' 'Kiss my ass.' 'Jack me off.'"

"And he did all this?"

"Like he was possessed."

I'd been dying to know something for years. "What was his dick like?"

"The biggest one I ever saw."

I opened my mouth to protest, horrified. Trevor smirked.

"Short and stubby. It looked like one of those Fisher-Price people. Did you have those? Anyway, he was masturbating so fast I could barely see it. It was pretty obvious he wasn't up to the job of doing me, so I ended up beating off and cumming in his face. It was so nasty."

I cast an oblique glance at Trevor's shorts and saw burgeoning evidence of seismic activity as we spoke. If this XXX confession led to us boffing on the sofa, I'd never feel clean again.

"I reached down and finished him in two strokes. He was moaning, 'Suck it, suck it.' As if. God, what a mess. He just sat on the bathroom floor completely spent while I got dressed. Then I gave him this bull about what an incredible fantasy adventure it had been and maybe we'd meet again and I was out the door and on my bike and I never saw him again. I swear."

"I believe you," I told him. "But apparently he figured out who you were. He had to have recognized you in *Advocate Men* to have called the magazine."

"He *had* that issue?"

"He probably has a huge collection. Nick told me he's a really voyeuristic lech."

Trevor shuddered, as if Barney getting all steamed up over his photospread was somehow more distasteful than Trevor shooting a load in his face in person.

"You're insane," I told him, as if it wasn't really a bad thing to be. Which it isn't.

He pulled his legs up and leaned over his knees. "I deserve a spanking." Couldn't argue with that. "Are you mad?"

"I don't know. Do you think I should be?"

"No."

"Why not?"

"Because you and I weren't . . . together when this happened and I didn't do it to fuck up anything for you."

"So why didn't you tell me about it?"

"If you were me, would you have told?"

"I would never have done it!" I almost laughed.

Trevor dug his fingers into the cushion and stared down at

his high-tops. "I guess I thought you might use it to try to get together with Nick again." How kooky. Perish the thought. "And I don't want that to happen. Because I love you."

I looked deep into his jawbreaker-size hazel eyes for some sign of sarcasm or irony and there was none and it was a little frightening.

"Trevor . . ." I said, thinking I had to say something. He stroked my cheek with his fingertips. I spread my arms and he moved in and I slid my hands over ridged lats and felt the marbled perfection of his bare back. His head was against my chest. I raked my fingers through his fifty-dollar haircut.

He lifted his head and gave me a shy, close-mouthed kiss. "I still feel kind of facially, so I'm going to have a quick shower. Then let's go to dinner."

"Okay."

He disappeared into his room. Jesus H. Christ. I tried to sort out what I'd absorbed in the past fifteen minutes. Barney had cheated on Nick. I believed Trevor. Why would he possibly make up something that sordidly bizarre? And here Barney was, in Santa Monica trying to establish contact with Trevor (or Randy Northcutt, as his *Advocate Men* fans knew him) and *do it again*. I had been thinking about it the whole time Trevor was spilling his guts, and had come to the conclusion that, even if faced with Trevor's nubile charms in a zipless fuck situation, if I was Nick's and he was mine, I would stay true to him.

Something occurred to me. While I had been locked in a passionate clinch with Nick at his office, Barney and Trevor were . . . that goddamn phone call from Barney . . . about the cookies! He was probably stalling for time while he mopped up jism. Oh, the salty irony. Even so, I refused to indulge the fantasy that Nick had come out here to be with me. The presence of Barney, duplicitous, nudie-modelfucker he may have been, nixed that fairytale scenario. Sara said Nick was worried about me, but I guess he'd never know that the tantalizing agony of his erratic interest in my life stung worse than a dozen tabloid cover stories.

There was no way to inform him of Barney's treachery, either. If I could ever make him believe it happened in the first place, he'd have to think that I put Trevor up to it, orchestrated the whole thing like I was Jill Abbott on *The Young and the Restless*. And Trevor would certainly have no further contact with the deadbeat in question for Nick to discover. After all, Trev had a prime-time family network series airing in a few weeks. And he was in love with me to boot. . . .

Another ant farm of problems to contend with. I felt instantly guilty for not telling him I loved him, too. But I just didn't. I was fond of Trevor and maybe that fondness was actually a love bud waiting to blossom at any moment, but for now it was closed. Not to mention the fact that even if I had been wildly in love with Trevor, telling him so after the Barney story would have made me feel like a chump. And if we loved each other, did that mean we had to start having anal intercourse? How could I trust him enough for me, properly condomed of course, to assume a Greek active, let alone passive role? Jesus help me.

I was running out of time to phone Nick. Soon Trevor would be out of the shower and we'd be on our way to some dark, trendy restaurant where chicken came in medallions. I fumbled out my PacBell card, just in case Santa Monica was a toll call that would show up on Trevor's bill. As I punched in the digits, I wondered if I should play a prank on Barney if he answered. No, he'd have a miserable enough time his entire visit waiting for Randy Northcutt to call him back.

"Hello?" It was Nick.

"Hi, Nick. It's Alex." I carried the cordless receiver out onto the balcony.

"How's everything goin'?"

"Just fine."

"Can you believe I finally made it to L.A.?" No, babe, I'm having a real tough time swallowing it, if you want to know the truth. "We gonna be able to get together tomorrow?"

I set my trap. "Actually, I've been under a lot of pressure at the show and was thinking about heading down to San Diego for a day or two. Get away from it all. Why don't you come with me?"

"Oh, I've got a couple meetings to go to. I don't think—"

"When are they? We can just go down afterward. No expectations. No catch. What do you say?" This was awful of me, but knowing his answer made me momentarily grateful that I wasn't setting myself up for another emotional freefall.

He sounded achingly sad, but if he was as sad as I about the way things had turned out, they wouldn't have turned out this way, now, would they? When was the last time a phone conversation with him *hadn't* been steeped in trauma? "I just can't, Alex," he said.

"Do I even have to ask why? He's here, isn't he, Nick? You brought him to L.A." He didn't answer. As the hot, prickly flow of tears rose higher and higher, I wondered how things could have gotten so fucked up when all I'd ever wanted was just one chance at happiness with him. "Tell me Barney's here," I spit.

"Yes. I couldn't come unless—"

"How can you say you care about me at all?" I clicked off, aghast that I'd spoken to him like that, feeling like I'd just run over a cherished pet. I could call him back and make plans to see him tomorrow. Tell him the whole story—*I'd* done nothing wrong—emphasizing Barney's adultery and his feverish desire for a repeat offense. He would believe me. He would—

"What's up?" Trevor asked at the doorway, the fluffy white towel slung over his well-defined shoulder dangling precariously in front of his free-swinging equipment.

"Just beeping in at home," I told him.

"Everything cool?"

"Sure. I have that new number and only those very special to me know it."

"What should I wear tonight?"

"Bicycle shorts and axle grease. Maybe you'll get lucky."

"I already did." He forced me down onto the couch.

Parking downtown at noon was simply out of the question, so I begged Sara to drop me off at Mezzaluna, the restaurant where Nick had asked me to meet him for lunch about "something important and kind of exciting."

"This could be it," I babbled, as she drove south on Red River and brushed her luxuriant black tresses into submission.

"Stop it!" she growled, trying to sound annoyed. "You have no idea what this is about."

"Yes, I do. He's going to tell me Barney's moving out. And then we're going to stop by Big Sur Waterbeds for a waveless king-size."

"I hope so, darlin'. Okay, we're here."

"Bye. Do I look okay?"

"Like a little angel."

"Thanks for the ride." I hit the sidewalk.

"Alex! Your backpack." She tossed it to me and I went into the tony restaurant, a favorite among handsome yuppies in three-piece suits, including Nick, who waved at me from a table by the wall.

"Hi, there. I went and ordered us a couple of antipastos. I hope that's okay."

"It's fine," I smiled warmly. "What's up?"

"Right to the point, huh?"

"Well, you said it was important. And exciting."

"Well, potentially."

"Stop. You tease me."

This wasn't about dumping Barney. Still, I wondered what the hell he was up to when he reached into his briefcase and pulled out a sheaf of papers.

"I've been trying to launch your movie career," he said, handing me what turned out to be a script.

"*Teenage Brides of Christ?* By Fisher MacDonald? Who's Fisher MacDonald?"

"Well, his real name's Ed Cohen, but he changed it for this 'cause he thought folks might get upset that a Jew wrote a movie about nuns getting massacred by this slasher loose in a convent. Gary Van Owen, one of the partners at the firm, is producing it with him."

"This is going to be a real movie?"

"Oh, yeah. They're filming up in Dallas in just a little bit. This one gal who was in *Playboy* and does a lot of horror movies is starring in it. The thing is, the fella they hired for the male lead kind of wimped out on them and they need to find somebody else quick. So I skimmed the script and thought you'd be perfect. And I told Gary about you and he thought it was worth a try. What do you think?"

"Sure. I mean, I'd love to. They'd want some kind of audition . . ."

"Uh-huh. Gary talked to Ed and he said for you to Fed Ex your picture and resume to Dallas. I brought you an envelope all filled out from work, so just drop it in the box in front of the Tower on campus. The director is coming to Dallas from L.A. this weekend and you can drive up and meet him and Ed."

This was so sweet of him. Watching his animated, kissable face as he told me made me want to cry. "Thanks, Nick. You have no idea what a chance like this means to me."

"I think maybe I do." His eyes were hypnotizing me. Must—say—words: I love you I love you . . .

"Nick, I—I wonder, do you know exactly what they're looking for, for this character?"

"Blond and real nice-lookin'. Like you. Around twenty-two. You gotta be okay with doing a couple scenes in your underwear. You're having sex with one of the nuns."

"Those nutty, busty convent sluts."

We ate big creamy pasta dishes for lunch, then split a wedge of amaretto cheesecake. I waited until he was driving me back to school to ask, "Would you be able to go up to Dallas with me Saturday morning?"

"Maybe, Alex."

When I read the splattery script, I estimated that my part, Paul Hunt, was the third lead (after Sisters Corky and Bernadette). It went on and on until he had a pitchfork run through him on page seventy-seven. The screenplay was outrageous in a deadpan, offensive way I kind of liked: wayward young nuns "punished" by a psychopathic ex-altar boy in a variety of creative death scenes. I desperately wanted to be a part of it. Fortunately, I had to spend only twenty-four hours in a tension frenzy. Ed Cohen called Nick late the next afternoon and told him to send me up. I was to meet Ed and director Carl DeAngelis at the Marriott in Dallas Saturday at 1:00.

Of course, Nick couldn't make the trip with me, but Valerie and Chuck had been planning a visit to her mother's in Fort Worth and offered to let me tag along. We arrived past midnight on Friday and slithered into the majestic mock-Colonial house, easily the jewel of the subdivision, as quietly as possible, to discover that Valerie's mother had prepared a huge feast carefully Tupperwared in the two-door refrigerator-freezer with automatic ice-maker. "Thought you kids might be hungry. See you in the a.m. Love, Mom" read the note stuck to the fridge with Sesame Street magnets. We pigged out on fried chicken, potato salad and pecan pie, then drank sangria in Val's old room until we were all sprawled on her bed, reading Dr. Seuss books out loud and laughing our asses off.

The next morning we enjoyed a hearty breakfast prepared by Valerie's large Texan mom, who made me perform several scenes from the script, then cheerfully proclaimed, "You're gonna git that part, sugarplum." Valerie and Chuck drove me to the hotel, wished me luck, and went to play in the pool. I went into the men's room and fingered my gel-job. I was wearing black pants and a charcoal-gray T-shirt bearing the slightest arcs of dampness beneath my arms. I turned on the blower and took care of that problem. Fortunately, I was always odor-free. I was ready for my meeting with the director of such hits as *Camp Panty Raid* and *Cyborg Slayer*.

I rode the elevator alone to the tenth floor, any fears I might have had about being lured into international bondage in some gay Arab sex ring alleviated by a misty-edged, cameo-size mental image of Nick in his little office making phone calls, trying to boost my acting career. I knocked on 1017, a conscientious three minutes early. A short bald guy with a black beard in mismatched Hawaiian beachwear answered. "Alexander?"

"Hi, it's great to meet you," I said, Pepsodent smile and butch handshake at the ready.

"Ed. Ed Cohen. Gary Van Owen had some great things to say about you." I had never even spoken with Gary Van Owen. Ed motioned me to a chair. "Want a beer?" he asked, pawing through the fridge.

"Oh, no thanks. I'm fine."

In walked the most flaming queen in history. "Christ, this heat is gonna finish me off!" He had thinning blond hair slicked back on a conical head, John Lennon sunglasses and a lacy white shirt he pinched between two fingers and billowed in and out, fanning himself. "Texas in March? Who knew? Hi! Who's this?"

"Alexander Young," Ed said. "And this is our director, Carl DeAngelis."

We exchanged pleasantries and Carl arranged himself on a little sofa and examined my resume. "I don't know if Gary told you what a *bind* we're in. This actor's piss-licking agent held onto our contracts hoping this series deal would work out, and it did, and they screwed us. We start principal a week from Monday. No male lead. *No problem!* Anywho, you look the type, don't you think, Ed?"

"Absolutely."

We read the first scene—Bernadette telling Paul that she's taken a vow of chastity before he rakishly persuades her to ride the baloney pony in the attic. "Very *nice*," Carl cooed, clapping his hands together three or four times. Ed nodded. We proceeded to the dramatic highlight wherein Paul discovers two dismembered nun corpses then runs into Sebastian, the social misfit, and starts to realize he may be the killer.

"Very good," Carl said. "Annelise Collins cast the movie in L.A. Do you know her?"

"No," I replied. "I've never worked in Hollywood."

"Oh, yes. I *love* it," he said, scanning my resume again. "You plan to, don't you?"

"As soon as I graduate in May," popped out of my mouth, news to me. They said I'd done fine and asked about my availability for two to three weeks. I assured them I could swing it and they showed me to the door.

I plodded toward the pool, fairly bewildered. Had I gotten it or not? Shouldn't they have had me read the lines more than once? Maybe not. I'd been prepared. Being recommended by Gary Van Owen must carry quite a lot of weight, too. Nick had said he was putting up "a chunk" of the movie's budget. And they'd told me to hold on to the script. But what were they going to say? "Give it back"? That would have been pretty undiplomatic, even if they'd hated me. Who knew how many more actors they were seeing? Southern Methodist University's joke of a theater department certainly boasted a few hunky thesps to choose from. And wasn't it conceivable that Carl would hit the Dallas gay scene and wind up plugging some boy-toy discovery into the role?

Holding all these gnawing rhetorical questions back behind the door of my conscious brain functions proved an impossible task, but all I could do was wait and try not to drive my friends batshit in the process. When I got back to my apartment Sunday night I had zero messages. (Nick had very sweetly called me at Valerie's mother's house Saturday afternoon for a full report.) Monday was infernal. I called my machine after every class, then slammed down the phone, messageless, when it didn't pick up on the first ring. That night, I resisted calling Nick and did four hours of class reading, masochistically willing the movie job into existence by preparing for my two-week absence from school.

It worked. I was toweling off Tuesday morning when Nick called to tell me the part was mine. "Congratulations, movie star. You report to the Best Western motor hotel on Sunday. Two thousand a week for two weeks, plus forty bucks a day for meals. Sound okay?"

"I don't know how to thank you, Nick. This is the most exciting thing that's ever happened to me."

"I was talking to Ed Cohen and he says it's gonna be at the theaters for at least a week before it hits the video stores."

"Too bad all the good drive-ins are closed down."

"You're on your way, Mr. Young. Ed said you were the hands-down choice for the part." Then why the Christ did they torture me for seventy-two hours? "Gary's pretty excited, too. He wants to take us for dinner Saturday."

"Great! Are you free tonight for a little celebration?"

"This week is no good, Alex. Tell ya what—we'll go to the lake on Saturday. Get Sara to take off the bikini top. If you're not too busy."

He killed me. "I'd love to."

"I'm real happy for you. And I'll make sure Gary takes us someplace real expensive."

" 'Kay. You know, you'll be getting a commission for this."

"Aw, no. Forget it. You're not giving me a cent of that hard-earned horror money."

"Money wasn't what I had in mind."

He hummed enigmatically. We hung up and I went to school. I had to inform all my teachers that I would be out of town for two weeks due to either a film role or dire family emergency, depending on how cool they were.

Dear Mrs. Wanda Blake,
You should know that Simon Arable is the one who tried to kill Cyrinda, not Sean! I can't believe no one has figured this out, but Simon is a liar and a murderer! Don't hire him to be the managing editor for your newspaper. After today's show, I'm pretty sure he will try to kill Cyrinda again, probably on Friday. That's why I am overnighting this letter to you. You have to get her out of that hospital!

I will be happy to testify at Simon's trial, any day but Thursday because that's when I have custody of little Ashlynn and Billy Joe Jr.
Michelle Martin
Roanoke, VA

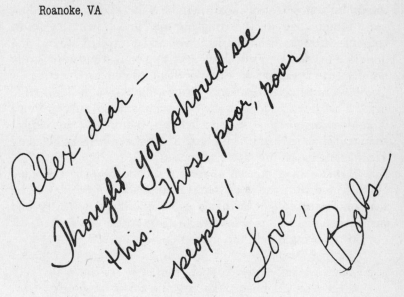

*Alex dear—
Thought you should see this. Those poor, poor people! Love, Babs*

Right after Trevor wrapped the sixth *Dino & Muffin* episode, I had a week in which Simon did not appear on *Hearts Crossing*, although I'd still be paid $2025, my minimum weekly rate. We flew down to Puerto Vallarta and spent five flesh-filled days at a *muy* quaint and tropical little hotel Trevor's model friend Lars recommended, that turned out, to my amusement, to be one hundred percent *maricones*. Trevor soothed his agitation by disguising himself in a Body Glove cap and shades whenever he left the room.

Our next-door neighbors were a hilariously "straight-acting" couple of USC frat hunks on a top-secret romantic hideaway. After we all became chummy, Trevor proceeded to annoy me by less than half-jokingly suggesting no less than four times that the two of us initiate a four-way with Dave and Kip, an idea I pretended to be more appalled at than I actually was—Dave was a hairy-chested fireman type with what looked like a four-alarm length of hose crammed into his Boca Chica Slide Thong. But I was better than that. (Not much.)

By our last night in Mexico, I was beginning to relish the imminent solitude of my apartment, at which I'd been spending mere minutes per week getting my mail and leaving checks to coincide with the maid's visits. Trev and I strolled around and bought a few Catholically ultra-tacky souvenirs, then impulsively bopped into a ramshackle, touristy café for an early dinner. A *monchichi* on steroids showed us to a wobbly, rough-hewn table next to a hanging parrot cage. The occupant, an unkempt bird with glamour-length claws, crawled up and down the side closest to us, cackling in Spanish and sending periodic drifts of blue and green feathers wafting onto our basket of greasy, razor-crisp tortilla chips. Trevor poured us each a second margarita while I absently fingered the shark's tooth necklace I'd been wearing the whole trip. I'd told the ever-curious Trevor that it had merely been part of my *Psycho Beach Party* costume, leaving Nick out but thinking about him more than a little.

"God, I love it here," Trevor said. "Mexico, I mean. It's like a black velvet painting come to life. How are the fish tacos?"

"Pretty weird. The drinks make up for it, though."

"I have this overwhelming desire to tear that tank top off and ravish you under the parrot cage."

I gasped. It had been a while since his last playful streak. "I'll have to ask you to restrain yourself. You know, the jails down here . . . not a pretty thought."

"Yeah, they'd love to get their hands on you and that big blond penis of yours. They'd ream you six ways to Sunday dinner." He ran an experienced tongue over his lips and lustfully clutched one pec.

"Trevor—*what* has gotten into you tonight?"

"I don't know. We're lucky, aren't we?" I nodded. He whipped out his platinum card. "Let's blow this dive."

We tottered onto the festive streets, drunk enough to put ourselves at risk of abduction by bloodthirsty black-magic cultists on the prowl for human sacrifices, but nothing worse than diarrhea ever happened in Love Boat Land. The Mexican moon beamed down at us, looking for all the world like a precisely rounded scoop of French vanilla ice cream suspended in the invigoratingly starry sky. We ambled in the general direction of our seaside hideaway, but were distracted by a gaudy movie theater with a blazing marquee advertising *Basic Instinct* in Spanish.

We bought tickets and creaked up red-carpeted stairs to the balcony, where we found a couple of seats on the end, behind three Vallartans in curlers and housecoats whose nonstop giggly whisper-chatter during even the most mildly torrid scenes was slightly more entertaining than the cruddy film. Not that we cared. Trevor discreetly slipped an arm around my waist and shoved one of his big hands into the pocket of my shorts. During the appropriate scene he leaned over and squealed, "I do believe I forgot my panties!" then kissed my ear and neck until he started laughing and a couple of the women in front of us turned around.

"I love you," he said to me.

"I love you, too." Maybe it wasn't an all-encompassing, breath-stopping force of nature, but maybe holding out for another love like that would be the stupidest, most hurtful thing I could do to myself. What Nick had evoked in me, the scary, exhilarating, sensual feeling of swirling boatless through the rapids of a warm yet powerful river—wasn't it possible that it could never again exist outside the transient, deciduous garden of First Love?

I had to enjoy what was here and real and now. Which was a midnight romp in the surf after we got back from the movies, with Trevor yelling, "Jellyfish! Jellyfish!" and attacking me, pulling off both our bathing suits so we had to run naked back to our ground-floor beachfront terrace. We torpedoed into bed still wet and didn't go to sleep for two hours. I woke up in the middle of the night, cold and disoriented. I felt like I shouldn't be alone, but for some reason I was, and I couldn't figure out where I was until Trevor emerged from the bathroom and slipped back into bed.

We took separate flights out of Mexico: Trevor to Seattle on a modeling gig for Guess (he'd kissed and made up with his print agent, at least until *Dino & Muffin* was put on the fall schedule), me to Burbank. I shuttled home to the Hollywood hills and cordlessly returned calls while unpacking. Every single person—Allison Slater Lang, my parents, even my maid—had a machine on. I took a hot shower and hit the sheets, looking forward to a leisurely weekend alone. Grocery shopping with a Walkman, a few chapters of *The Oldest Living Confederate Widow Tells All*, maybe a sauna—the world was my oyster.

And now for the mail. I had received an invitation to the Daytime Emmys in New York. Actually, an invitation to pay an outrageous ticket price then sit through a black-tie circle-jerk in which *I wasn't even nominated* for Outstanding Younger Actor in a Drama. *Hearts Crossing* had received a total of four nods— three technical and Brent Bingham for Best Lead Actor, which pretty much invalidated the existence of the Television Academy. I stuffed the Emmy crap back into its glitzy, gold-lettered envelope and tossed it, turning to the packet from the studio containing the three scripts I'd be doing next week. I picked up Tuesday's episode and skimmed the synopsis, the two-page scene breakdown prepared by college interns who were paid absolutely nothing and were not even allowed to touch the bagels and cream cheese laid out every morning for the crew.

Simon was breaking up with Jane, and not a moment too soon, if you asked me. Before I went to Mexico, Simon had copied the computer file containing the sex-potency drug formula, then introduced a virus into Jane's program, ruining it. Now he was blaming Jane for the mistake and using her "carelessness" as an excuse to banish her from his life, while he of course had the secret formula Jane had worked so hard on as well as an experimental batch of the stuff stolen from her lab, ready to unleash on the unsuspecting residents of Harts Crossing.

This was a busy episode. I had four scenes in my office at the newspaper with Anna Ford, but I got to bark awful things at the ignorant slut, so it was okay. Then it was over to Allie's Alley, as we called the inexplicably long set that served as Natalie's living room, for a fun fight in which she told me I had to move out. It couldn't be too much of a surprise to the home audience—I had been blackmailing her since Thanksgiving, not to mention destroying her romance with Sean by framing him for Cyrinda's attempted murder. After all, a girl can only take so much. I was also in the last scene of the show:

ACT VII
SCENE 3
INT. SIMON'S BEDROOM   SIMON, MOVER

My blood froze as I read the synopsis:
SIMON instructs a sexy young MOVER to pack up his belongings. When the MOVER strips off his shirt, SIMON displays distinct interest. Tension builds as SIMON chats with MOVER then embraces him for an O.S. kiss.

This had to be a lame joke. That must be it. Some smartass in the production office tacked it on the end of the synopsis as a prank. I turned to the end of the script. Oh, my God. There it was:

SIMON
(MOVING CLOSER)
I've seen you around, haven't I?
MOVER
It's a possibility.
SIMON
I doubt I'd forget.
(They are standing face to face, eye contact smoldering—it's a dangerous, unsettling moment. With slow deliberation, Simon runs his fingers across the mover's muscular chest . . .)

MOVER

Go for it.
*(They lock into a steamy embrace, then collapse onto the bed,
eyes closed in anticipation of an offscreen kiss)*
Fade out
End of Act VII

Nobody would go to the trouble of writing a phony four-page scene for my benefit. This was real. I started reading it from the beginning with a glazed, horrified fascination, automatically saying Simon's lines to myself in character. The phone rang and I jumped, almost tossing the script into the air.

"Hello?"

"Alex! Thank God you're back. It's Allie Lang."

"Hi. Have you seen Tuesday's script?"

"Yes! That's why I called you last week. Don't you ever beep in?"

"No . . . I mean, Linda's secretary had my number in Mexico and so did my agent. Anyway . . . Jesus, Allie, what the fuck is going on?"

"Simon's gay. That's what's going on. It was all everybody could talk about last week."

"So what are they all saying?"

"That it's ridiculous! Not to mention personally offensive to you. This whole thing is even stupider than the time they sent that eight-year-old brat to boarding school and she came back three months later as Nori Ann Marshall."

"Look, Allie. I think I'll call Jerry Reynolds and see what he has to say."

"Fine. But try to stay calm. You're great and whatever shit they churn out and call writing, you're going to always be better."

"Thanks."

"Did you have fun in Mexico?"

"Yeah."

"Don't tell me you went to a lush paradise all by yourself."

"I'm not telling you that."

"Okay . . ."

"I'll bring you a picture of him on Tuesday."

"Bye, Alex."

I located my *Hearts Crossing* phone sheet (wouldn't Juliana Butts give her left tit for a peek at this, I thought randomly) and dialed Jerry at his Marina del Rey condo.

On the first ring: "Hello?"

"Jerry? This is Alexander Young."

Stuttering: "Uh . . . h-h-hi, Alex. . . . Back from your trip?"

"Yes, I just got in actually and started to look over my scripts and I haven't been able to get past Tuesday's episode. Do you know the one I'm talking about?"

"Oh. Yes. Simon and—"

"Why is this happening, Jerry?"

"Alex . . . we've been wanting to—hold on, let me turn off the computer." He was writing soap opera scripts on Friday night? Good lord. "Okay, um . . . you see, a gay storyline is something we've been wanting to try for, uh, quite a while, and we also weren't that happy with the Jane-Simon romance. . . . the viewers didn't really buy into it. . . ."

"What do you mean?"

"The letters we've been getting indicate that it seems really false."

"Well, it is. He's using her to get the secret formula, right?"

"Yes and no. See, we like to leave our options open about the relationship. But sometimes the chemistry isn't right, you know . . . the viewers aren't . . ."

I had to be careful. He was the co-executive producer and shared control of my fate. Ah, hell. He was a wimp. "So what you're saying, Jerry," I replied into the awkward silence, "is that nobody sees me as heterosexual. It's beyond my range."

"No! Alex, that's—it's not . . ." Of course it was. "It's just a bizarre new twist. Not that being gay is bizarre. . . . I'm writing the Simon plotline out now. I really think it'll be fun." Yeah. Like an Amy Grant concert. "I hope you're not mad, Alex." He sounded frightened.

"So what *is* going to happen, plot-wise?" I asked.

"Oh, well, you know. I can't really say yet . . . it's just—"

"Thanks, Jerry. See you Tuesday." *Click*.

By the end of the week, Simon had moved into an outrageously faggy apartment that seemed to have been transplanted whole from a Conran's Habitat Showroom. I thought the plaster Roman busts were an especially nice touch. I couldn't wait to see what they'd come up with for my bedroom. Maybe some tasteful Mapplethorpe prints from *The Black Book* and a wrought-iron bed equipped with wrist and ankle shackles.

I complained bitterly to Connie at lunch that Friday at Johnny Rockets. "There's absolutely nothing you can do, hon. They write it, you do it. It's a one-way street, y'know? Jesus, have these fries always been so big?"

"I don't suppose I have any outs in that contract," I said, unsheathing my chicken burger.

"Please. You're chained to that show for two-and-a-half more years. And don't go getting fired. I got bills to pay."

"Connie, what's this going to do to my career?" It sounded pathetic, but that's why you had an agent.

"To be honest, being on a soap is more hazardous to an actor than playing gay. Who works more, William Hurt or Stephen Nichols?"

"Who's Stephen Nichols?"

"Exactly."

"I'm a little worried about the double whammy," I told her.

"Look, you're fabulous. Keep it up. Stay easy to work with. Linda Rabiner and Reese Jacobs love you. They say you're a doll. You know who they hate, don't you? Brett Butthole or whatever his name is. The stories I hear . . ." She wadded up a napkin and dabbed the corners of her mouth. "Fuck, my lipstick. You're gonna be okay, Alex. I have no doubt."

Trevor had doubts. He didn't freak out when I told him Simon would soon be daytime's most prominent homo, but I felt our relationship cool a degree or two. I couldn't expect him to be happy about it, but it seemed paranoid and insulting that we suddenly only went to movies at really off, empty-theater times and restricted our dining out to restaurants where they could have handed out flashlights along with the menus.

Contrary to what he'd always said, Trevor was more insecure about his career than ever in the wake of *Dino & Muffin*. No one would know the series's fate until the six episodes they'd taped aired in early summer, and in the meantime, he was climbing the walls. He dumped the small agency that put him on *Dino* and signed with CAA, did a guest-star shot on a trendy detective pilot in which he played a promiscuous artist who meets a bloody end (quite a stretch) and then was unreasonably crushed when, after two callbacks, he wasn't cast in a Disney adventure about Yukon sled dogs. "I really need you tonight," he told me, before requesting a massage then immediately falling asleep.

A few days before my first queer episode was on, *Soap Opera* magazine ran a little item in the gossip section: "Rumor has it a major gay storyline is about to start at any moment on *Hearts Crossing*. . . . All we can say is a current regular character will be revealed to have homoerotic tendencies the likes of which have never been seen on daytime. . . . Without mentioning names, our bets are on a certain young supervillain of recent tabloid fame. . . ." Those bitchy hacks. I'd never cooperate with them again unless I really needed the publicity.

The day before that show was on I called my mom and told her. It made me feel really awful, like I was admitting the consequences of some irresponsible and shameful action. She was sweet and supportive, as always, which in a way made me feel worse. Neither one of us brought up my grandparents. I supposed she'd come up with something to tell them. It really sucked that their enjoyment of *Hearts Crossing* would be irrevocably tainted from this moment on.

I didn't have the energy to formulate a way to ease my relatives into my special new stardom. As soon as I pulled that hard-bodied Italian mover out of the frame and onto my bed, the *Hearts Crossing* phone started ringing and didn't stop for days. Viewers were shocked, outraged, delighted and titillated in various combinations, as my avalanche of mail indicated. Connie talked to Linda Rabiner and Jerry and relayed to me that they were "pleased" with the "interest level and intensity" of the public reaction to the new twist.

Soap Opera Weekly and *Soap Opera Update* were pretty damn interested, too, and prepared lightweight pieces on the minus-cule history of gays in daytime drama. I had Connie decline their requests to interview me; my "schedule absolutely did not per-mit." I had nothing good to say on the matter. The orientation flip-flop was stupid and my private homosexual life certainly had no parallels with that of the murderous, power-crazed manipu-lator I portrayed (though Barney might have disagreed), but bad-mouthing the show's writing and character development was a sure way to reduce my weekly salary from around three grand to zero. My new phone number had luckily remained airtight, so *Edge* and that other journalistic potpourri of gay news, views and S & M personals, *Frontiers*, had to filter their repeated re-quests to interview me through Connie. Again, my schedule would absolutely not permit.

Trevor and I rarely discussed the show—it upset him—which helped me maintain a precarious, imaginary shell to keep reality out so I could bullshit myself those first couple of weeks that I could just go to the studio, play my part, come home, and ignore what anyone said or thought about it.

Sara called and told me the rag that outed me was currently running a dishy item about Simon's new improved sexual ori-entation along with a smaller reprint of the notorious kiss-photo. "But if it's any consolation, a lovely profile of you written by someone very special goes to press tomorrow." I'd completely forgotten about the *Paseo del Rio* article. "I'm going to have it framed and drop it by your mom and dad's."

"You don't have to do that . . ."

"I want to. I think it'll make them happy. Your mother called to invite me over for dinner and I want to bring it with me."

"Okay, but let me reimburse you for the framing. I'll send you a check."

"Who are you now, Richie Rich? Don't worry about it, Alex. How's Trevor?" I told her. "That son of a bitch. Like there's any doubt in anybody's mind that he's gay as a debutante. Who else would have Taylor Dayne in permanent rotation on the CD player of his Miata? If I were you, I'd cut him loose.

Fuck him if he's not mature enough to handle it. You're too good for him. Now what the *hell* is going on on that soap?"

This is what was going on: Simon was becoming quite chummy with Ollie Tarlton, former husband and current boyfriend of Gwen Tarlton, society columnist for the *Crossing Herald*, still suffering from a severe intimacy disorder brought on by her subconsciously suppressed rape by Chip Blake, Cyrinda's drug-addict adopted stepbrother. Very chummy indeed. Chummy enough for even the most half-witted viewers to deduce that a certain temperamental Emmy-nominated Christian stud would soon be Simon's new playmate. Naturally it took the Mercedes-owning performer in question a bit longer to figure things out, but whether fellow cast members clued him in or he read it in *Soap Opera Digest*'s "What Will Happen" corner, the screaming fight that took place in Linda Rabiner's office between Brent and the executive producers was the buzz on the set for days.

Phalita explained the situation to me during a Thighmaster session in her dressing room. "Brent hates being on the show, but his contract isn't up for eight months. I don't know where the hell he thinks he's going to go, Emmy or no fuckin' Emmy." She hadn't been nominated in a while.

"Why don't they just buy him out if he's such a pain?" I asked.

She grimaced, partly from muscular exertion. "Too cheap. He's getting thirty-five hundred a show with a two show per week guarantee. Those year-long option cycles are a bitch. But if he walks out of his contract, they don't owe him a dime. I personally think they're using that wacky shit with you to ride Brent's ass, no pun intended. To see how much he can take."

"No pun intended," I cracked.

She burst out laughing and the Thighmaster popped into the air.

"Hello?"

"Uh, hi. Alex?"

"Who's this?"

"Oh, sorry. It's Brent. Bingham."

Why, Brent. I was just thinking of you. How could I not be since we're supposed to kiss live on videotape tomorrow morning? I was lying on my stomach in bed all alone, reading that very scene. Trevor and I had had an entirely mindless argument about returning a bag of movies to Video West four days ago and we hadn't spoken since. I decided to wait and see how long it would take him to call me. Considering his stubborn streak, this was akin to lighting our relationship on fire and watching it slowly crinkle and blacken into a fine gray ash. Still, I couldn't wholly quell my inherent perky optimism and honestly expected it to be Trev every time the phone rang, which was a lot less often than you'd expect for someone as cute and successful as myself.

"What's up, Brent?" He'd been very civil to *me* since we started working together, but as a rule we had nothing to talk about. Christ only knew what would prompt a phone call now.

"We've got a lot to cover tomorrow, and I was wondering if you'd mind rehearsing a little tonight."

"Okay," I said, shocked.

"You want to just come by?"

"Malibu, right?"

"Yeah, the address is on that home list thing. You have one of those?"

"Yes. It's around here somewhere. Okay, got it. Should I leave now?"

"Sure. Park in the space next to my car. You know, the Mercedes. It says 'reserved,' but they're out of town."

"Okay. I'm on my way."

"See you, bud."

I put on a sweatshirt and grabbed my script and took off down Sunset Boulevard without giving myself a chance to consider how nuts this was. What if he'd flipped out after reading tomorrow's episode and was planning to murder me? They'd find my body in a ditch in Trancas Canyon and a TV movie would follow starring Rick Schroder and Stephen Baldwin.

I retrieved 10,000 Maniacs's newest CD from under the seat and popped it in. I'd used my cruise cancellation money to splurge on a pull-out player but rarely had any discs on hand because I was afraid they'd melt if I left them in the car. By the time I got to Brent's, the album was almost over. How could he drive this every day? It took less time to fly to Vegas. The house was a waterfront duplex on Pacific Coast Highway. I squeezed into my assigned parking space, recognizing the shape of Brent's low-model Mercedes under a tan dropcloth.

I passed through an open wooden gate and took a flagstone walk down the length of the house. At the end there was a redwood terrace divided by little fences on either side of the jacuzzi that was in the center. The entire back wall of the house was glass, affording me a surprise view of shirtless Brent scratching his balls. I waited until he took his hands out of his sweats, then hit the buzzer. A few seconds later, he came to the door in a Gold's Gym tank top from which his gorgeously mounded pecs erupted beneath a garden of black chest hair. "How you doing, Alex?"

He showed me in. Lots of ugly white furniture, a Crate & Barrel dinette with wet, sand-encrusted swim trunks on it, a nonfunctional fireplace sporting his Viewer's Choice Soap award and a couple of baseball trophies on the mantel. A golden Lab with a red bandanna knotted around its neck snoozed in the corner. I took a seat on the sectional sofa.

"Sorry about the mess," Brent said. "It's the maid's day off." He noticed a dried salsa stain on the hideous oval chrome-and-glass coffee table and covered it with the latest issue of *People*, which had been at the top of a foot-high stack of literature including a hefty leatherette Bible with Brent's name actually embossed in gold on the cover. Brent plunged his hand between the couch cushions and located the remote control for his giant-screen TV. He muted a classic Tears For Fears video on VH-1 then asked me if I wanted Diet Pepsi or a wine cooler.

We got right to work on our scenes, which involved some nonsense about me assuring Ollie Gwen's job would be protected when I started restructuring the newspaper staff in yet another cold-blooded power play. What mattered was the subtext, which seemed to whizz completely over Brent's head. I couldn't play out my half of the sexual tension if he was going to be so dense. Should I be directing him? I asked myself helplessly, annoyed at the futility the evening was amounting to. We ran through everything twice, up to but avoiding the actual kissing scene, which was of course the last segment of the show.

"This isn't going anywhere," Brent huffed. He got up and shuffled to the kitchen.

I followed a bit hesitantly. The Lab was sniffing around an empty food dish. "Maybe you'd rather work on it at the studio in the morning," I suggested.

He overfilled the bowl with Purina Dog Chow from a fifty-pound sack he extracted from the walk-in pantry and ignored the nuggets that skidded across the saltillo tile floor. "Fuck. Excuse my language, Alex." He put the dog food away and took out a giant Tupperware canister that must have contained three bags of Oreos. He slumped into a chair at the dinette and started eating. "I'm just so bummed out about the show. Have some. They know I'm walking after my contract's up the first of next year. So they're trying to screw me out of my Emmy with this stupid storyline. No offense." He opened an Oreo and tongued out the cream. I experienced an involuntary erotic shudder.

"It's okay. I think it's pretty stupid myself."

"My manager's telling me not to cause trouble, but he's not the one that has to put up with assholes like Reese Jacobs and that bitch Linda Rabiner, pardon my French. I'm one of the big reasons that show is popular—I've been on *Soap Opera Digest*'s Ten Hottest Hunks list for five years in a row. That's more than Don Diamont. I'm going to beat them at their own game, though. Whatever they write, I'm going to kick butt with. I'm going to win that Emmy." Not if what I had just witnessed was any indication. "Is Jerry Reynolds gay?" He looked at me very seriously.

"I don't know," I said. "He could easily be."

"I thought you guys automatically knew." He was almost charming in a juicy, ox-like manner.

"I wish," I blurted, then wanted immediately to retract it. I watched him for some untoward reaction, but he seemed to be studying the kibble on the floor.

"Let's run through it again," he said. He got up and

reached over his shoulder, pressing fingers into his middle back. Everything in the vicinity bulged. "Ouch. I strained a muscle or something working out. I'll have to get a massage tomorrow."

Oh, God. Don't even think about it, Alex. Not for one second. Lead us not into temptation and deliver us from Malibu unbashed. We adjourned to the living room and picked up our scripts. And all of a sudden, he was right on, subtext and all. We re-did the four short scenes we'd previously rehearsed and then he barreled straight ahead into virgin territory, Act 7, Scene 3.

"It's getting late. I don't want to keep you up," Brent/Ollie told me/Simon.

"Don't be silly. It's been a fascinating evening, Ollie." Could my lines be a little faggier? "Gwen isn't expecting you, is she?" I knew damn well she had moved in with Brittany, who had been ironically married to Gwen's rapist at the time of the attack.

"I wasn't going to mention it, but she's staying with Brittany for a while," Ollie said.

SIMON: "I'm sorry to hear that." (BUT HIS EYES GLEAM WITH SECRET ENTHUSIASM) Yeah, big secret.

Brent got up and paced to the middle of the room, exactly as indicated in the script. "I think it was her therapist's idea. For some reason, I don't feel that upset by it. Our problems were . . . very complicated."

"But you tried. I know that." (HE RISES AND CROSSES TOWARD OLLIE) and damned if I didn't do just that.

Brent turned to look me in the eye. "You've been a great friend through all this, Simon. It means more to me than you know. In fact . . ." He trailed off, but maintained eye contact.

"Yes?" I prompted him, moving a fraction closer.

"It's confusing, but lately I've had some very strange thoughts about you."

"Tell me about them."

"I'm not sure I can explain them. In words."

"Then show me," I whispered through clenched teeth, hoping to lighten the mood with a little camp since it was the last line of the scene. But before I knew what was happening, Brent's hands were on my shoulders. As he pressed his mouth against mine, I tasted chocolate from the Oreos and felt the hardness of that Top 10 chest against me. Holyshitjesuschrist what was he doing?! I was paralyzed. His grip on me tightened, and I was afraid that this was it, he'd really lost it, and the next thing I knew I'd be flying through the glass wall.

But instead he released me and asked dryly, "How was that?"

"Fine," I said.

"Thanks for coming out. I think tomorrow'll be cool."

"Okay, bye." I gave him an easy smile and got the fuck out of there before he took off his clothes and tried to baptize me in the jacuzzi or something. With that bizarre interlude echoing through my system, I drove home, chalking the evening up to artistic license on Brent's part and nothing more, although I couldn't help wondering if I wouldn't cross his mind for just a nanosecond the next time he felt his adherence to the Commandments weaken and broke down and beat off.

I walked past my answering machine with "0" flashing on the message readout and hit the rack without further ado. At some point in the night I dreamed I was on the Simon's Apartment set at *Hearts Crossing* trying to remember my lines and waiting for Brent to come back so we could tape the kiss. Then I looked up and Nick was standing on Brent's mark. We'd taken a break in the middle of the scene but now they were ready to roll and the stage manager was barking, "We have speed. Very quiet please." I couldn't understand what Nick was doing there, so I looked around and saw Jerry Reynolds and went to talk to him.

"Didn't you know? We let Brent out of his contract. He's been replaced," he said, gesturing toward Nick.

"But that's—" I started to argue, and suddenly we were doing the show and I was face to face with Nick.

"It's confusing, but I think I'm falling in love with you," he said.

I didn't think that was right, but I said my next line anyway, thinking that it was really awful that we were going to have to play boyfriends on TV when he didn't want me in real life but wanting to kiss him badly just the same. And we did. I kept expecting the director to "cut" over the intercom because the scene was going on too long and Nick was fondling my crotch, which was definitely not allowed on TV. I realized we were alone and that it wasn't the set but Simon's actual apartment, which made sense in the context of the dream for some reason. Nick and I retreated to the couch and he held me so tight and sweet and kept whispering in my ear, "See? I told you it'd be okay." He'd finally come for me.

I awakened in darkness, the image of Nick in my arms dissolving into a dull, cool disappointment that settled over me like a shroud. I heard voices through my window. "You're wrong, Yip," my gay downstairs neighbor chortled. I hopped out of bed and crept over to the window. My neighbor was in his kimono and boxer shorts, sitting at his patio table and enjoying a candlelit tête-à-tête with an Asian youngster in a sleeveless Keith Haring T-shirt. "*Kevin Glover* is the porn star with the smallest cock."

Yip chattered something I couldn't make out. I compressed my own turgid penis between my stomach and the wall and moved my head closer to hear the outcome of the debate.

"Didn't you see *Top Man*?" my neighbor asked Yip. "Let's go in and cue it up, shall we? Video doesn't lie."

They got up and I jumped back so they wouldn't see my shadowy outline hovering at the window. I climbed back into bed and hugged one of my foam-filled pillows, letting my mind wander back into the passionate dreamworld fantasy I'd just left. I could call him. First thing in the morning. Just pick up the phone and dial his office number and tell him what's been going on. It wasn't like we couldn't see each other. All I had to do was fly to Austin. There was that hotel directly across from Nick's building. I didn't even work this Friday. I imagined phoning Nick and making up some clever reason for him to come up to Room Whatever then when he opened the door, I'd be standing in the middle of the room. And I wouldn't say anything. I'd just stand there until he put his arms around me and then I'd whisper so my voice wouldn't crack. "I love you, Nick. I love you." I didn't call.

Trevor surfaced toward the end of the week, the day I was

asked to be Grand Marshal of the Long Beach Gay Pride Festival. I was flattered, and intrigued at the possibility of being so civic-minded while meeting loads of cute guys, but I wasn't sure if I wanted to ride a pink convertible or worse, a Lambda-shaped tissue-paper float down the center of town at high noon. Connie nixed the idea: "Don't make a spectacle of yourself, Alex. Go to Long Beach, party, frolic, bond with the kids. But none of this Grand Dragon crap. You're gonna have enough notoriety on your hands when you start screwing Mr. Sunday School weekday afternoons at two. That friggin' show. They want sick? They ought to make a soap opera out of my life. Bye, Doll." Hopefully, it wasn't too late to check RuPaul's availability. I was handwriting the Festival organizers a charming rejection letter when the phone rang and my machine immediately clicked on. I'd forgotten to reset it after playing back the day's mediocre messages.

"Alex, it's Trevor. I know you're home, so please pick up."

Yessir, on the double. "Hi," I said.

"Hey."

"So."

"What are you up to?"

"Well, I'm just working quietly here at home. But you know that obviously."

"I was in the neighborhood and I saw your car."

A drive-by. That was interesting. "Yeah? What's going on with you?" I was so low-key. My eyes drifted over the apartment and settled on my *Making Mr. Right* poster, which Ann Magnuson had autographed when I was a day player on *Anything But Love*. I re-read the credits over and over and wondered what screenwriters Floyd Byars and Laurie Frank were doing right this minute and if they knew what a classic film they'd help create and if Trevor was going to break up with me right now.

"Things have been pretty dead, career-wise. And otherwise. Look, Alex, if you're planning to stay pissed at me forever you might as well tell me now. I wasn't even going to call, but . . ."

"I'm glad you did, Trevor." He had made the first move. Why be difficult?

"Why don't you come over, Alex?"

"I've got to get up early tomorrow . . ."

"I'll make it worth your while."

When I got there, he was spread naked on the couch, slowly traversing the length of his golden, rippled torso with a dripping bottle of Sauvignon Blanc. "I was reading *Playgirl* magazine earlier," he explained. "For the articles. Great ideas in there . . ." I could see right away a heart-to-heart about the direction of our relationship wasn't too plausible. We had white-hot sex, did a little name dropping, then snuggled under the red satin comforter to watch *The Mrs. Mouth Show* on public access. A thoroughly normal couple by West Hollywood standards.

Later on, people would ask how it felt to perform what were to become known as some of the most outrageous scenes in soap history, and I'd have to say that I had a pretty great time— fighting with Natalie, doing Ollie, kidnapping my ex-lover Frederic (an ex-*Santa Barbara* contract player who now recurred on *Hearts Crossing* solely to take my abuse), spewing passably campy dialogue. ("You're as transparent as prison bedsheets, Natalie. And just as besmirched.") And the costume designer, Mitch (Mittens to his friends), who was eager to prove right the cliché that homosexuals dressed better, came up with some real smart ensembles for me to terrorize the town in.

Unflagging ratings and *Entertainment Tonight* coverage notwithstanding, there were those not entirely happy with the new Simon. The Gay and Lesbian Alliance Against Defamation was a tad ticked off by the negative image conveyed by my sadistic, ruthless, sexually active, stylish, homicidal character, especially when it was revealed Simon had used the mysterious sex potency drug to *change Brent's orientation from straight to gay*.

"Homophobic science-fiction . . . This irresponsible and ludicrous soap storyline presents us with the only gay character on daytime television and makes him as wicked and perverse as broadcast standards allow. . . . The participation of gay actor Alexander Young in this hateful claptrap is particularly unconscionable. . . ." Unconscionable was one of the show's dialogue writers' favorite adjectives, too. Readers of the GLAAD newsletter from which the above quote was culled were encouraged to express their disapproval by writing and/or phoning the network, the production office, local TV stations and myself. I'm sure GLAAD didn't *officially* suggest that people call me at home, but somehow those irrepressible anonymous activist moppets got hold of my number and left messages like "Take a stand! Quit the show!" and "You make me sick, you gutless fucking traitor," so I had to change it again. I sent a funny postcard to Nick's office with just my initials and the number scrawled on the back. Just in case.

I couldn't help wondering what he thought of the new controversy. GLAAD had strong ties to the Gay-Lesbian Services Center in Austin and I knew he'd helped organize a petition drive when *thirtysomething* was getting flack for showing two men in bed together. Was I a monster for going along with the cultural overlords' heinous propaganda dissemination? The show was so over-the-top, I found it impossible to get personally offended. And anyway, Simon had been utterly villainous long before his gayness came into the picture. It wasn't as if he had been specifically created the world's most diabolical queer.

Oh, no, a condescending, political little inner voice replied. Simon didn't turn gay until Alex's orientation became public knowledge. And we certainly shouldn't construe that artistic decision as a personal slam or *punishment* of any kind, should we? Heavens, no. It was just a wacky soap opera coincidence, much like Michael Damian starring in *Joseph and the Amazing Technicolor Dreamcoat* on Broadway at the exact time his character did the same thing on *The Young and the Restless*.

But what was I supposed to do, quit? Sorry, Connie, I just can't play a gay psychopath anymore. Not unless they add to the cast a masculine, friendly, well-adjusted gay hero with discreet, vanilla sexual tastes as a positive role model. And Simon *must* volunteer at least three hours per week to AIDS charities. Those are my demands. See you at the arbitration hearing. Then there was the option of acting like such a dickhead at work that they fired me. Either way, I'd be lucky to ever get another audition. But there were some things more important than buckets of money and a career in show business—moral and ethical fiber counted for something.

Call me a whore, but I believed none of it. And I had a sneaking suspicion Nick was sitting home after Barney had gone to sleep, enjoying my taped antics with a grin on his face, if not a lump in his pants.

Predictably, the show ignored the initial GLAAD squawk and proceeded as written by Jerry Reynolds. Monday—Simon installs a listening device in Cyrinda's office. Wednesday—Simon informs Gwen that Ollie is moving in with him.

S: "It's a one-bedroom apartment. And I don't have a futon couch—if you know what I mean."

G: "Are you trying to tell me that you and Oliver—that Ollie is . . . ? Oh, my God, I don't believe you! You're lying! You're lying!"

Thursday—Simon torments Frederic with a live rat. Friday—Simon makes a covert end-of-show phone call indicating he plans to use the sex drug for widespread domination.

Allie and I were in my dressing room between scenes signing stacks of 8 by 10 glossies the fan mail office had dropped off along with a fan letter for me from prison and an offer for me to endorse Wet brand lubricant, when Babs Flanagan showed up carrying the new *Entertainment Weekly*.

"Just look at this!" she brayed excitedly, handing me the open magazine. My eye was immediately diverted by a photo of Corey Haim, Trevor (nude under overalls) and a couple of other hunks clustered around the dimpled baby diva who played Muffin. Below was a semi-sarcastic announcement of the ridiculous new sitcom's place on the summer schedule, to be kicked off by a live MTV party at a UCLA frat house. By comparison, the *Hearts Crossing* blurb on the opposite page was quite favorable, with a shot of me, Babs and Megan and a winky recommendation calling the show "daytime's edgiest and most shameless traumarama."

"What on earth am I wearing?" Babs took a little pair of cat-eye spectacles out of the pocket of her caftan and squinted at the picture. "Ah, what the hell. Alex, you look adorable, honey." She picked up one of the photos I'd autographed. " 'See you in Hell'? Oh, Alex, you go too far!" she tittered.

A bit later, we were taping a scene at the Blake Mansion

and I noticed a tremor of unrest among the crew that went above and beyond their usual annoyance with Babs for screwing up shots by obviously reading her unmemorized lines from the cue cards. When we took a five-minute break, I asked our three-hundred-fifty-pound stage manager what was going on. "There's some kind of protest out front," he said, swiveling his headset around to avoid getting chocolate from his Kit Kat on the microphone. "Everyone's in the booth checking it out."

I hurried back there. It was full. One of the monitors in the viewing bank was tuned to the closed-circuit camera at the studio gate. An indeterminately large crowd was marching around waving picket signs. One flashed on-camera long enough to read: HEARTS = HATE. STOP SIMON NOW!

"It's those GLAAD kooks," the associate director said.

"They're gunning for you, baby," Reese Jacobs told me, clapping me on the back.

I was ready to spaz out, but the mood in the booth was surprisingly lighthearted. Anything to break up the monotony of another taping day. Everyone chatted and speculated about whether or not it would be on the news until it was time to go back to work. We got through the scene, my last of the day, and Allison accosted me en route to the Natalie's Office set where they were now positioning cameras.

"Hey, Alex, if you wait, I'll walk out with you. I've only got a couple short ones and I'm through."

"Okay," I said. I showered and changed and assumed the fetal position on the sofa on the now-dark Simon's Apartment set at the other end of the stage as Natalie wound up some emotional moment with her legally married lover. I wondered how long it would be before my storyline became more trouble than it was worth and I got axed.

Suddenly, a pair of ripped Levi's and a hairy washboard stomach under a cropped Nike T-shirt was dominating my field of vision. I looked up. It was Brent. He sat down.

"What's up, Alex?" he asked quietly. I clutched my forehead and shook my head dejectedly. "That big stink downstairs? I don't get it. They're gay, right? You'd think they'd want more gays on TV. And I don't see why they're called GLAAD if they're p.o.'ed all the time."

"The name is an acronym," I foolishly tried to explain. "You know, the first letter of each word put together to spell something."

"Oh, okay. Like FBI."

He was trying to be supportive. "Exactly."

They wrapped and Allison came over. "Ready? Hi, Brent."

"Hey, Allison."

"Don't you want to take your makeup off?" I asked.

"I'll do it at home. Come on."

We said goodbye to Brent, who was polishing his large gold cross with his T-shirt. We went into her dressing room and she changed clothes in front of me. "If those protesters hassle you, don't even talk to them. You don't owe them any explanation." She gathered a few stray items and stuffed them into her bag.

"They think I'm a traitor to the homo race."

"Fuck them. I know plenty of queens more evil than Simon. Most of them are casting directors. You're just doing your job."

"So was Eichmann."

We walked past the *Date Bait* isolation booth sitting for-lornly on wheels in the studio corridor and got on the elevator. "How's Trevor?" she asked. He and I had recently had dinner and a video screening of *Baby Doll* at Allison and her husband Danny's beautiful Spanish home on Commodore Sloat Drive.

"A little self-obsessed."

"When you look like that, who can blame you?"

"The timing's really off."

"What timing?"

"The fact that I'm becoming real notorious just before he becomes a star. I mean, he tries to understand, but it's . . ." I didn't know how to describe the omnipresent tension that hung like a haze over even our cuddliest moments without making Trevor sound like an asshole. Which was rather telling, I suppose.

"If you ever want to change your surroundings or just hang out and watch obscure black-and-white films, we'd love to have you. Alone or attached. Just call me, okay?"

"Thanks, Allie. I will."

We left the building and headed for the parking lot. There weren't any game-show lines today, thank God, but we wouldn't be able to see if the picketers were in front of the studio until we were driving out. Allie got into her navy blue BMW convertible and raised the top. "Stay close behind me," she ordered.

I started my car and we pulled around the building together. The GLAAD kids, about twenty or thirty of them, were parading around the main gate, which Allison and I were approaching at the prescribed speed of fifteen miles per hour. A news van from another network's local affiliate was parked across the street, eager to discredit their rival with a live scoop.

We were close enough to actually see the picketers by now—mainly plain-Jane activist types of both genders, thirty-fivish, with a smattering of the shaved 'n' pierced Club Fuck set thrown in for variety. They were chanting something. I lowered my window a crack to hear. "Positive images now! Positive images now!"

Allison was at the gate. The mechanical wooden arm raised and she drove through, preparing to turn onto the street. The protesters swarmed around her car, trying to thrust leaflets at her. She kept the car moving and spurted into traffic at the first opportunity.

The crowd turned their attention to my car, now passing beneath the wooden arm. I spasmodically checked to make sure all four windows were up and noticed my white knuckles clenched around the steering wheel and relaxed my grip. They had probably never actually watched the show. Plus I was wearing Trevor's enormous sunglasses.

They converged on the car and a fat guy with Dr. Cyclops glasses and an Endora T-shirt shoved a computer-printed pamphlet titled "Heartless Crossing" up to my window. Five or six sign-wielding people were directly in front of my car, but I continued to roll forward. Then someone slapped the hood of the car and I distinctly heard him scream, "It's him! *That's* Alexander Young!"

Holy shit. Now they were all pressing up to the windows to get a peek at me, a cacophony of yelling audible through

Saf-T-Glass. I slammed the horn down and the mob rebounded slightly. The studio guard was arguing with a couple people to my left, but it wasn't clearing the way any faster. I started to plow through anyway. Later I found that someone had crook-edly affixed a SILENCE = DEATH pink triangle sticker to my bumper. (I left it there.) Just as I was ready to make a right onto the avenue, a goateed maniac leapt onto the hood and started waving his fist and bellowing something defiant.

Thoroughly agitated, I pulled out with him still on the car and accelerated down the street with a trail of protesters running behind. Probably remembering how vile he'd been told I was, the guy on the hood slid over to the edge and shakily assumed a launch position before I decided to hit the freeway or shoot him. I put on the brakes ever so suddenly and he toppled off. In the rearview mirror I watched him careen into a curbside garbage can, shrieking obscenities.

Somehow this wasn't how I'd pictured stardom.

May 1991

I had until May 31 to be out of the apartment, but Sara's summer job at *Paseo del Rio* started June 3, which meant we had to leave San Antonio on Tuesday the 28 if we wanted to have the weekend in L.A. My parents had been up to Austin Friday and we moved all my stuff back to San Antonio and ordered pizza and my dad made a little speech about how proud he was that I was pursuing my dream and moving to Hollywood to act. I happened to know this required him to swallow quite a chunk of disappointment over the law school thing (the tuition deposit was fortunately refundable), so I was especially shocked when he whipped out a check for $20,000 (one-fourth of his settlement from the recently ruled-upon assault case) and told me it was a graduation present from him and Mom.

"If you're going to be out there busting your ass to be a

movie star, we don't want you worrying about holding down some piece-of-shit day job," he said.

Sara was all for it. She'd spent a couple days in Dallas with me during *Teenage Brides of Christ* and said, "This is what you were meant to do." And despite the nineteen-hour days, cat-fighting alcoholic co-stars, and director Carl DeAngelis pawing me on two separate occasions, I knew she was right. I'd never felt this alive, not even with Nick. It was two weeks of exhausting, nerve-wracking magic and I'd do anything to recapture it. The other cast members fueled my fantasies with promises of places to stay and introductions to agents.

Leaving Nick in Texas was the only run in the pantyhose of my plan. But I didn't know what else to do. Our relationship couldn't progress without his dumping Barney, and if he had any plans to do that, they were a secret from me. Whenever I envisioned the coming fall semester, I shuddered. It would have been madness saddling myself with the gauntlet of first-year law school on top of the stress of constantly wondering if *this* would be the week he'd tell me he loved me and that he wanted to be with me alone, or if my one free evening would tragically co-incide with some mandatory hours of Barney maintenance. How could I concentrate on memorizing a thousand-page tort text when all I could think about was Nick?

And he'd never try to stop me from going to L.A., not even if it was just the two of us here, if Barney had been dropped as an infant and taken a job at his parents' furniture store and never went to college and never laid eyes on Nick, who wanted great things for me (himself apparently excluded). This was the right move at the proper time, before I started to wrinkle around the eyes. If only Nick wanted great things for himself. He'd pack up his safe, fatally bland existence in Austin and take a chance and come with me. I knew how impossible this was, but it still saddened me to realize that I'd been unable to demonstrate that my love for him was something he could rely on.

Between finishing the movie, graduation, and tying up the ends of my life in Austin, we hadn't seen too much of each other. There were a couple wonderful evenings right after I got back from Dallas, but he hadn't been willing or able to stay the night with me since that single, epiphanous milestone back in March. We had a long-standing engagement to spend my last day in Texas together, so I drove up from San Antonio the morning of Memorial Day with an air mattress and my portable CD player in the back seat and waited for him in my empty apartment.

He knocked and I answered and there he was at my door for the last time, in a white cotton button-down and khaki shorts, his arms and legs tan from a recent trip to the lake with Dogface.

"All cleaned out," he said.

I nodded without saying anything, not wanting to cry before we'd even had sex. We looked at each other for a long moment, then he kissed me like no one has ever been kissed at eleven in the morning. "I think I miss you already," he said.

"Don't," I whispered. "Today's gonna last forever. I decided." I made quick work of his shirt and palmed his bare shoulders and fabulous chest before blasting into nipple-sucking, stomach-licking overdrive. I felt his hugeness against my chest and slid a hand up into his shorts, squeezing and stroking the hot bulge through his briefs. I channeled his stiff cock through the leg-hole of his underwear and pushed his khakis up high enough to reveal the first two or three inches against his hairy, well-muscled thigh. I wrapped my lips around it, teasing with my tongue while he pulled my Flying Fish T-shirt over my head. "Your pants, too," he half-growled in that butch bedroom voice that could have turned Rambo queer. While I complied, he forced his own down past his raging erection, then lowered me onto the air mattress, which was conveniently blown up and sheeted with my mother's fresh linens in the middle of the living room.

Fifty minutes later, my head was resting on his chest and I was wondering if this was the last time making love would feel like this. From the Undergraduate Library to here, I marveled, loving the way his big penis didn't become less than half hard for most of the refractory period. Loving him. I burrowed my face under his arm into the warm muscle of his lat. Would I get him wet if I cried? How could I leave this behind?

"Hungry for lunch yet?" Nick asked, rubbing his index finger over the small of my back.

"That Nickburger whet my appetite," I said, toying with the meat in question.

He laughed.

We walked across the street to Hyde Park Bar & Grill and ate tons while discussing the logistics of the drive to L.A. and the busty trash-film stalwart who was "totally psyched" that her *Teen Brides* co-star would be crashing at her Studio City apartment for the next couple of weeks. The rest of the afternoon was eaten up by a matinee of *Truth or Dare* at the luxurious Arbor Cinema in north Austin. We kept up a lightweight conversation about the merits of the film on the way back to my place, but I could feel the crushing specter of goodbye hurtling at us at the speed of light. I'd promised my mother I'd be home by 8:00 for a major dinner. That didn't leave much time. Not much at all.

We went upstairs. I took Cokes and peppermint patties from the barren, Mom-scrubbed fridge. We sat on the air mattress because there was nothing else but the floor. I had been dying to tell him something for a year and a half. So I did.

"Nick . . . we didn't ever meet at Human Rights Activists at law school. I've never been to one of those meetings."

"I know."

"You do?"

"I always knew, Alex." He smiled and put his hand on my shoulder. "I knew that the first time I came over here."

"Were you mad?"

"Oh, no. I guess the word would be intrigued. So where was it? My hypothesis is one of my rare outings to a gay bar. The Boathouse?"

I shook my head. "UGL. I saw you there one time. Actually, I saw your backpack and the copy of *Jock* magazine hanging out of it. You know, the Joey Stefano issue?"

Nick shook his head, amazed. "I remember. Barney had me pick that up for him at Hastings." Thank *you*, Barney Gagnon. "Then I did go to the library! But how'd you know my name?"

"I read it off a folder next to the magazine. I looked you up."

"Why?" He was looking at me as if he'd never seen the whole me before. My heart trip-hammered a sudden, hopeful beat.

"Because you were the handsomest guy I'd ever seen."

He took me in his arms. "You're an angel, Alex," he whispered.

Sara, forgive me. I made sure we were eye-to-eye and said it. "I love you. I've loved you from that first night in the restaurant. And I always will. I promise."

I leaned in to kiss him, but he pulled back, stood up, covering his face. He made no noise, but I saw his shoulders heave a little and heard the velvety splat of tears on carpet. I tried to embrace him.

"Please don't," he choked.

"Why?" I was crying myself and didn't even realize it until I heard my own clotted, fragile voice.

"Because I've loved you as much as I can and now it's killing me." I couldn't believe it. He'd said it, too. I put my arms around him. He resisted for a moment then pulled me to him and held me tighter than ever. Before, during and after a searing hot kiss. "What's happening to us, Nick?"

He shook his head. We sort of slumped onto the mattress on our backs. "I can't go to California with you, Alex. As tempting as it is. And I've been thinking about it for quite a while now."

"I've got twenty-four thousand dollars, Nick. That's enough for the two of us for a year, easy. As soon as I get a place to live—"

"Alex." Robo-Nick. "I can't leave Barney. He needs me."

"I need you, too."

"You don't get it, Alex. If I left, he'd never find anybody else. I can't." I wished like hell that red-headed ball-and-chain could have been under *my* bed to hear that last choice line. Was even Barney's self-esteem low enough to live with such an assessment?

Nick stared at the ceiling. "Someday you'll understand, Alex. You will."

That was the only lie he ever told me.

Dear Mr. Young,

I am a regular viewer of <u>Hearts Crossing</u>. And I like your character of Simon Arable, an excellent villain on <u>Hearts Crossing</u>. I <u>don't</u> like what you did to Cyrinda. I <u>didn't</u> like the way you framed Sean. And then lying to Jane and stealing the secret formula and then hypmotizing Oliver to be your gay love slave and then threatening Natalie if she reported you to Rutherford after blackmailing her and poisoning Cyrinda and framing Sean and lying to Jane and stealing the secret formula and hypmotizing Oliver to be your gay love slave.

Yours truly,

Gigi Polanski

Lincoln, NE

By the time we went on a two-day hiatus for the Daytime Emmys, the Simon storyline had been covered in varying degrees by *The Advocate, Buzz, Details, Genre, Inches, The L.A. Weekly*, MTV, *The National Enquirer, Newsweek, People, Playboy, Playgirl, Rolling Stone, Soap Opera Digest, Spin, Spy, TV Guide, Us* and *The Village Voice*. Basically everything but *Humpty Dumpty*. I'd turned down requests for interviews from all that asked, plus the E network's *Inside Word, Oprah Winfrey, Jane Whitney, Montel Williams, Arsenio Hall* and most regretfully, *Ricki Lake*. Connie insisted I keep a low personal profile. "It'll make you more of an enigma, Doll. Nobody'll feel like they really know you, in spite of all the hooplah, and you'll still be interesting and fresh when this blows over."

This theory also excused me from having to offer any personal or political justification for my part in what GLAAD continued to call "a daily mockery of 22 million gay Americans." They hadn't let up on the show and had managed to get some fairly widespread publicity themselves. The upshot of all this was that *Hearts Crossing* had climbed to the number 4 Nielsen slot and even tied for third a couple of weeks.

No amount of media exposure could win Brent Bingham the Emmy, though, and when he got back from the awards in New York, it was one tantrum after the next. None of his nastiness was specifically directed at me, but when I had to stay until ten or eleven at night to post-tape scenes because he'd called in sick two days in a row, I suffered along with everyone else.

One particularly late night I got home and found Trevor's Yale sweatshirt (yeah, right) casually tossed on a living room chair. I penetrated deeper and discovered Air Jordans outside the bathroom door. I flicked the hall light on and peered into the depths of my bedroom. He was a black-and-white postcard waiting to happen—sheet pooled around his thirty-inch waist, one athletic arm flung over his head. Absurdly touched, I padded back into the living room and checked my messages.

"Hi, it's Sara. It's urgent you phone me back pronto. Bye." I speed-dialed and she picked up on the sixth ring. "Hello?"

"It's Alex."

"Jesus. What time is it?"

"You said it was urgent."

"Oh, yeah. Give me a second. Did you just get home?"

"Yes. I spent the last six hours trying to convincingly portray anxiety over the possibility of Ollie cheating on me with my own sister."

"I thought you turned Ollie gay with the sexual wonder drug."

"There may be a problem with the secret formula. Now, enough of that shit. What's up?"

"This is horrendous, so you might want to take a seat." I stayed standing, but put the container of crab salad I'd extracted from the fridge down on the counter without opening it. "Remember Juliana Butts?"

"How could I forget?"

"Guess who's making local headlines with the Baptist censorship group she started with her fat mother Eunice?"

"Are you kidding?"

"No! And the fuckin' idiot newspaper here just printed this nauseating feature on them. The group's called Clean Airwaves.

Isn't that cute? And they have this hit list of TV shows they want to get rid of and *Hearts Crossing* is number one with a bullet."

"That hypocritical slut," I said. "She and her goddamn mother have seen every episode of *Hearts Crossing*. They told me. This is all because I told her to fuck off."

"They hate other shows, too. *Sisters, Roseanne, Silk Stalkings*, the Fox lineup. The scary thing is how efficient and mobilized they are. They're affiliated with Wildmon's American Family Association and this nationwide network of churches, and they've started a massive letter-writing campaign to sponsors and networks."

"And they're getting a lot of press in San Antonio?"

"All of a sudden. A few days ago they picketed the TV station here. They want them to stop showing *Hearts Crossing* in San Antonio."

"Sara, if I see or get wind of one more *protest* of this show, I'm going to be on Prozac. It's a fucking soap opera! Am I the only one able to handle it?"

"You know how right-wing San Antonio can be. Despite my efforts to the contrary. Call me at work tomorrow and I'll fax you the news article. I hope the lovely photo of Juliana and Eunice reproduces. How's Trevor?"

"I just came home and found him in the bedroom."

"Naked?"

"How else?"

"That's more than I can say."

"Where's Richard? I keep forgetting you're shacked up. You still are, aren't you?"

"Yeah. The band's playing a gig in San Marcos tonight. I'll have to send you their demo. They're kind of like the Ramones meet Morrissey. I gotta get back to sleep, babe."

"Okay."

"I'll fax you tomorrow. Oh, and Alex? You better hire a publicist or something. I didn't see anything about you in the latest *Modern Maturity*."

"The real hell of getting all this press is that I haven't had one single offer to do anything else. Acting, I mean. Except this horrible play for no money at this 'gay-positive' theater in West Hollywood."

"How could you do anything, anyway? You're under contract to the show."

"There are ways. And it's just nice being asked."

"Goodnight, media slut."

"Bye." I clicked off in time for Trevor's bed-headed entrance.

"Who was that?" he asked.

"Sara."

"Everything okay?"

"Yeah." I didn't want to get into it. Actually, I was afraid to get into it, afraid of push coming to shove and Trevor's squirming coming to bolting, forcing me to confront the emotional attachment to him I swore wouldn't happen.

Was a supportive, well-adjusted boyfriend who kind of *got off* on dating daytime drama's "evil gay mastermind" so much to ask? But who in Queer Nation had an ass like this, I thought shallowly as Trevor bent over to pick *Vanity Fair* off the floor to show me his Guess ad. I was sure everyone in Queer Nation hated me, anyway. I listened to Trevor babble about the photostylist who'd wanted to fuck him. Maybe Terry Sweeney was single.

Juliana's administrative training as a student office aide during her Roosevelt High School years was apparently paying off in spades, as I followed with morbid absorption the Clean Airwaves saga via Sara and my mom, who was quoted in every San Antonio paper re: the brouhaha over the South Texas network affiliates possibly dropping *Hearts Crossing*. "If these people don't like what's on TV, let them turn it off," Mom said, when reached by phone at her northeast San Antonio home. I found it loathsome that station management even agreed to meet with Eunice, Juliana and "other key members of the group, including two deacons from Trinity Baptist Church," much less consider their demand to replace *Hearts Crossing* on the afternoon schedule with "family-oriented programming that reflects the Christian values of this community." Despite a petition and a slew of anti-*Crossing* propaganda that used ultra-lurid plot synopses to convince the city how reprehensible and scandalous the show was (but probably only enticed more to tune in), the proposal was nixed by the TV station just after Sara published a great editorial in the San Antonio *Express-News* and just before the ACLU was about to pounce on the situation.

Naturally, all Eunice and Juliana's hard work to undermine free expression did not go unnoticed by those in even closer direct contact with Jesus Himself. In short order, the Clean Airwaves gals found themselves awarded the highest of born-again media accolades, a guest appearance on that pinnacle of Christian infotainment, *The 700 Club*.

I cut my strictly pore-therapy sauna short and sped home from the gym on the appointed night, turning on the set just in time to hear Pat Robertson say, "These little ladies from Texas saw a problem on our airwaves and they're busy cleaning it up as we speak. Please welcome, all the way from San Antonio, Eunice and Julie Ann Butts!"

And there they were. As I quite well knew, the video camera added twenty-five pounds, so, to be fair, Eunice Butts probably actually weighed in at around two-forty. She sported a rosy-pink pants suit and a big eighties perm and plenty of makeup, including drawn-on eyebrows reminiscent of Divine in *Polyester*. Juliana had a hellacious blond do happening, complete with a frizz pinwheel the size of a pie plate over her forehead, although her blue eye shadow did match the dress she'd recently purchased at North Star Mall.

"Hello, Pat. We're so happy to be here," Eunice purred.

"It's our pleasure," Pat assured her. "And you both look lovely, I might add. Now tell everyone at home what Clean Airwaves is all about."

"Well, you see, Pat," Eunice began. I was glad to see she was already starting to sweat. "I work out of my home—I'm a regional distribution manager for a major cosmetics company—and one day my daughter had an afternoon off work and we happened to have the TV on and we simply could not believe what we were seeing on this soap opera. Two men kissing right on the air. Frankly, I was shocked."

Juliana piped up. "Pat, we personally believe homosexuality is a sick and perverted lifestyle in the eyes of Jesus, but I don't judge what people do behind their own closed doors. It's when they start advertising it on TV that we get offended."

"Absolutely." Pat nodded in total agreement.

"We weren't big TV watchers," Eunice claimed (oh, sure), "but we started watching as much as we could, day and night, just to see what kind of filth was out there, Pat. We kept a diary and found that fifty percent—"

"Sixty percent," Juliana corrected her.

"Thank you, hon. *Sixty* percent of all shows deal with or joke about or refer to premarital sex, adultery, sex perversion, bathroom functions or just outright smutty sensuality."

Pat continued to shake his head, the wickedness of the world a bottomless lake of anguish for him. "And this is regular broadcast TV, too," Juliana shrilly reminded the would-be presidential candidate. "We're not even talking about cable or movie channels or anything like that."

"Oh, my goodness, don't get me started on movies," Pat said. "The pornography they're passing off as 'art.' It's outrageous."

"We're very concerned about the state of today's movies, Pat," Eunice said. "But we feel it's a losing battle. I mean, when they nominate a transvestite for the Academy Award, Christian values are obviously *not* a priority in Hollywood. We're concentrating on TV because we think the viewers have a much better chance of controlling it."

"Well, it's so important to stay focused," Pat concurred. "And it was one daytime soap that started all this for you?"

"Yes. *Hearts Crossing.*" Eunice attempted to smile and purse her lips simultaneously in a dainty display of disgust.

"It has homosexuality, voyeurism, rape, promiscuous sex, bondage. Practically every perversion you can think of," Juliana added. Speak for yourself, honey. I was a little in awe of the vocabulary she'd gotten together for the national TV debut I was one hundred percent directly responsible for. I thought I'd hallucinated what Pat said next:

"We've got a clip from this soap opera, and I think you all

at home who don't watch daytime TV will be unpleasantly surprised at how *graphic* this is."

They cut to a scene of me cuddling my ex-lover Frederic into a false sense of security before whacking him in the head with a candlestick and locking him in a cage in a secret corner of my loft. How the hell had this fascist show gotten permission to use a clip? That fucking network really had their heads up their asses. Either that or they were so publicity-crazed no request was refused. "Don't be so gloomy, Freddy," I snipped at the unconscious, underwear-clad prettyman. "You used to love this sort of thing."

Cut back to Juliana, Eunice and Pat performing a ballet of head shaking. "To think any child home sick from school could see this," Eunice said.

"Ladies, what can we do to get this garbage off our airwaves?"

"It's very simple, Pat," Eunice insisted.

"But everyone needs to do their part," Juliana said.

"Exercise your right and your voice," Eunice continued, "and send letters to the network saying you don't approve of this type of program. And write the sponsors of these trashy shows and tell them you're not interested in being a customer of their products so long as they pump money into advertising on these programs." Her jowls rippled as she became more adamant.

"In a second we're going to put our toll-free number on the screen," Pat said, "and we'd like you to all call in if you're interested in joining Clean Airwaves in their fight for decent family television. We'll take your name and address and send you an information kit, won't we, Julie Ann?"

"Yes," Juliana chirped. I watched her for some sign of annoyance at Pat's continued mispronunciation of her name. "What's in the kit is a list of the worst shows and their sponsors and all the network addresses, and some tips on how to start your own Clean Airwaves chapter from your home or church."

"While we flash that phone number on the screen, you ladies please join me in a prayer, won't you?" They bowed their heads. I clutched mine, biting back a scream. "Oh, Lord, please be with us and help these good Christian women in their mission to make—"

My phone rang. "Hello?"

"Oh—my—Christ." It was Sara. "I hope you're taping this." I wasn't! Damnit.

"I'm not."

"Okay, I'll copy mine and send one to you to treasure always. Those lying twats. You don't know how bad I want to expose them," she seethed.

"What's to expose?" I asked. "Ignorant bitchiness? They're not exactly keeping that a secret."

"There's gotta be something," Sara said. "Traffic violations, child molesting, dancing on Sunday. I bet Eunice has a giant vibrating dildo with Julio Iglesias's picture taped to the shaft. If I could just break into their house . . ."

"It's not worth it. Trust me."

She growled. "Okay. But I'm going to call that toll-free number and let them have it. Richard, hand me a pen. Richard says hi. When are you coming back here?"

"Probably after I get fired."

"Stop it. You're the only interesting thing on daytime TV and everybody knows it."

"Soaps weren't made to be this controversial. I feel like I'm on a toboggan ride that's gonna end in this icy chasm of death."

"Just hang on. Love you."

"Love you, too."

Not everyone hated Simon's shenanigans. Some even admitted it publicly. Barry Walters wrote a terrific piece called "Simon Sez Chill the Fuck Out: Why I Never Miss *Hearts Crossing*" describing me as "angelically handsome and wonderfully expressive" and basically calling the show enjoyably campy nonsense that nonetheless brought an unapologetic homosexual into millions of homes daily and thus paved the way for openness previously impossible on soaps. *The Advocate* ran it opposite a statement from the National Gay and Lesbian Task Force condemning the show. I always liked that Barry.

Tommie the makeup man brought in an issue of *Spunk* and showed me an ad for Revolver, a video bar in deep West Hollywood. Wednesday was *Hearts Crossing* night—"Your favorite soap from 10-2 with Simon Specials (dollar well drinks) all evening!" I wondered if this was happening other places in the country and wished a graduate student would investigate and write a thesis. This was about the same time the first bootleg T-shirts started appearing on Melrose and Santa Monica featuring a crudely screened but cute picture of me, the words "Simon Says," then one of a variety of queer slogans. I wasn't able to get my hands on one for the longest time, then two different fans mailed a couple to me right after I stopped a guy wearing one outside Marix Tex-Mex and offered him fifty dollars for his shirt. He was ecstatic to meet me and stripped it off immediately, refusing payment, then dragged me into the restaurant shirtless and made me drink margaritas with his friends until I shoved two twenties and a ten into his shorts pocket and escaped.

As *Dino & Muffin*'s debut drew closer, I was only too happy to let the flood of media attention for it overshadow my own infamy. Trevor almost wrecked his car upon first sighting a billboard on Sunset Boulevard featuring his pecs and other cast members in a splashy ad for the show. Then it was off to New York for *Live With Regis & Kathie Lee*, where the whole gang trotted out precious clips and hawked the big premiere party at the UCLA Sigma Chi house, to be hosted by Duff on MTV directly after the sitcom aired.

I picked up Trevor at the airport when he got back from New York. We were discussing the shindig and how funny it would be if "Muffin" somehow got blitzed on trash-can punch and ended up having a three-way with those twins from *Full House* when Trevor said out of the clear blue, "I don't think I can bring anybody with me to the frat party. You don't mind, do you?"

Yes, I did mind, actually. Had I been presumptuous in assuming that my boyfriend (who *loved* me) would want me around to celebrate the launching of the series that could very well make him a star? Did he think I would embarrass him with some tacky display of public affection in front of MTV? No guests at a premiere party? Did he think I just fell off a turnip truck? And even if the producers *had* told Trevor this, I wasn't just *anybody*. I was Alexander Young, damnit! the diva in me screeched. In all seriousness, I was hurt, but I didn't argue. I just shrugged and said, "That's fine" fairly convincingly and turned up the Utah Saints on CD maxi-single to subtly discourage further conversation till we got home.

It was past midnight and Trevor had an 8:00 a.m. photo shoot for *Sassy* the next morning so we went straight to bed. He was asleep in minutes. This wasn't the way things were supposed to work out for me—dicked around by the show, a joke in the national press, and now lying awake in my bed miserable because Trevor Renado was treating me like shit. It was time for me to regain control of my life. Hot sex with a great-smelling, witty hunk wasn't worth feeling like this. I studied him in the darkness for a few minutes, just to be sure. He'd brought me back a present from New York—stone gargoyle candle-holders from a curio shop in the East Village. He said their names were Hecate and Jecate. I would give him the benefit of the doubt about the party—for the time being.

He was dead meat. I'd sequestered myself in my dressing room after hair and makeup and called the *Dino & Muffin* production office. Pretending to be Trevor was only minimally risky. He was at Griffith Park charming some photojournalist from *Sassy* who most likely graduated from Sarah Lawrence about a week ago.

Me: "Uh, hi, this is Trevor Renado."

Bubbly P.A. Gal: "Hi, Trevor!"

Me: "Who's this?"

BPAG: "Amber! What's happening? You'll be there tomorrow night, won't you?"

Me: "Yeah, actually that's what I'm calling about. Am I allowed to bring anybody?"

BPAG: "God, yes! Didn't you get Andy's memo? They want to rock the house. Just let me know by tomorrow morning so I can put them on the list."

Me: "Okay! Great! Bye!"
Okay. Great. Bye.

The live MTV broadcast was scheduled from 5:30 to 10:00 Pacific time to encompass *Dino & Muffin*'s premieres across the nation's time zones. (It was, of course, an 8:00 show.) Trevor would be leaving for Westwood around 4:00, I guessed, but I waited until rush hour was over to drive to his apartment with a flight bag and a handwritten note.

I let myself in and tried to feel angry as I went through the bedroom gathering articles of my clothing. He's a selfish, arrogant creep, I reminded myself, scooping up *Confederacy of Dunces* and *Boys on the Rock* and *Requiem for a Dream*, books I'd loaned him and he'd never cracked, and shoving them in my bag along with a dozen CDs I'd anally kept on a separate shelf from his collection. Goddamn him, I paid for that Absolut Citron, I sneered, adding the bottle of vodka, purchased to celebrate some little career victory of his, to my loot.

I didn't start to cry until I hit the bathroom and plucked my toothbrush from the silver holder next to the sink. I sat down on the edge of the tub with one hand gripping a bottle of Tangerine Grapefruit shower gel and the other roughly flinging away tears wept for the torrid embraces we'd shared and would never share again under the hot pounding Water-Pik spray. I salvaged a few more personal items then went down to get the parking pass from my rearview mirror. I placed it and the key on top of the note I'd agonized over for hours the previous evening, eventually boiling down two pages of psychodrama to this:

Trevor,
    I'm sorry this is in note form, but we've never been able to talk about how my situation affects you and our relationship. In a word, fatally. And I can see no short- or long-term future with someone so uncomfortable with major aspects of my life. I do care for you, but with things as they are, I'm better off alone.

If I don't hear from you, I'll assume you agree with
me.
Alex

Leaving him the option of contacting me was questionably un-
self-actualizing, but I was too much of a romantic to utterly
banish the notion of an enlightened Trevor crawling to me, big
brown eyes wet with tears of repentance, for forgiveness.

I went directly to the gym and did my Tuesday and
Wednesday workouts combined. When every major muscle
group was pumped to soreness, I trudged to the third floor to
Stairmaster those endorphins to prescription-strength distribu-
tion. Twin TV monitors displayed a crowd of kids shakin' it to
"Roam." The song ended and Duff popped into the frame.
"Someone just spilled something *all* over me!" she squealed.
"Was it you, Trevor?"

Angle on Trevor Renado, unbuttoned Hawaiian shirt,
two—count 'em, two—bimbettes hanging off him. "I'm not the
one who got you all wet!" Trevor retorted naughtily. All three
girls shrieked with laughter.

"Trevor Renado, who plays Ky on *Dino & Muffin*, what do
you think of our little party tonight?"

"Do you mind if I change the channel?" I asked my sole
co-aerobiciser, a bottom-heavy blonde on a bike. She didn't. I
switched over to "Sex Symbols" on VH-1, which was playing
"Addicted to Love" for the twelve hundredth time. I slipped on
my headphones and fired up Bananarama's *Greatest Hits* (import
version featuring "Help!") on my Discman. This was one of
Trevor's favorites, but he'd never gotten around to copying it
for himself. Tough shit. I exercised until I could barely walk
downstairs.

I thought about the last time I'd talked to Nick. How could
I have hung up on him? He had been right here and he wanted
to see me. What if he hadn't had any choice about Barney coming with him? Barney was obviously hellbent on hooking up with
Trevor, aka Randy Northcutt, again; that must have been an
enormous motivational factor. (It was weird, but my bitterness
toward Barney had mutated into something disturbingly akin to

sympathy. How could I feel anything but sorry for someone who had what he had—brains, a practical degree, a man like Nick—and still was unable to put a life together? That was profoundly sadder than a dozen failed romances. Well, two, anyway.) Whatever the circumstances, it had probably been my last chance to hold Nick.

I was scurrying through the studio corridor wearing a suit, which I hated doing almost as much as thirty pages of trial scenes, the most boring soap opera component (with the possible exception of weddings and baptisms) and the most hellish to tape, wherein talented contract players like myself sit around a courtroom set like goddamn extras all day, intently focusing on some vitally important, snail-paced legal proceeding, in this case Sean Nortonsen's trial for Cyrinda's attempted murder, and, in my case, getting paid around $375 per tiresome reaction close-up.

I postponed my between-scenes trip to the commissary long enough to stop and read a pink poster tacked up on the glassed-in bulletin board next to the men's room. "Annual Fan Club Gala," a headline in calligraphy trumpeted. I'd forgotten all about this, but there was my name at the bottom of the list of actors who'd agreed to attend the banquet two Saturdays from now. I couldn't believe the club was too cheap to spring for the Mondrian or the Hollywood Roosevelt and was throwing the star-studded luncheon at a Stouffer's in Woodland Hills.

I'd wanted to carpool to the party with Allison, but she and Danny were spending the Thursday and Friday before the Gala in Santa Barbara and would be driving down Saturday morning. So I met her in the makeshift green room along with nineteen other series regulars and recurring actors, including such obvious filler as Beth Maitland, who played Rutherford Blake's nosy secretary about one episode per month, and Cliff Shivers, who'd been a lifeguard on the show *last* summer and wasn't cute or especially talented but was, more importantly, Linda Rabiner's nephew. Imagine the chagrin of the fans assigned to *their* tables. Imagine the chagrin of the cast when we discovered there was assigned seating. Twelve fans and two actors per table—I was at Table Five with Nori Ann Marshall, who I liked but would probably be unable to speak to because we'd be separated on either side by six soap addicts.

Linda Rabiner, looking severe in a Satan-red tailored number, popped in to formally introduce the fan-club president, Naylene, a blond-streaked Tustin control-freak and housewife, who had already made Allison's shitlist by objecting to Danny's unscheduled accompaniment.

"We can squeeze another chair in, can't we?" Allie had asked pleasantly.

"Well, I—I wish I'd known he was coming," Naylene replied.

"We're on our way back from a little second honeymoon in Santa Barbara, aren't we, honey?" Allison asked Danny, struggling, I could see, to keep her Irish temper in check. Her husband, quiet but elfin and prone to mischief, nodded earnestly.

"It's probably too late to put in an order for another person," Naylene fretted.

"He can share mine," Allie said.

"I guess that'll be fine. . . . I just wish people would let me know what's going on before everything's all organized," Naylene semi-huffed, already stalking away.

Allison said, in a voice slightly louder than normal: "Thanks. I appreciate your consideration. It's not like the fans are here to see me or anything." Naylene spun around on her sandal and had this delightful expression on her face—half blank, one-quarter appalled, one-quarter mortified. Allison had already moved over to a cluster of cast members and was paying Naylene no further attention, but Allie rolled her eyes and twisted the upper lip of her smile into a "the nerve of that bitch" grimace and we all laughed, including Cary Rietta, Allison's tablemate.

She had confided to me the week before that she'd had an erotic dream about the scrumptious, wet-eyed twenty-year-old hunk. Considering how he looked now, open black jacket over a scoop tank top and jeans tight enough to compress the carbon in his buttock molecules to diamond, I'd probably have one myself tonight.

Our entrances into the dining area had been choreographed, by Naylene presumably, to be as tacky as possible. After a fatuous opening address from Linda Rabiner, the *Hearts Crossing* announcer called us out two by two. Nori and I joined hands and proceeded to our table amid wild applause. Fan-club ushers wearing name-tag labels retracted our chairs for us. On our plates were identical tags with our real names and characters. Mine had been written in fluorescent pink magic marker. I smiled and said hi to the fans seated next to me and slowly affixed the name tag, scanning the table to see if I was the only one with pink. It looked like it—but I was momentarily distracted by the table's centerpiece, a hideous ice sculpture of the show's logo.

Nori was captivating everyone at her end of the table—they were touching her shoulders, shaking their heads at each other, open-mouthed with glee. My closest neighbors were an elderly woman studying her program and a young black matron engaged in a heated conversation with the girl next to her about the civil service exam. Since everyone was ignoring me, I started looking around the banquet room, hoping to establish sarcastic eye contact with Phalita or Allison. Oh, my God. Babs Flanagan was holding her iced tea below table level and pouring an unidentifiable liquid into it from a little silver flask she promptly deposited in her purse. This was almost as good as Megan DuBois whipping out a gold lamé bib and tying it around her porcelain neck without the slightest twinge of irony.

But were there any hot guys here who weren't part of the cast? There we go—at the Megan/Reggie Van Wyck table, in the *Jurassic Park* baseball cap. So what if he had his arm around his fluffy blond fiancée? He was like a WASP version of Robert Beltran from *Eating Raoul*. He was looking at me. He'd caught me staring at him. How humiliating. I smiled and nodded my head as unpredatorily as possible. A neutral elevation of the eyebrows, then he whispered something to his girlfriend. I pretended to be looking over them at the next table, but saw her check me out then whisper something back to him and giggle. I caught her eye and waved. Christ.

Waiters served a pale, flaccid salad garnished with inferior, bleachy-tasting cherry tomatoes. I rescued a green pepper slice from a pool of house dressing and felt a tap on my arm. It was the old lady. "Excuse me," she said, "but will Anna Ford and Brent Bingham be here later?"

"I don't think so," I told her.

"Oh," she said. "You're the one that put my little Cyrinda in the hospital. The fruity one."

I looked at her, amazement canceling out offense. These people ultimately paid my salary. Maybe she didn't know I was "fruity" in real life. After all, the intertextuality of it all was rather sophisticated. "I like you. You're good. Give me an autograph, would you please?" She handed over her program and Stouffer's souvenir pen.

"Sure," I said, signing it to Vonda per her name tag.

"You're a good bad guy," she continued. "Remember that one on *Young and the Restless*? Shawn? He buried Lauren Fenmore alive."

"I've never really followed that show . . ." I stupidly began, resulting in a full recounting of the mid-eighties storyline in question by Vonda during the entree, a classically uninteresting piece of hotel cuisine involving chicken à la king in some sort of pie-crust dumpling contraption. After coffee and green Jell-O (I swear) with Cool Whip, the fans started to fidget and Naylene adjourned everyone to the lobby and adjacent patio area for "mingling and autographs."

Allison and I gravitated toward each other as the majority of fans thronged around Megan, Phalita and Cary Rietta. "I don't ever want to do this again," she said in my ear. "These people are wackos. They sit and grill me about these episodes I don't even remember taping. You know how they all blend together. And then they want nasty gossip about the other stars. It's just like being at my biological mother's. Danny, can't you say hello to Alex?"

"I already did," he protested. "I'm going to go find a TV before that lady comes back."

"What lady?" I asked them.

"That one that wanted to read her tarot cards." He scuttled off as Allison shook her head.

"How was your little weekend getaway?" I wanted to know.

"He read the whole time. A book. It's my own fault. I
bought it for him. Let's sit down." She pulled me onto a round
sofa with a bonsai tree planted in the middle and we stayed there
while she chatted with a limitless supply of adoring viewers and
cracked me up using expressions like "God bless you" and kissing everybody on the cheek.

I wasn't entirely forsaken. A couple of tawdry record company receptionist types asked me to take pictures with them, and
I had to spend several minutes convincing roly-poly identical
marrieds that I'd never been on *Ryan's Hope* under any hair color.
For the most part, though, I stood around neglected. I decided
the reasons were in order as follows: 1) Villainous character off-
putting; 2) Eclipsed by presence of more stellar cast members;
3) Homosexual character off-putting; 4) Actor's homosexuality
off-putting. I spun a resentful glance toward Beth Maitland, who
actually had a line queued up to pay tribute. The only thing
worse than being harassed and picked over by gibbering, star-
struck couch potatoes was being ignored by them. And I didn't
even have a boyfriend to go home and commiserate with. I wandered over to the bar and ordered my seventh Diet Coke of the
afternoon.

I never really believed that crap about *knowing* someone was
watching you. It was a device from early eighties horror movies
with Jamie Lee Curtis. Besides, my own voyeuristic experience
with the always-naked swim-team member in the next apartment
building the first two months of my junior year had proven the
theory false in the most rewarding manner possible. Still, standing by a potted ficus tree wondering if I could possibly evade
both Linda Rabiner and the dreaded Naylene while making a
getaway, I felt a paranormal creepy sensation I traced directly
back to the gaze of a dark, thin guy at the other side of the bar.

He was all in black—hair, goatee, button-down shirt, jeans,
Doc Martens—and reminded me of an arsonist. Either that or
somebody who worked on Melrose. He was around thirty, holding a manila envelope. He was also coming toward me with too-
quick strides that resulted in him having to stop abruptly, as if
encountering a force field, to avoid smacking into me.

"Alexander," he said. His eyes were so dark they seemed pupilless. The heavy patchouli smell reminded me of the pasty misfits in my film class at UT.

"That's me," I said, stepping back into the ficus tree like an idiot. He continued to stare at me. His lips parted and his tongue flicked out to moisten them. "Do I know you?" I finally asked.

He nodded. He had some kind of silver talisman in his left earlobe, but I was getting too agitated to notice exactly what it was. "I'm Astaroth," he said.

Astor Roth? The only Roth I knew was the cinematographer who had lensed my second movie, a straight-to-video Roger Corman phone-sex comedy. I shook my head. "I'm sorry . . . I really don't remember . . ." These people killed me. You say hello to them once because they're visiting the studio or you bump into them at Book Soup and they expect you to retain *names*.

"Ray Lanville," he muttered intensely, placing a long, olive-skinned hand inappropriately on my forearm. "You've been writing to me. You signed my movie poster. Raymond Lanville, from Silverlake. Astaroth."

Oh God, *that* nut. The one with the nipple-ring and the witchcraft poetry and the big "endowment." I slid my arm out of his grasp under the pretext of shaking his hand. "Oh, hi. It's nice to meet you. I'm glad you made it, 'cause I'm just about to leave," I smiled, setting the stage for an immediate exit while involuntarily scanning Raymond's narrow chest for protruding jewelry.

"I've got something for you," he told me. I bet. He handed me the manila envelope. "I think you should open it upstairs."

"Huh? What are you talking about?" Out of the corner of my eye, I saw Allison and Danny talking to Phalita and heading this way. Thank Christ.

"I reserved a room for us here. Come. Let me show you." He was practically on top of me. I felt his breath on my ear and recoiled.

"Look, Ray, this isn't really the time for that. Isn't there anybody else from the show you'd like to meet? Why don't we circulate a little bit and, uh . . ." You can find the men's room and beat off a few times. "I'll see you again later."

"Yes, Alex. You will."

He gave me one last Mansonite stare and was gone, literally. I got tapped on the shoulder and turned to find Allie standing beside me. "Who the hell was that?" she asked. I glanced over my shoulder to see where Ray was. He seemed to have vanished. I untensed.

"I can't believe I never told you about him," I said. "He's like a warlock from Silverlake who's sexually obsessed with me. Let's see what this is." I slit open the envelope with a fingernail (not biting them was the hardest part of being a TV star) and pulled out a pen-and-ink sketch of me, naked and apparently suspended in space, getting fucked by a winged creature that bore an uncanny resemblance to Raymond Lanville, or Astaroth, as he had signed this particular original.

Allison took it from me and regarded it gravely, shaking her head. "You're enabling this," she said, mock-stern. Danny appeared and gasped at the depraved drawing.

"Astaroth?" he asked.

"That's his underworld name, I guess," I said. Allison thought it sounded familiar.

"Yeah, it's the wizard in *Bedknobs and Broomsticks*," Danny informed us.

"Hey, you're right. That was my favorite coloring book in nursery school," I confessed.

Allie gave the picture a final once-over. "I guess a Disney warlock is the best kind to have stalking you," she remarked, passing the sketch to Phalita, who had escaped to the bar for a Crystal Geyser.

"He sent me a charcoal rubbing of his penis a couple months ago," I told them.

"When I was doing the national tour of *Dreamgirls*, this crazy dude from Cincinnati left me two dozen roses backstage along with a full-color blow-up buck-naked self-portrait with his phone number written across his face," Phalita recalled, oblivious to the permed chubbette fan in the smoked bifocals who stood a few feet from us, transfixed, her leatherette autograph book dangling from one charm-braceleted paw. "Well, next weekend we were in Dayton and he sneaks his ass into the hotel laundry room and steals my bra and panties."

"How'd you know it was him?" asked Allie.

" 'Cause the next day I get another two dozen roses, this time with a new picture of him wearing my goddamn lingerie. Honey, I was fit to be tied. Mick Jagger gave me that bra. Anyway, I think he wanted to do my part in the show more than he wanted to do me. You get what I'm saying? Don't be shy, baby, hand that li'l ol' book over," she purred to Bifocals. Phalita of course had her own autograph pen uncapped and ready for action.

A short time later I was heading east on the 134, disturbed by the whole afternoon. Soap fans disturbed me, and not just the certifiable ones like Astaroth. They shattered any drama school pretensions I might have entertained about how an acting career meant connecting on a higher level of emotion or consciousness with your audience. My audience moved their lips while reading Harlequin *Temptations*. They saw no reason to argue with a Bible that forbade homosexuality. They thought *Three Men and a Little Lady* was "cute." They volunteered their names and numbers on Sally Jessy Raphael's answering service when the upcoming topic was "Spouses Who Won't Shut Up."

Being a professional actor was about making enough money at it to not have to wait tables or sell health-club memberships or kiss ass in retail hell at the Beverly Center. It had about as much to do with artistry as grocery checking, and was a lot less reliable.

Ray Lanville disturbed me for different reasons, like the fact that he reinforced the stereotype that all gays were perverts who'd have sex with a stranger at the drop of a Boy London cap. Moreover, it was depressing that out of all the eligible bachelors in the area who *might* have had a peripheral interest in the show, Raymond was the only one who'd made an effort to meet me today.

At least the freeway was clear. I'd been compulsively checking the rearview mirror for weeks since seeing a news exposé about criminals who bump up behind you in traffic then carjack you when you pull over to investigate possible fender damage. No matter how rich I became, I'd never drive any car in L.A. flashier than my current Honda. I made a mental note to order the darkest window tint allowable by law Monday morning, then exited in Burbank to pick up some food at the Pavilions near the studios.

I kept my sunglasses on to skipper my purple cart through the spacious, upscale aisles, enjoying the impulsive, list-free kind of shopping afforded by my generous paycheck. I had paused, trying to decide at what point certain brands of granola bars insidiously cross over to full-blown candy status, when a cart coming up the aisle clattered into mine, displacing two bottles of Perrier, which somersaulted out of their six-pack in the child passenger compartment onto a bed of pasta. I reflexively slipped off the shades and found myself face-to-face with a freckled girl with a haphazardly barretted cascade of brown ringlets wearing a one-piece leopard-print swimsuit and hot-pink jams. *"Oh, my God!"* she screamed. "Simon! I can't believe this—Holy God Almighty! Mom, come over here! Oh God, hurry! I'm sorry— you must think I'm nuts," she said to me, extending her hand over two lengths of shopping cart. I shook it, inwardly thrilled at this relatively wholesome ego-boost.

"Hi, I'm Alex," I said.

She turned around and hollered, "Mom, it's Alex Young from *Hearts*!"

"For crying out loud, Tina, I know who he *is*." A Linda Evans–type Valley mom had joined us. "We just love you. You're such a wonderful villain. I hope they keep you on forever."

"I cannot believe you are shopping in *this* store," Tina panted. "Do you live around here?"

"No," I quickly clarified. "I was just driving by."

A Mexican woman with a tarted-up infant girl in her cart slowed to a stop and asked Tina's mother, "Isn't that the soap opera guy? Simon?"

Mom nodded and continued ferociously buttering me up.

"You're so wicked on TV it gives me the shakes sometimes, it really does. For God's sake, Tina, remember that episode where he attacked Natalie and drowned her in the fountain?"

"That was only a dream, Mom."

"I *know* it was a dream, dear, but the *suspense*, it was *shocking*."

"Oh, please, sir, can I get an autograph?" The Mexican lady had retrieved a marker from her purse and now thrust it at me. "Just sign this!" She handed me a box of Kix. "My girlfriends, they will be so jealous!"

By now we were attracting quite a crowd. Two minutes later I was fielding questions from an all-girl traffic jam of shoppers I would have thought much too jaded to give a soap star a second look. But no, they wanted to ask me how they could get "tickets" to the show and didn't I see a future for Sean and Cyrinda and they knew how hard it must be to play the bad guy and that the gay storyline was just so creative and different and was it true that Brent Bingham had quit the show and they were using a lookalike?

An assistant manager forced his way through to my side and asked if I was okay. I said everything was cool. "Because sometimes these situations can get ugly," he told me confidentially as I signed the back of one woman's checkbook. "Just a couple of weeks ago that retarded kid from *Get a Life* came in for a bag of ice and we had to escort him out the back. Real mob scene."

"I'm going to be heading out in just a minute, but thanks," I said, a real pal he could add to his figurative Rolodex of chummy celeb customers.

But before I could gently break up the group, I observed something strange at the end of the aisle, by the dairy case. Was that—? Someone moved directly into my sightline and I pulled Tina closer and said, "Can you do me a favor? Just check out the end of the aisle and tell me if you see a thin guy dressed all in black hanging around? He's kind of like this weird fan who's been following me today."

"Sure, Alex!" she gurgled, zipping away, leaving me feeling pretty pompous and paranoid. I started to extricate myself, purposefully heading in the opposite direction from where I could have sworn I'd seen Ray Lanville lurking.

An older woman put a gnarled hand on my upper arm and asked if she could have a kiss. I obliged, practically tasting the potion of face powder, Aspercreme and Avon sachet on her disarmingly overrouged cheek. Tina was back. "I couldn't see anybody who looked like what you said," she reported. "And I checked three aisles over both ways."

"Thanks," I said, clapping her on the back. "Thanks to everyone for watching the show. It was great meeting you all." I gracefully resumed my shopping as the little knot buzzed about *Hearts Crossing* and how *nice* I really was. They seriously ought to hold the next Fan Club Gala at a grocery store, I reflected. Maybe that huge Ralph's on 3rd and LaBrea. Think of the money they'd save on a hotel rental. We could all just eat those self-serve bags of yogurt-covered raisins that nobody ever pays for. I'd have to send a memo to Naylene.

In the checkout line, I ran into Tina and her mother again. "We're the only ones who didn't get your autograph," Mom mock-pouted.

"So we bought these," Tina said, displaying copies of every soap rag currently on sale that mentioned me. I dutifully inscribed all six issues before requesting paper not plastic.

The one space in front of my apartment house was occupied by a motor scooter so I had to park in my carport unit in back and make three trips upstairs with my dry cleaning and grocery bags, the heaviest of which I used to prop open the front door and then forgot until I'd put away the frozen items. I went down and got it, and when I came back Ray Lanville said, "Hi, Alex."

He was standing in the center of my living room. I dropped the bag of juice bottles but caught it before it hit the parquet. "What are you doing here? How did you—" But of course it was obvious how. And as for what . . . flashes of Rebecca Schaeffer from the Hollywood Atrocity File went off like crimson-tinted video bombs in my head.

"We needed to be alone," he said, moving between me and the door. "So I followed you. It's what you wanted, isn't it, Alex?"

"No. It's not what I wanted. I want you to leave. Okay? Right now." My entire upper body felt clenched in a vise of tension and I had to struggle to keep my voice from squeaking into a higher register.

He shook his head and began unbuttoning his shirt. He tossed it over his shoulder and started toward me. He was slender but corded with muscle, hairless except for one dark triangle at the center of his chest. A large silver ornament dangled from one of his nipples, which were almost black and the size of heavy-duty pencil erasers. I debated lunging across the room for the phone, but what if he had a knife? Instead I bolted deeper into the apartment and locked myself in the bathroom.

And immediately felt like an idiot. He was alone in my house. If he touched one goddamn thing, I'd kill him, I growled to myself, enraged. I shoved the window up all the way. It was too small to escape through.

"Alex, come out here." He rapped on the door. Fuck him. "I need you," he said. That didn't sound too menacing.

I heard opera from downstairs. *The Mikado*. Which meant my neighbor was home. I yelled out for help and got no response. I did it again. Did the music just get *louder*? All right. I'd had it. I pulled my head back in and scoured the room for some type of improvisational weapon. The best I could come up with was a large glass mouthwash bottle. I pressed my ear up to the door. Nothing but goddamn Gilbert and Sullivan. I felt surprisingly calm considering my actions in the next few minutes could determine whether I lived to deny this story to Janet Charlton.

"Raymond?" I called through the door. "Raymond, are you there?" As noiselessly as possible, I unlocked the door, then stood back against the tub, ice-blue Listerine sloshing around inside my sole defense against the rampaging Astaroth. When nothing ghastly occurred, I leaned forward and twisted the knob then simultaneously threw the door open and splayed myself back against the bathtub, bottle held high. No slavering death charge. Maybe he'd become embarrassed and left. I crept to the open door and put my hand back on the knob, ready to slam it behind me if Ray was lying in wait. I looked to my right—the hall was clear. Gripping the Listerine tighter, I stepped out of the bathroom and peeked left. Clear access from there to my open bedroom door. I decided the wisest plan was to get the hell out of Dodge and strode rapidly in the direction of my front door.

Ray Lanville scared the shit out of me for the second time that day by being in the living room, stark naked except for Doc Martens, anointing his reptilian body with patchouli oil with one hand and whacking off with the other. He hadn't been kidding about his "endowment." It was at least eleven inches long and, even more shockingly, had a major gold pirate hoop through the pierced glans. What the Christ did he expect me to do with that thing? I thought crazily, pausing for only a second to behold the scene before continuing to the door. "Get on the couch, Alex," he commanded. My hand shook as I turned the knob. Locked. Becoming a tad more frantic, I undid all three locks and opened the door. Home free! my mind gasped prematurely. Ray tackled me from behind.

"Goddamnit!" I screamed. He seized me by the arm and pitched me back into the living room then slammed the door shut. The mouthwash bottle had rolled into the corner next to my baker's rack, and I scrabbled along the floor like a toddler to retrieve it. Ray leaped on top of me and we wrestled on the floor.

"Submit! Submit!" he kept hissing.

"Fuck you, you sick son of a bitch!" I replied, yelling and pounding the floor with my hands and feet, trying to alert my neighbor. It was practically impossible for my fingers to gain purchase of Ray's greasy flesh and he quickly had me on my stomach with my right arm twisted painfully behind my back.

"Don't move," he said in a bland tone. He reached under me to try to open my pants but decided ripping the buttons off my new Geoffrey Beene shirt would be more rewarding. His hand was like a slippery bald tarantula scampering across my chest. He tweaked my nipple and thrust against my ass. That did it. I brought my foot up as violently as possible and kicked him in his lower back. He screamed and catapulted forward, over my head, releasing my arm. I put both hands around his neck and rose to my feet while choking him.

"You piece of shit," I growled, then commenced screaming for help. Raymond's lithe appearance belied formidable strength, though, and he regained his feet despite my strangulation attempt. I was certainly unprepared for the severe pinch he administered to the side of my neck, dropping me to my knees, a vital conjunction of nerves in agony.

"It doesn't have to be like this, Alex," Ray said. My head was level with his crotch and I saw that the fight had done nothing but inflame his lust—his monster prick stood at an ultra-tumescent acute angle. He splayed his left hand on my scalp and proceeded to wallop me in the face with his dick. And it hurt! Especially when his penis ring flicked into my eye. "You will swallow the staff," he barked, no Trevor when it came to pillow talk. I considered swallowing then biting the staff right off, but instead assumed the most glazed expression possible, then socked Ray in his flat, olive-hued stomach. He doubled over and hit the deck with the aid of a good shove, but snagged a handful of my hair on the way down and it was WWF time again. Having just gotten up close and personal with his phallus gave me an idea, however, and I reached down, inserted my index finger in the gold hoop and yanked. Ray shrieked and slapped at me.

I was peripherally aware of my door being thrown open. "Oh, my God! Alex, are you all right?" In an instant, my neighbor and an in-shape Asian were pulling me and Ray apart.

"Don't let that fucker get away!" I said. We were on our feet and Ray was in a defensive stance, staring around the room wildly like the caged animal he was. His pipi had deflated but retained respectable length and girth. "He followed me here and attacked me," I added, starting to feel concern that he might be seen as a trick I'd invited home who turned ugly.

My neighbor, whose silk kimono clashed horrendously with the green and orange micro-workout shorts his boyfriend du jour had managed to pull on before coming to my rescue, placed his hands on my shoulders. "I'm going to call the police," he said. I gestured spasmodically in the direction of the phone, my eyes riveted on Ray, who suddenly rushed the Asian. A mini-karate battle resulted, with my neighbor's buddy doing all the karate, complete with foreign-language war cries.

Thwak! Ray was buffeted against the sofa, which I would have to have steam-cleaned immediately. *Chop!* The Asian sent Astaroth to the floor and pinned him like a butterfly. I was stunned at the drama of real life.

My neighbor hung up the phone. "The cops are on the way. Are you both okay?"

"I'm fine," I said.

"How about you, Run Run?" The Asian nodded. "Do you have him . . . under control?"

"He not going anywhere," Run Run said.

"I'm sure I've got a pair of handcuffs somewhere. I'll be back." He left.

I wanted to say something. "Thanks a lot," I began.

"No problem. You TV star, right?"

"Yeah, I'm on *Hearts Crossing*. Sometimes it's dangerous to my health."

"Oh, *Hearts Crossing*. Very pretty show." Ray stirred under Run Run. Had he been knocked out? He mumbled something. "Quiet!" Run Run ordered, applying some Oriental pressure technique that made Ray yelp.

The L.A.P.D. was there before my neighbor returned. A George Kennedy–type heard my story, told Ray to get dressed, made fun of his piercings and manacled him. Then his back-up arrived in a separate car and I was in love. Officer Carvajal was like the Mexico City Chippendale's version of a cop. He confiscated Ray's wallet and they called in his stats. We quickly discovered Astaroth had a very unmystical assortment of unpaid parking tickets, including the one he'd received during the shenanigans chez moi.

This was good because the upshot was the police hauling Ray's nutty ass to jail even though I didn't want to press charges. I wasn't sure if a stalking law would apply, since the campaign of terror had been confined to one afternoon. Also, retestifying the absurd details of my attempted molestation held zero appeal.

And since I hadn't been harmed, Ray would inevitably be released to roam the streets, harboring a richly brewed resentment
of me that could only lead to tragedy.

"Stay the hell away from me," I contented myself with telling Raymond in my most threatening Simon voice as George
Kennedy took him out. I stopped Carvajal before he could follow them. "I don't have any real idea how these things work,"
I said, "but I'd love and appreciate it if this whole incident could
be kept out of the press."

He smiled adorably and put his arm around me. "I'll do
what I can. You shouldn't have to worry."

"Thanks a lot." I don't think it's a good idea for me to be
alone. What time do you get off duty and how do you like your
eggs?

"It was great meeting you, Alexander," he said. "I'm kind
of a fan, too."

"I need more fans like you, Officer," I actually said before
he split. I barely had fifteen seconds to bask in his glow when
my neighbor was at my door, insisting I join him and Run Run
for dinner. I accepted, not wanting to seem ungrateful. Although, it would have been much easier if I could have just
called the escort service with my credit card and paid my
neighbor's bill for the night myself, making certain of course to
include a large tip for Run Run.

Luckily I still had the *Hard Copy* segment on Clean Airwaves to look forward to. It was quite a beaut, too. A swirling
montage of titillating and/or "perverted" soap opera clips, foot-
age of Eunice Butts getting out of her Chevy Celebrity and wad-
dling into her French provincial tract home in San Antonio's
Royal Ridge subdivision where Juliana was overseeing a staff of
knuckleheads stuffing hundreds of envelopes. A surprise appearance by our exec producer Linda Rabiner, tersely defending the
show's content and offering this sound bite when the perceptive
reporter brought up (and the graphics department helpfully su-
perimposed) my tabloid kiss: "We don't write our storylines and
characters to reflect actors' personal lives. Period." Quick cut to
me faux-Frenching Brent. Perceptive reporter: "Alexander

Young, the openly gay actor who plays the seductively diabolical Simon Arable declined to comment." This was insane. I got my agent on the phone the next day.

"It's time to break the conspiracy of silence, Connie. I sound like a pissy little hemorrhoid."

"So what do you want to do?"

"I want to talk to somebody while anyone's still interested. Who's wanted to interview me lately?"

"*Interview.*"

"Yeah, you know, talk to a magazine, get a little photo action going."

"You little smartass. *Interview* magazine, honey. Ring a bell? It's big in New York. Actually, it's huge. I can't fit the damn things under my coffee table. Drives me nuts. Anyway, they called last week, wanted to talk to you, I gave them the standard spiel. But I'll call tomorrow and say you're interested."

"Great. Thanks. You think it's a mistake?"

"No. What the hell. At this point, it can't hurt. Be nice, though."

A few Trevorless days later, I had lunch with a hyperactive boy-writer who *Interview*ed me at Butterfield's then hauled me up to Fatty Arbuckle's ex-mansion for an outdoor photo shoot. I was nice. I was funny, clever, snappy about Simon and *Hearts Crossing* while remaining benevolent, warm and approachable. I was also off the show by the time the issue hit the stands.

I knew something was very wrong when Jerry Reynolds called me on Sunday night and asked me to meet him in an hour in Marina del Rey. He would give me no details, and his light, friendly tone showed signs of disintegrating into quavering kvetchiness when I didn't commit right away, so I had no choice but to jump into relaxed-fit jeans and valet park at The Red Onion, a sub-yup dockside disco/bar/nightmare straight out of a Sandra Bernhard performance piece. The frat boy at the door looked me over and said, "You do know tonight is Grateful Dead night," as if I might have mistaken the raucous cover of "Bertha" emanating from some unseen live band in the depths of the club for a Paula Abdul megamix.

"That's fine," I replied. "Is there a cover?" There better not be.

"Five bucks. But you get five drink tickets," he added brightly.

I forked over the cash and went in. The place was full of tie-dye, Day-Glo bears, macramé vests, granny glasses and flabby, ex-hippies' asses swinging on the dance floor or clustered around a buffet layout. I wandered through the crowd and found Jerry hunched over a table in the corner slurping down the last of some slushy red concoction. I took a seat.

"Hi, Alex," he said, myopically fumbling for his glasses.

"Hi. What's going on? Are you a Dead head?" I was leaning in close but still had to yell. He smelled like rum.

"Oh, no! I just wanted to meet somewhere no one would recognize us." I would have preferred Chuck E. Cheese. "Would you like a drink?"

I displayed my chain of school carnival paper tickets just as our waitress appeared. I ordered a margarita. "Another strawberry daiquiri, please," Jerry asked. "And five more tickets."

He'd already had four drinks? How much did a one-hundred-twenty-pound man (six feet tall or not) need to get plastered? My eyes fell onto a doll-size buffet plate with an assortment of coagulating Mexican zakuskas. "Have a flauta," Jerry suggested, pushing the plate toward me with a bony finger. To make him feel more at ease, I did, then felt it burn through my digestive tract for the remainder of the evening.

"You're probably wondering why I asked you to meet me," he began. I nodded mildly. "I've been sick the whole weekend trying to decide if I should do this, but I think you've got a right to know."

"Know what?" Anyone could tell this was going to be *really* bad.

"They're killing you off, Alex. In three weeks, you'll be dead. And the worst part is, they weren't even going to tell you until you saw the script."

Our drinks came and Jerry downed his in two swallows. I felt as if I'd been told I had to have something amputated. The show had been the skeleton supporting my entire life. Money, confidence, legitimacy—whatever crap I'd had to wade through on- or off-screen, the show had given me these things without fail for almost a year. "TV Regular" was a vital component of my self-perception. Without it, what was I but another scared, helpless actor whose most recent credit would probably do him a lot more harm than good resume-wise? How am I going to get another job *now*? I moaned to myself while an inner control-voice kept repeating like a mantra: "You have enough saved to last you two years. Thank God you didn't buy that thirty-thousand-dollar car."

"Why?" was all I could get out.

"It's gone too far," Jerry said miserably. "We lost two sponsors on Thursday. The network daytime people panicked and Linda and Reese agreed with them."

"Is it because of Clean Airwaves? Is it because of those boycott threats?"

"They didn't say that specifically, but I have a feeling . . ." Jerry was eyeing my drink from which I'd only taken one sip because it tasted like lime Za-Rex. "They've been getting a lot of pressure from GLAAD and the gay rights people, too." At least *those* poison pen letters are probably grammatically correct, I thought. "It's not a bad storyline, is it, Alex? It isn't hateful?"

He was crying. I saw him signal for another drink. "Jerry, it's a soap opera. It's a wild plotline. I don't think—" Why was I reassuring *him*?

"Alex, they're firing me! They're not renewing my contract. The network's blaming me for this whole mess. Linda had final approval over the Simon story—I just wrote most of it. They think I ruined the show. . . ." Now he was sobbing. He wrenched his glasses off and dabbed his tears with one-ply cocktail napkins.

"Is everything okay?" the waitress asked, plunking down another noxious-looking daiquiri.

"Death in the family," I explained. She looked mortified and scampered off. Seventies concert extras silently swayed on a projection television playing *The Grateful Dead Film*. Jerry tried to drink the daiquiri, but I put my hand on his shoulder and he set the glass down.

"Let's get out of here," I said. He had minor difficulty standing, but we managed to make it out the door. I spoke Spanish to the parking guys and they said it was okay for Jerry's Volvo to spend the night. We got in my car and he drunkenly mumbled directions to his nearby condo.

We went in and he tottered over to his office area and fell into the director's chair in front of his computer in a knobby heap. I suppressed a gasp realizing the horrible significance of what had happened to him: The entire room was a shrine to *Hearts Crossing*. A framed, poster-size current cast photo was surrounded by dozens of smaller mementos—magazine clippings, pictures of Jerry with a galaxy of daytime stars (including me), plaques, a *Search for Tomorrow* script cover that bore his name at the bottom of a list of writers. (Was that his first script?) I wondered if those shits at the network had ever seen this room. I wondered if *anybody* had.

Jerry had gotten something up on his computer. "I had to write the breakdown today. Cyrinda regains her memory and shoots Simon six times. Self-defense. I'm so sorry, Alex. You were a great Simon. I loved writing for you." He made no effort to halt the tears now.

"Jerry, you did a wonderful job. They don't deserve you. I know you'll find something better. I've really got to get back home now. Are you going to be okay?" The crying combined with the electrical equipment made me worry about the danger of shock. I couldn't imagine how things could get more awkward.

Then Jerry stood up. "Thank you for everything." He put his arms around me and I hugged him back, feeling every rib. He moved his hands over my shoulders and down my chest. Hey, wait a minute. "Oh, Alex, you have such a delicious body." He looked into my eyes for a second, then clumsily clamped his mouth over mine. I gripped him where his biceps should have been (my fingers touched) and gently broke us apart.

"Jerry, you're upset . . ." I offered stupidly. He turned and bounded up the stairs like a gazelle with cerebral palsy, still sobbing. I followed him to his room, where he'd crashed onto the bed. "Jerry, please . . ." Touching him wouldn't be a smart idea.

"Just go, Alex! I'm—" The rest was lost facedown in the pillow.

I went downstairs. The computer was a more sophisticated version of my parents', so I knew how to turn it off. I looked at the walls just a little longer before getting in my car and driving home with all the windows rolled down.

My first impulse was to leave town for an extended vacation the night I finished my last episode, but Connie convinced me to stay for all those roles I was now eligible for. Twelve auditions and seven callbacks later, I'd booked nothing.

I spent a lot of time working out and hired a personal trainer two days a week. I read everything I'd been meaning to for the past year and ordered postcards of myself to send to casting directors. Sometimes I watched *Hearts Crossing*, but it just wasn't as good after Cyrinda remembered everything and I tried to kill her again and she shot me six times. Without me to administer daily doses of wonder drug to keep him queer, Ollie lapsed back into heterosexual society and got back with Gwen. After a brief investigation, Sean was released from prison to find both his ex-girlfriends engaged to other men. Most of the other characters were embroiled in an uplifting summer storyline about crack babies. I wasn't sure what Jane was up to, because I switched over to TBN whenever Anna Ford showed her rotten face. Allison provided me with an interesting footnote when she told me Ray Lanville had been casting his runes in the direction of Cary Rietta, X-rated artwork and all. Cary freaked out and his manager brought in the FBI. Allie told me they had Ray, a word processor at a prominent real estate office, under surveillance.

Most everyone had been terrific during my final shows. Megan threw me a little farewell party in her dressing room with a cake from the Melrose Baking Company and presents. A VCR from Phalita and Allison, a Belinda Carlisle import CD from Nori Ann Marshall, and a really beautiful shirt from Brent Bingham. "To a totally cool and talented actor and good friend.

Good luck! God Bless! Brent." I was touched. Especially since his name had been evoked and his Christianity questioned by Clean Airwaves repeatedly in the past several weeks. Anna Ford stopped by for a piece of cake and to say goodbye, which took a lot of balls, if you ask me.

I smiled at her extra-sweetly. I'd called the guy from *Interview* a while ago and told him it was okay to go on record with the name of the homophobic bitch in the cast I'd discreetly referred to over lunch. Then I forgot to tell him I was about to be canned. Oh, well. When the issue came out next week, there'd still be almost three weeks of on-air Simon shows left.

Fired up by what they perceived to be a righteous victory in the war on depravity, Clean Airwaves intensified their assault. Their next target was *Roseanne* and its "coarse humor, teen sex and lesbianism." Big mistake. Efforts to alienate sponsors and enlist quality-television groups backfired horribly, Roseanne Herself took personal offense, went on *The Tonight Show*, called Eunice and Juliana "an inbred version of the Judds" and invited them to "kiss my ass. Censor that, Eunice!" Clean Airwaves' fifteen minutes were up. They faded into a local nuisance and were subject to frequent ridiculing in Sara's new *Paseo del Rio* column, "A Girl's Gotta Eat."

The summer wore on and *Dino & Muffin* became a major Top Ten hit and was put on the fall schedule. Trevor never called me and got the lead in a TV movie and started appearing all over town with a twenty-one-year-old cutie-pie film actress (and dyed-in-the-carpet Sister of Sappho, to those in the know). Could Scientology be far behind? I wondered how long it would take for the Hollywood Kids to come across a certain *Advocate Men* back issue.

My downstairs neighbor went to Thailand for ten days and asked me to come in and water his plants. I couldn't help snooping and discovered a Louis Quatorze armoire containing an electric butt plug still in the box, a family-size jar of something called Elbow Grease, various flavors of Orville Redenbacher microwave popcorn, and a single magazine featuring a tumescent Asian coverboy entitled *Kung Pao Pork*. I stayed caught up with my letter-writing and toyed with the idea of asking out my trainer. Sara and Richard made plans to visit me in late August. I was determined to have a job by then.

I was clandestinely perusing *Dramalogue* when the phone rang. Fully reverted to the popular Desperate Actor mode, I snatched it up on the first ring. It was the Executive Director of GLAAD. He wanted to know if I'd consider joining them for a special project. He said he was sorry to hear I was off the show. I expressed what I thought was a little well-deserved cynicism at this. He told me I was an excellent actor and asked if I'd come in the next day for a meeting. "I think we're both in favor of the same things," he said. I said I would, a sucker for polite guys with deep voices.

At 3:00 the next afternoon I showed up at their office attired in a coolly L.A.-formal dark blue jacket with matching pants and socks and Italian loafers. I wasn't some dumb blonde TV bimbo about to be fancy-talked into becoming an activists' puppet, not me. I waited patiently, legs uncrossed, until a female intern with that Bud Bundy haircut showed me into a small, chaotic office with a VCR/monitor unit and a desk entirely covered with magazines and torn out daily calendar pages. "Nick will be right with you," she said.

I was bound to run into another one sooner or later. I reached over and picked up a soap mag dated after my demise. I hadn't kept up with press reactions to my departure. It was just too depressing. What a horrible picture of Linda Dano. The poor thing looked like Mephistopheles. . . .

"Mr. Young?"

My head snapped up like a roughly treated marionette's. Only one man in the world sounded like that. It was. "Nick? Oh, my God. What are you doing here?" This was the biggest surprise I'd ever had, except for maybe the first time I ejaculated. A tempest of conflicting emotions spun into a cyclone deep within me, then attacked my brain. Tears of happiness were clobbered by disbelief and resentment that he could have come to L.A. and not even called me, which were in turn swallowed up by a feeling of relief and hope so intense my muscles seemed to have turned to Jell-O. I stared at him, his Kevin Kline's–Texan cousin beauty, those blue eyes destined to haunt me through as many Trevors and *Hearts Crossing*s as there could be until the end of time. He was in jeans and a comic-art T-shirt that read, I DON'T MIND STRAIGHT PEOPLE AS LONG AS THEY ACT GAY IN PUBLIC.

I made no move to get up or do anything, the memory of Barney's co-starring role in Nick's last L.A. engagement suddenly burning me like a red-hot poker. Nick leaned on the corner of his desk, smiling. "I wanted to surprise you," he said.

"You did."

"I started here about a week ago. Volunteer stuff. I got laid off in Austin. I believe they refer to it as downsizing."

"I'm sorry," I said.

"Aw, it was time for a change. I'm collecting unemployment, getting ready for the California bar this fall. The folks here think they'll be able to get me set up somewhere working in our field."

I nodded, wondering if this whole thing had been a ruse to get me down here to see Nick, and if so, what that might mean. "And you," he said, tapping me on the shoe with one of his cowboy boots. "You've been causing *all* sorts of trouble. Scandal boy."

"That's why I'm in this business," I quipped.

"I know GLAAD was giving you a pretty hard time for a while. But if you're not too mad at us, we'd like you to be the keynote speaker at a media conference in Chicago this October."

So the meeting was legit. "I don't know if I'd have anything that incisive to say," I replied. "I mean, during everything that happened, I never felt that political. I don't know what the moral of the story is."

"You were always honest about who you were," he said.

I nodded, nonplussed, then picked up a pen and gestured at Nick with it like a lecturer. "And we must keep that in mind no matter what reactions we get from others," I said.

"Sounds good to me. Just as long as you don't let that network off the hook too easy."

"Those fucks." Nick smiled at my foul mouth. "I guess I'd be interested . . ." I began, still feeling spacy at Nick's being three feet away from me, much less the prospect of working on a culturally relevant out-of-town project with him. Nick's phone beeped.

"Nick, your roommate's on line two," someone intercommed.

" 'Scuse me a sec." He picked up. "Hi . . . yeah. I bought some cat food last night. It may still be out on the balcony, come to think of it. . . . No problem. . . . I'll see you a bit later." I heard him hang up but I wasn't looking at him. My gaze was riveted on a section of the tile floor that I could make swim in and out of focus by relaxing my eyeballs. The best thing to do was end this quickly and get out. I could have Connie call them later and tell them I'd reconsidered and wouldn't be participating. How could he? How the fuck could he? He didn't even know what he was doing to me. That was how pathetically askew our perceptions of each other were.

"To-Bel," Nick said. I forced myself to look at him. Just pretend he's Brent, an inner voice helpfully suggested. "I'm staying with a friend from undergrad down in Redondo. Temporarily, anyway. Nice fella, but he doesn't know a thing about cats."

I didn't even bother to let my wheels go through a single spin before blurting out, "What about Barney?"

Nick folded his hands and looked down at them for a moment before answering. "Barney's not here."

"Oh." I was pushing it, but I was also way too tired for games. So I asked him: "What happened?"

He shook his head, looking past me, then meeting my furiously measured gaze. "I guess sometimes you just wake up and all of a sudden everything looks different. I tried . . . but, uh . . ." Big sigh. "California's not a good place for Barney. So he's staying in Austin. Without me."

What was I supposed to say? Congratulations? I stayed quiet, nodding my head almost imperceptibly.

Nick got up and sat behind the desk. He started absently arranging the mess in front of him. "I know you're probably real busy, Alex. Maybe we could get together and talk about the conference and all over dinner? Tonight?"

I stepped out of the shower and went straight into the kitchen for a swig of Tropicana Twister ("Flavors Mother Nature never intended"). I still had no idea what to wear tomorrow for my meeting with—get this—Gus Van Sant. Oh, shit. The package. I put on shorts and dashed downstairs and found it at the front door. It was the script, as promised by Tim, my film rep at the agency who'd left the most delightful message on my machine while I was at GLAAD.

Gus Van Sant and his producer wanted to meet with me at 11:00 regarding their new movie. Not read, not audition, but *meet* and *discuss*. Tim said they'd seen me on the soap and especially liked the *Interview* piece and would messenger me a script. I'd have to read it later, though.

I doffed the shorts, selected underwear and started dressing. Then stopped to spread styling gel evenly through my wet hair. I'd just turned on the dryer when I heard the knock. I shut it off and listened. My imagination. Then, again. I went out and used the peephole. I opened the door. "Hey, how'd you get in?"

"Your neighbor was just coming home. The Chinese fella."

"I think he's just visiting."

"Those directions were perfect. Still not really used to finding my way around the big city. This is a fantastic apartment."

I closed the door and gestured to my hair and lack of pants. (My shirt hung tastefully below briefs-level.) "It'll be a couple of minutes, Nick."

He looked at his watch. "I'm sorry I'm early."

I tried to look into his eyes with the utmost solemnity but ended up cracking a smile. "Early?" I repeated. "The way I see it, Mister, you're incredibly late."

And then he kissed me.